THE PROPHECY

THE PROPHECY

The Fulfillment Series

Book One

Erin Rhew

Tenacious Books Publishing

Published by Tenacious Books Publishing

Copyright © 2013 Erin Rhew

Published by Tenacious Books Publishing in 2018
tenaciousbooks@gmail.com

This book is a work of fiction. Names, characters, places, and incidents are either the product of the author's imagination or are used fictitiously.

Library of Congress Cataloging-in-Publication Data
Rhew, Erin.—Third edition.
The Prophecy/ Erin Rhew
ISBN 9780998951867 (print)
ISBN 9780998951881 (e-book)

Cover Image: © iStock
Cover Design: Anita B. Carroll www.race-point.com
Book Design: Ellie Sipila www.movetothewrite.com

Printed in the United States of America

www.tenaciousbookspublishing.com

For everyone who's ever had a dream…keep believing.

CHAPTER ONE

Layla

Beware of gray skies; they can be an omen. Layla Givens had heard those words her whole life, part of an ancient maxim amongst her people—the Vanguards—and wholly unsanctioned by the religious Ecclesiastic group. Such silly superstitions, she decided as she looked at the gloomy clouds above, snickering to herself. Gray skies meant rain, nothing more. Any farmer worth a sack of potatoes knew that.

The crisp chill of the early autumn air nipped at Layla's nose as she raced through the flower fields separating her farm from the center of Medlin, the closest town. Walking the distance took an hour, but today she ran. Her feet couldn't seem to carry her fast enough to reach Samson Mantar several paces ahead. Layla could practically taste the baker's cinnamon bread in her mouth. He made it twice a year, so if she didn't get there soon, she knew he'd be sold out. She pressed forward.

At the top of the hill, Samson bent over, panting. With laughter in his light brown eyes, he glanced back down the incline. Layla, pushing her way up, her face ablaze from the effort, envied the ease with which he traversed the distance. He offered his hand, but she slapped it away. He laughed—his amusement evident in his glinting eyes.

"Come on, slow poke," Samson teased.

"I'm coming." Layla flicked her black hair back out of her face. "You didn't tell me we were racing."

"We aren't racing. You're just that much slower than me."

Layla gave him a playful push, surprised to see his legs buckle. When Samson grabbed onto her for support, they both laughed and fell to the ground side by side.

"You're a real jerk sometimes, Samson. You know that, right?"

"I can't help it." He snorted. "The Day of Dawning is my favorite holiday. Besides, if the baker sells out of that cinnamon bread, we'll have to wait until King's Day before he'll make it again. That's six whole months away. I don't know about you, but I intend to eat at least one piece today."

"Well, let's go," Layla said, leaping up.

She sprinted away before he even had the chance to realize what was happening. Layla heard Samson grunt, and she glanced back to find him chugging along behind her. She would have chuckled at his red, puffy cheeks if her own lungs didn't burn so much.

Samson. Thinking about him made her forehead ache. They'd lived together their whole lives, raised like brother and sister, yet she knew the townspeople expected them to marry one day. Layla honestly didn't know quite how she felt about that. Of course she loved Samson… she always had. But did she *love* him?

As they approached the edge of town, Layla slowed down, enjoying the festive air that had overtaken her otherwise boring town. Ribbons, brilliant in their kaleidoscope of colors, decorated every storefront in a myriad of different ways—wreaths, flags, wind chimes. Her gaze swung back and forth, up and down, unable to settle on any one place in particular. She loved The Day of Dawning.

"Put up your hood," Samson warned as he approached from behind. "Mother and Father didn't want you to come at all today, and you promised you would stay out of sight."

"Fine." Layla yanked up the hood, which had fallen back during their run. "I still don't understand what all the fuss is about. It's not like I'm the only person in Vanguard with black hair."

Samson grabbed her by the arm and stared into her eyes, his brow furrowed with concern. "But you are the only person with black hair and purple eyes…"

"Which no one will see because I put the drops in before we left the house."

"You've been told about the dangers your whole life, yet you blow them off like they mean nothing," he growled.

Sighing, she pulled Samson along by the arm. "Come on. You know everyone will head for the cinnamon bread first."

Just as Layla feared, a long line snaked along the front of the baker's shop. Samson groaned as they took their place in the back, but Layla appreciated the extra time to stand and watch the preparations. When she inhaled the intoxicating scent of cinnamon, nutmeg, and yeast, her mouth watered in anticipation.

A little girl squealed as she raced by with a young boy giving chase. Layla smiled at their obvious joy, remembering how she and Samson had done the same not so long ago. She took in his dark brown hair and light brown eyes, missing the carefree days of their shared childhood.

In the open field past the butcher's shop, Layla spotted the circle. Ribbons—red, blue, orange, purple, and green—lay unmoving in the green grass, awaiting the dance that would give them flight. Of all the activities on the Day of Dawning, she looked forward to this one the most. Visions of leaping in the air, waving the ribbon circle high above her head with Samson laughing at her side, floated through Layla's mind. Excitement, tinged with sadness, shot through her. With their eighteenth birthdays approaching, this year would be the last she and Samson could participate.

Layla turned to see the donkey races, apple bobbing, and hair braiding all being set up along the town square. Next year, instead of fidgeting while a patient woman twisted her hair, weaving the Day of Dawning ribbons in and out of her strands, Layla would be the one doing the braiding. Would the celebration lose some of its appeal when she finally viewed it through the eyes of an adult?

"Look," Samson cried, drawing her attention. "The Ecclesiastics are arriving."

Layla, placing her hand over her eyes to block the sun, scanned the horizon to find a long procession approaching the town. Hundreds of men in long black and purple robes, the signature garb of their religious sect, labored toward Medlin on horseback. She could hardly believe it. The men who'd been nothing more than mythical figures before now marched toward her. Layla's stomach churned with a mixture of fear and eagerness. She knew what the Ecclesiastics could do if they found out about her, but at the same time, she couldn't resist seeing them firsthand.

"I knew I'd find you here," a deep voice came from behind them. Layla recognized it in an instant.

"Grant." She squealed, turning to jump into his open arms.

Grant Mantar chuckled as he drew her into a hug. She squeezed him hard. To her annoyance, Samson adjusted her hood, which had fallen as soon as she pulled back from the embrace. In an effort to distract and calm herself, Layla studied Grant's face, noting the slight flush in his cheeks and the green tint in his otherwise brown eyes. She recognized the subtle signs. Grant was happy, and she had a sneaking suspicion as to why.

"You were supposed to be here last night," Samson said. Layla detected a slight hitch. He had already told her how much he'd looked forward to Grant's arrival and how disappointed he'd been when his brother wasted a portion of the three-day leave. She started to reach for his arm, to comfort him, but halted in midair.

"I had to make a stop before coming home," Grant said. His lips twitched, hinting at a grin that died before it started.

"I knew it. You went to see your lady love." Layla gave Grant a triumphant smile while Samson rolled his eyes.

"I admit nothing," Grant said, but the green sparkle in his eye and blush on his face continued to give away the truth. He lowered his volume, speaking so quietly Layla had to strain to hear him. "So, Father still won't attend the festival, huh?" He clearly wanted to steer the conversation away from his personal life, though he'd swung it in a direction Layla would rather avoid. "Even today, when the Ecclesiastics are here and Layla could be in danger. Which brings up a better question, why is she even attending the Festival?"

Samson leaned in, murmuring like Grant. "Mother and Father didn't want her to come, but you know how stubborn Layla can be. If they had forbidden her, she would have just snuck out and come on her own. After all, this is our last year to participate in the events."

Layla looked back and forth between them, incensed. "Stop talking about me like I'm not here, and quit being so protective. I'm a Vanguard, same as you."

Grant lifted Layla's chin, gripping it when she tried to pull away. "Hopefully, she will be safe with those drops in her eyes."

"The drops have worked just fine for the past seventeen years," she reminded them. "Why would today be any different?"

"You know why," Grant whispered.

"I wish Father would tell us why he never comes," Samson said, breaking the tension and shooting Layla a weary look. "He is at home, as usual. Mother left the house with us, but we ran on ahead to get the cinnamon bread. I don't know where she is now, but I'm certain she'll be here soon, for Layla's sake."

Grant nodded. "I'll try to find Mother soon. You know how Father is, Samson. He has his secrets."

"And it appears you do too." Layla hoped to redirect their discussion away from her and back to Grant's mystery woman.

"Nice try," Grant teased.

"Next!" The baker's call shook them out of their reunion. He smiled as Samson, Layla, and Grant approached. "Well, if it isn't the Mantar brothers and their little tagalong." The man waggled his eyes suggestively.

Layla flushed. Tagalong. She turned away to avoid the baker's leer, his implication that there was more between her and Samson than friendship. Layla stole a quick glance at Samson, surprised to find him regarding her as well. Her face grew warmer, a mortifying shade of pink based on the burning sensation in her cheeks, so she turned away to hide her bizarre reaction. Of late, a new kind of strangeness, like discomfort, had crept into her relationship with Samson, altering their behavior toward one another. Layla didn't like it. She blew a stray strand of hair out of her face in frustration.

Samson finished purchasing the slices of bread, two for the three of them and a few for his parents. They moved away from the baker, to Layla's great relief. Samson handed her the long awaited treat. Unable to wait a moment longer, she slid the warm bread into her mouth, savoring the rare combination. Layla moaned with pleasure. As she held the delicacy, hoping to make each moment with it last, snippets of conversation swirled around her. A tense atmosphere replaced the festive one.

"...Elder Werrick said our version of celebration is too overt. What does that even mean?"

"...wants us to take everything down."

"...no donkey races, no ribbon dance, no nothing."

Layla's gaze settled on the black and purple robes now infiltrating every part of town. Who did these solemn men think they were, coming into Medlin and changing their most sacred holiday? This town celebrated the Day of Dawning in the same way every year. A sudden desire to protect their traditions overtook her. With the Ecclesiastics here, forcing a new and different celebration, the holiday no longer held its traditional appeal. She considering going home—all of the Mantars would approve of that choice—yet she remained planted in place, staring.

"Everything must be taken down." A rotund man, with beady black eyes, surveyed the town, disdain in his expression. While he did not appear distinguishable from the other black and purple clad men, he spoke with authority. "The First Ones and their great Prophecy must be honored properly." He sniffed, his actions indicating the very existence of Medlin and its occupants offended him.

Layla wondered what this man considered a "proper honoring" of the First Ones. The First Ones...they'd been dead for centuries, and, as far as Layla could tell, hadn't done much in life except start a never-ending war. She knew nothing more about them except that she was to thank them for good things, curse them for bad, and celebrate them on this day.

"That's Elder Werrick, head of the Ecclesiastics," whispered Samson, glancing back at Grant. Layla noticed the look that passed between them.

Grant nodded his assent. "Get her out of here, brother."

Samson tried to steer Layla away, but she held her position to get a closer look at the man whom her family so feared. She knew they had good reason to worry—her black hair and purple eyes marked her as a Fulfillment candidate, one with the potential to bring about the long awaited peace. But she couldn't quite bring herself to believe Elder Werrick would notice her on the crowded streets, especially with her eye drops and hood. Could he really be responsible for dragging candidates from their homes, forcing them to undergo strenuous, sometimes gruesome, testing for the sake of the Prophecy? To Layla, he looked like nothing more than a short, fat, unhappy man. The very notion that he could strike such fear into the hearts of her people seemed almost laughable…almost. As his gaze swept over the crowd, she glimpsed a sinister undertone that made her shiver.

Waving his pudgy arms at the awaiting townspeople, Werrick commanded, "Take it down."

Suddenly, his body stilled and his tiny eyes grew wide. They briefly connected with Layla's, narrowing with calculation. The Elder turned to his nearest black-clad companion.

"Do you feel that?" Layla heard Werrick ask.

The other man looked skeptical. "Feel what, Elder?"

Werrick leaned in as the two whispered, stealing furtive glances in her direction. When the Elder's companion pointed at Layla, Samson grabbed her arm. She heard his breathing change from rhythmic to jagged as he pulled her away from the men.

"We have to go now." His urgency spurred her into action.

Grant moved to block them from the Elder's view. "Get her away from here, Samson."

The Elder looked up to see everyone staring at him as if frozen. He repeated his demand, "I said take everything down."

The townspeople, joined by the Elder's minion, scampered to remove their decorations, anxious to "properly" celebrate the First Ones. Their flurry of activity concealed Layla as Samson and Grant escorted her away. Layla scanned the streets, horrified, as the people of Medlin stripped the town's center barren. In no time, everything appeared as it always had, devoid of any celebratory adornments. She looked up at the sky with its gray clouds lingering overhead. A bad omen...

On the hill, a safe distance away, Layla watched a group of Ecclesiastics erect a monstrous stage where the donkey races should have occurred. She heard the braying of the angry animals, harnessed and corralled on the orders of the Elder to avoid interfering with the "true" Day of Dawning celebration. Her ire rose. Who did they think they were coming in and changing everything?

An icy, phantom finger traced a frigid line down her spine. After hearing warning after warning from the Mantars her whole life, Layla knew exactly what the Ecclesiastics could do, what they had done to others in the past. Maybe Samson and Grant had been right. Maybe she should never have come, especially today. Layla turned her back on the town, resolved to go home, to safety.

"Layla!" Samson's alarmed tone sliced into her, and she swung around toward him.

To her horror, two Vanguard soldiers forced Samson to the ground. She knew just how much strength he possessed, yet he couldn't free himself. Her hands balled up into fists, shaking with their desire to unleash the full force of their fury.

"Run!" Samson screamed before a soldier's fist smashed into his face.

His body stilled. Panic, coupled with indecision, crippled her. She should run like Samson commanded, but she couldn't leave him lying there. To her relief, Grant sprinted toward them, his eyes full of rage.

"Run!" Grant echoed Samson's warning.

With a final glance at the two boys who'd been as close to her as brothers, Layla fled. She flew down the hill, swinging her head from side to side in alarm. Ecclesiastics swarmed throughout the city, making a clear escape route difficult to discern.

Terror rose within Layla. Why hadn't she listened to her family? She'd been foolish to believe she could sneak around under the ever-watchful eyes of the Ecclesiastics, and that hubris put Samson and Grant in danger as well. She choked back a sob.

"Run," she whispered.

Willing her feet to move forward, Layla darted toward the back of the baker's shop, hoping to take a shortcut through the alleyway. She swerved to miss a wooden box and stumbled, arms flailing to right herself. Unfamiliar hands reached out to break her fall. Once stable, Layla looked up to find Elder Werrick staring down at her. She screamed but no sound came out of her open mouth.

"I've been looking for you," he said, a wicked smile on his face.

A strange vibration passed between them. Layla jerked her hands away, stepping back. Given his weight, she calculated she could easily outrun him. Layla took another step backward.

"If you are thinking of running again, I wouldn't," Werrick warned.

Two Vanguard soldiers stepped out of the shadows. What had the Elder told these soldiers to convince them to turn on one of their own? Layla tried to slow her racing mind and regain control of her breathing. Based on what she'd seen with Samson, she couldn't use brute force to extract herself from this situation. She would need her wits.

"Why are you looking for me?" she asked, pretending to be nonchalant.

The Elder smirked. "I think you know. Now, you can either let me inspect you willingly or..." He narrowed his eyes as his gaze fell upon the nearby soldiers. "I can make you."

Despite her racing heart, Layla nodded her assent. She'd been diligent about applying the eye drops before she left the house, as always, though the thought brought her no real comfort. Layla refused to become another casualty in the Ecclesiastics' relentless pursuit of their fabled Fulfillment, but she didn't know how to prevent it. For the second time, she lamented her choice to attend the Festival.

The Elder stepped forward and yanked down her hood. Layla's long, raven black hair spilled out. Grinning like a man observing a prized horse, the Elder picked up a strand and massaged it between his fingers. Layla barely contained her disgust. The tremor she'd experienced before hummed through her hair into the Elder's beefy hands. His grin widened.

When he began his inspection of her eyes, made blue by the drops, his smile faltered. The fluttering in her chest slowed. Maybe the drops would work; maybe she could escape the Elder after all. A movement to her right drew her attention. Another black and purple robed man walked with faltering steps toward the Elder.

"We're almost ready for the ceremony, Elder," the man said, submissive. "Is she someone we should consider?"

The Elder's eyes narrowed into slits. "She has the hair, but her eyes are blue."

"Then she cannot be the one," the other man said.

"I felt something, Amster." Werrick looked stumped. "The First Ones are trying to tell me something."

"Perhaps they are telling you that it's time to start the ceremony," Amster offered. The poor soul's eyes lit up like he'd actually stumbled upon something his superior might deem useful.

After sending the other man a withering glare, Elder Werrick returned to his careful observation of Layla. She stared back, the stubbornness Samson bemoaned earlier replacing her fear. If she stood her ground, maybe the Elder would back down. She had no other options.

"She ran from us, and those boys defended her. Something doesn't fit." Werrick gnawed his lip, chewing on it and the problem like one working out a complicated puzzle.

Layla cursed herself yet again for coming to the Day of Dawning Festival. As usual, she should have listened to the wise counsel of the Mantars. She glanced at Amster, hoping the man could convince the Elder to attend the ceremony, leaving her alone. The moment she did, Layla realized her mistake.

"There," Werrick cried out, pointing to her face. "Look, there, in the corner of her eye. They are purple. The color change is some trick by those blasted Voltons, I know it. They mean to foil my quest as they always have."

Voltons? The faces of Layla's aging physician and boring tutor swam through her mind. As far as she knew, the Voltons devoted their lives to medicine and learning. Other than wearing robes—green instead of black—and sharing space in the Borderlands, the Voltons had nothing in common with the Ecclesiastics. Why would they be interested in obstructing the plans of someone like Elder Werrick?

Amster leaned in, his curious green eyes boring into hers. "I'm sorry, Elder, I only see blue."

Werrick shoved the other man back. "Go, prepare the stage for me. This Day of Dawning will be like no other."

Even though she had no chance to escape now, Layla shoved the Elder with all her might. The blow sent him flying into the baker's door, which splintered under the force, and she darted forward. The Vanguard soldiers moved to block her.

"We are all Vanguards," she pleaded. "Please let me go."

For a moment, they hesitated. Layla used the opening to slip around them. She ran as fast as her legs would carry her, but they proved to be too slow. Within moments, the soldiers leapt upon her, knocking her to the ground. Wrenching Layla up by her hair, they dragged her back to the Elder, whose face now bled from his encounter with the baker's door.

"I see you're going to be trouble." He brushed the dirt off his robes. "You can't escape your destiny, girl."

Werrick made a motion, and the soldiers from earlier dragged a half-conscious Samson into view. Horrified, Layla clamped a hand over her mouth to keep from crying out. Blood seeped from a gaping wound on his head.

"You will do as I say, girl, or he dies." Werrick didn't bother to conceal his fury. "I've searched for you my whole life, and I will not let you ruin this moment."

"Elder, you don't mean to announce her," Amster said, his mouth left open in shock. "We haven't done the proper testing. We don't know for sure."

"No testing is required," Werrick snapped. "I know she's the one. The First Ones made it clear to me."

"Elder—" Amster tried again, but Werrick silenced the other man with one look. "As you wish."

"Follow me," Werrick commanded the soldiers.

They hauled Layla and Samson to the back of the platform the Ecclesiastics had erected earlier. Motioning for them to stop, the Elder surveyed the masses. The townspeople waited in solemn silence for his arrival. When he smiled to himself, a shiver of disgust rocked Layla. If Samson's life weren't in danger, she would have gladly ripped the Elder apart.

Werrick turned to the soldiers. "Do not let her out of your sight, and if she tries to escape, kill the boy."

Without another word, the Elder spun around and dawdled to the top, gathering everyone's attention. A reverent hush befell the crowd. The most important moment of the Festival had arrived...the reading of the Prophecy. Most years, Layla suffered through the reading, anxious to get to the more enjoyable activities, but the presence of the Ecclesiastics, combined with the now barren town, brought a new somberness to the event. Despite her current situation, she found herself listening with a single-minded focus she'd never had during any other ceremony.

"Today, we celebrate The Dawning, our origins." Werrick's voice rose, his words descending upon the townspeople like a hawk swooping in on prey. A shiver ran through Layla.

"We celebrate the First Ones, those who came before, those who made us all." The Elder spoke in a deep tone that resonated through the square. "We Ecclesiastics have devoted our lives to worshipping the First Ones and to studying their great Prophecy. Today, in celebration of our ancestors and the peace they foretold, I will read the sacred words of the Prophecy."

A murmur went through the multitude. In Vanguard, peace was a divisive word. For centuries, Layla's people, endowed with superior strength, had been in constant strife with their neighbors, the Ethereals, empowered with the ability to control minds. Yet there were those from both sides who longed for this elusive peace, those who believed in the Ecclesiastics' promises and the Prophecy of the First Ones.

"Silence." Elder Werrick commanded. The crowd fell mute. "The Ecclesiastics are a neutral people, serving both the Vanguard and Ethereals without prejudice. We seek peace as we always have, and the First Ones have shown us the way through which this conciliation will come. Through the Prophecy."

"The Prophecy," hundreds of black and purple robed men hummed.

"Blessed be the First Ones." Townspeople chanted the words in response to Elder Werrick, but they spoke by rote instead of with zeal. Layla shivered again.

"The Prophecy reads, 'In a time of war, when the land is divided amongst the two, she, with raven black hair, purple eyes, and a special blessing from the First Ones shall bring peace. She, from one side, shall marry royalty on the other, and peace shall reign from that day forth.'" His proclamation, spoken originally by the First Ones and passed down through generations, hung in the air.

In unison, all four soldiers turned toward Layla. They appraised her, truly seeing her for the first time. A flush rose to her cheeks at their newfound scrutiny. She wondered again how the Elder had gotten them to cooperate. Samson's head lolled as he let out a mournful sound. Struggling against her captors, Layla reached for him.

"Please stop," a soldier whispered in her ear, "or we will be forced to kill him. I don't want to do that."

"Today, our centuries long search has ended," Werrick said. A surprised murmur rose from the crowd. He turned toward Layla. "Step forward, child." His tone left no room for argument.

To preserve Samson's life, Layla willed herself to put one foot in front of the other, though her legs shook so hard she was sure she would fall. Her heart slammed against her chest.

Somehow, she made it to the raised platform without falling, though her quaking legs threatened to give out. Layla took a deep breath and walked over to the Elder. He studied her meticulously, just as he had done earlier, though he seemed to look through her this time.

"Who are you?" he asked, booming as he performed this charade for the benefit of the crowd. His breath smelled sour. Layla tried not to gag. The Elder spoke under his breath so only she could hear. "You will answer me, or the boy dies. Do not make a fool of me, girl, or I will destroy you and everything you love."

Pushing down her desire to spit in his face, she managed, "Layla Givens."

"Who are your parents?"

"I don't know." Layla dipped her head. Almost everyone in the crowd knew her story, yet she still felt exposed sharing it here, on a platform with the Elder. "I was found as a baby by the Mantar family, and they took me in."

"And your name, Givens…how did you come by it if you were found by the Mantar family?"

"My adopted parents gave me the last name Givens because they believe I was given to them."

"Layla," he muttered. "Layla means dark beauty." She didn't know what to say to that, so she remained quiet.

As she stood across from this loathsome man, who held several lives in the palm of his hand, anger renewed itself inside her. Layla could hurl the Elder off the platform if she wanted. Given her Vanguard strength, the action would be simple, yet Samson held her in place. Even if his life didn't hang in the balance, the townspeople would never understand her actions. The Ecclesiastics' religious fanaticism toward the First Ones and the Prophecy afforded them special deference, allowing them to wield an unusual authority within both Vanguard and Etherea. So, no matter how much the idea of heaving his body into the butcher's roof appealed to her, Layla would simply endure the Elder's performance.

"Dark hair, purple eyes, no parents…" Elder Werrick muttered, peering up at the sky with such hope on his face. Layla recognized his grandstanding, but the mystified crowd looked toward the heavens with him like they believed the First Ones themselves might appear there.

"I am no one special," Layla said, to convey there must be some mistake.

"Oh, I believe you are very special, my dear."

The old man took her hand and raised it far above her head. She hoped the crowd couldn't see how hard she shook. Layla glanced up at the gray clouds in the sky...a bad omen...she never should have laughed at the idea.

"Finally, the Prophecy has come true. She has arrived at long last. Layla Givens is the Fulfillment."

Layla

Layla slumped against the seat of the carriage the Vanguard soldiers had thrown her into on the command of Werrick. A dangerous mixture of confinement and fury boiled inside her. Across from her, the guard watched her every move, tracking even the most subtle of shifts. His eager gaze suggested he would attack at the slightest provocation. Vexed, she wondered again how her own people could turn against her in favor of the Ecclesiastics. If the soldier weren't a Vanguard, she would have already escaped by now. She crossed her arms and glared.

"Are we going to move sometime today?" Layla offered him a tight, sarcastic smile.

"We go when the Elder says to go."

"And Vanguards have always done what the Elder said from the beginning of...wait, never. Until now. Why is that?" She turned her head to the side, awaiting his answer.

The soldier snorted. "There are plenty of people out there who want to see you dead." He jerked a finger toward the heavily draped window. "Maybe I should just throw you and your smart mouth out there to them and see how long you last."

The chanting outside grew louder, almost like the people heard his threat and chose to respond. Layla's leg twitched, but she kept her arms locked against her chest. She wouldn't show weakness.

A knock on the side of the carriage startled them both. Casting Layla a warning glance, the soldier opened the door. Grant stuck his head inside, his face hard. Though she wanted to sigh with relief, Layla remained stoic.

"The ranking officer told me to relieve you of duty because you're needed elsewhere." The ease with which Grant lied jolted her. When they were younger, he often spouted the great virtue of honesty. Had his time in the military adjusted his values, or had he chosen to forgo his moral code for her?

The other guard, who to Layla's relief failed to connect Grant to Layla, nodded and jumped up from his seat. Her adoptive brother slid into the vacant spot, shutting the door with a resounding bang. Once they were hidden from view, he wrapped Layla in his arms and flattened her against his barreled chest.

"Samson?" Layla asked, barely able to force out the name.

"He's being taken by carriage to the Ecclesiastic compound in the Borderlands." Layla grimaced. Samson—in trouble because of her—the notion tortured her. Grant pulled back just enough so she could see the mischievous sparkle in his greenish-brown eyes. "But they failed to place any Vanguard soldiers in the carriage with him. Before they even get close to the Borderlands, Samson will have reduced his transportation into a pile of shattered wood fragments."

"You're certain?"

Grant displayed no hint of concern. "You know Samson."

Layla nodded against the rough fabric of his soldier's uniform. Grant seemed so sure of his brother's safety that she shoved her fears down. He sat back, creating space between them. Where she'd seen impishness just moments before, she now saw distress.

"I know Samson will be fine, but I'm worried about you. Are they taking you to the Borderlands to perform Fulfillment testing?"

"I don't think so. Elder Werrick already proclaimed me the Fulfillment. To test me now would cast doubt on his declaration."

Grant blew out a frustrated breath. "I hope you're right, Layla, because people have died during those tests."

"I know."

"That's a big part of why we've kept you hidden for so long."

Layla pinched her lips together. "I know that, Grant, but you have to trust me. I think the Elder is more interested in being the one to find the Fulfillment than he is in ensuring I'm the correct choice."

"But that's blasphemous." Grant's eyebrows furrowed. In that moment, he looked just like Samson.

"I honestly don't think Werrick cares." Layla skipped ahead to the part that bothered her most. "He's going to force me to marry the Ethereal prince. An Ethereal, Grant. They'll take the first opportunity to wipe my mind so that I'm nothing but a blubbering idiot."

Despite their dire situation, he chuckled. "You don't have anything to fear from the Ethereals, Layla. They are not the monsters we were made to believe."

She drew back, her eyes wide. "What are you saying? You're a soldier in the Vanguard army, sworn to fight against the Ethereals. How can you say such a thing?"

Grant looked down at his hands and remained silent for so long that she didn't think he'd speak again. "I just know. They won't hurt you."

"If you say so…" Layla let her doubt hang between them, watching as Grant frowned. He sat back against the seat with a thud. A myriad of expressions passed over his face. She watched him struggle, trying to figure out what to say next. When his gaze landed upon her again, he regarded her in a new way, like a stranger. She squirmed.

"Do you believe you are her…the Fulfillment, I mean?"

Layla considered his question, the same one she'd been asking herself over and over. "The Fulfillment has to have black hair, purple eyes, and some special gift from the First Ones. Not even the Ecclesiastics know what that last part means. I wasn't lying when I told the Elder that I was no one special. I'm sure he's got the wrong girl."

"Then you escape the first chance you get." His protective growl further endeared him to her.

"But Samson…"

"I will get word to you once Samson is free. In the meantime, I'll move Mother and Father to a safe location so you won't have to worry about them as well."

Layla nodded, relieved to have her older brother provide her with sound advice. Her own thoughts swirled so violently she had trouble grabbing hold of just one. His plan could work, she decided. With her family away from the Ecclesiastics, the Elder would no longer be able to force her cooperation.

"Layla!" Someone screamed from outside, interrupting their conversation.

Grant and Layla exchanged terrified looks. "Mother." Her brother forced out the word with a strangled breath.

He pushed back the curtain blocking their view of the crowd. A line of black-robed men, with Vanguard soldiers at their sides, pushed back a swelling group of townspeople. Layla scanned the faces, finding true believers, who gazed at her reverently, mixed in with peace opponents, who sneered at her with murderous eyes. Finally, her gaze landed upon her adoptive mother. Layla raised her hand, compelled, and reached out toward Lia Mantar.

"Let her go." Lia's usually soft voice held uncharacteristic strength.

Elder Werrick stepped into Layla's view, his backside almost obscuring Lia from sight. "Madam, step back. The Fulfillment has a duty, a responsibility, and no one will stand in her way."

Layla heard the warning in the Elder's claim. The hairs on her arm stood up. She'd seen what Werrick had done to Samson, so she harbored no illusions about her mother's safety. Layla started to stand, but Grant placed a hand upon her arm.

"There are people out there who would rather kill you than make peace with the Ethereals," he whispered.

Layla yanked her arm away. "Werrick is dangerous."

"She's my daughter." Lia's conviction rang out, rising clear and true.

Werrick turned just enough for Layla to catch a glimpse of the smile plastered upon his face. "Madam, with all respect, she is not your daughter."

"I have raised her and loved her from the moment she appeared on my doorstep seventeen years ago. I may not have birthed her, but she's my daughter all the same. Let her go. She belongs with her family."

Werrick barked out a hard laugh. "She belongs to the First Ones, not you. The Fulfillment will go at once to Etherea, marry the Ethereal prince, and usher in the peace that has been absent for centuries."

"No." Lia lurched forward.

"Mother!" Layla and Grant screamed in unison.

A large Vanguard soldier stepped forward and bashed Lia on the back of the head with the hilt of his sword. She crumpled to the ground as a soft groan escaped her lips.

"Mother." Layla croaked out the endearment while tears sprang to her eyes. She jumped up, ready to take on the whole Vanguard army to reach her fallen parent.

Grant pushed her down hard against the carriage seat. She kicked him with more viciousness than intended, her fear and anger providing extra force. Her brother knelt before her, grabbed the sides of her face, and forced her to look him in the eye.

"Stay for now and do your duty, Layla," She heard his protective ferocity, loving and hating it in the same instant. "I'll take care of our parents and alert you as soon as Samson is free."

"I can't leave her like that." She stabbed an accusing finger at the window for emphasis.

"You don't have a choice right now. They still have Samson."

Layla closed her eyes to still her raging emotions. Her brother was right. If she wanted to save her family, she'd have to play along with Werrick for a little bit longer. She nodded her assent with a heavy heart.

"Remember what I said earlier. The Ethereals aren't what you think." Grant leaned in, planted a rough kiss on her cheek, and stepped out of the carriage.

She reached out to grab his hand. He stopped, turning around. With a tense look upon his face, her brother nodded, understanding her unspoken plea.

"I'll take care of them all." Grant shut the door, leaving only his oath to comfort her.

From the window, Layla watched as mayhem erupt-
ed outside. The unjustified injury of a much-loved and
respected person like Lia Mantar sent the mob into an
uproar. Others, who wanted to kill Layla more than they
wanted to honor the First Ones, moved toward the carriage. Just as she reached forward to close the curtain
against the scene, Elder Werrick flung open the door and
jumped inside.

He beat on the wooden wall separating the coach from
the driver and roared, "Go!"

▽▽▽▽

In the carriage, the Elder said very little except to explain they would be stopping by the castle of the Vanguard king, Rex, on the way to Etherea. After arriving
and being greeted with little fanfare, Layla stumbled
along as two of the king's guards pushed her forward.
To her smug satisfaction, a second set of soldiers shoved
Werrick roughly down the hall beside her. The thought
of standing before her king, whom she'd seen only once
from a vast distance when she was seven, set her nerves
on edge and made her stomach roil.

As the guards pulled her along, she tried not to gape,
but the sheer grandness of the palace overwhelmed her.
Rich, dark tapestries hung on the windows while painted
children danced on the ceiling above her. Scowling faces
of former kings glared down at her from their perch on
the wall to her right. As in Medlin, vibrant ribbons lined
the hallways in celebration of the Day of Dawning. Layla concentrated hard on every detail because focusing on

the castle's grandeur helped keep her mind off the real reason she was at the palace in the first place. The Fulfillment...

When the audience chamber door swung open, King Rex's guards shoved Layla and Elder Werrick through it, throwing them to the ground in front of the throne. Layla stayed on her knees, though she stole a quick glance to observe her king. He stared down at her with formidable green eyes. She lowered her head in submission, her body quaking.

Elder Werrick rose to his feet, making a great show of brushing off his robe. "Why, King Rex, I've never received such horrible treatment. I am the Elder of the Ecclesiastics."

"And I am the King of Vanguard. One of my riders preceded your arrival, so I know all about the riot you caused in Medlin."

Layla's lips twitched, threatening a smile, as the Elder started and stopped before settling on the right words. "Surely you don't blame me for the unruly behavior of *your* subjects, King Rex."

"You failed to follow the proper protocol for a Prophecy candidate, and you bashed an innocent woman on the head. I do not take these offenses lightly, Elder Werrick. We afford you Ecclesiastics a certain liberty because of your neutrality and your desire to find the Fulfillment. However, I am prepared to imprison you right now if you do not explain yourself to my satisfaction." The king's threat echoed throughout the room.

Despite Rex's warning, Werrick appeared unaffected. He smiled the smarmy, conniving smile Layla had seen several times during their onerous journey together. The Elder paced back and forth, holding the conversation in a pregnant pause. Layla got the impression he enjoyed keeping his audience captive.

"Speak, Werrick, or I'll have my guards throw you in a cell right now." King Rex rose, drawing himself up to his full, intimidating height. Even from her position on the floor, Layla could feel the power he radiated.

"King Rex, I broke protocol because this girl..." Werrick paused, sighing as he offered his hand to Layla. Though she loathed the idea of touching him, she took it and stood. "This girl is the Fulfillment. No testing is required because the First Ones told me themselves."

One of the king's guards snickered, attempting to cover his action with a cough. King Rex shot the man a hard look. Nearly falling in his haste, the guard shuffled out of the room.

"The First Ones told you?" Even the king couldn't hide his disbelief.

"Touch her, King. You will feel the power of the First Ones flowing through her," Werrick insisted, shoving Layla's hand forward.

The king observed her with his piercing gaze. At the risk of incurring his ire, she lifted her eyes to connect with his. Layla tried to convey to her king, her potential savior, the abuse she had suffered under the Elder's care, but King Rex did not seem to understand her message. His hesitation clear, he reached out and touched her outstretched palm. The king's large hand engulfed her smaller one. He squeezed, forcing her fingers together time and time again with no success. He frowned, and she knew he'd failed to activate the sensation Elder Werrick insisted she possessed.

"I feel nothing," King Rex said after several tense moments.

Unfazed, Werrick continued, "My years spent studying the holy texts combined with my position as Elder gives me a unique ability to detect the often subtle messages from our First Ones."

"I suppose so." The king's statement did not match his expression, which conveyed a clear lack of conviction.

"And as for the regretful situation with the injured woman, I truly believed she meant to hurt the girl. It's my job to protect the Fulfillment until I turn her over to the Ethereals."

"Liar!" Layla screamed. "That woman was my mother, and she posed no threat to me."

"Silence."

Layla shrank back from the force of the king's words. She had hoped for assistance but instead managed to anger him. If nothing else, Layla prayed she had at least been successful in casting a shadow of suspicion across the Elder.

King Rex's skeptical regard of the Ecclesiastic assured her that she had.

After allowing Rex the silence he demanded, Werrick spoke again. "My duty to the First Ones requires me to transport this girl to the Ethereals where she will marry the Ethereal prince." He swallowed and lowered his head. Layla recognized the Elder's false meekness, but did the king? "May I have your permission to do so?"

Layla's focus vanished as the full impact of Werrick's words hit her, erasing all other thoughts. She had known the Fulfillment would marry into the other side. She knew it, yet still the enormity of it, the sheer revulsion of it, overwhelmed her. Wife of the Ethereal prince? Her head swam over the ridiculous notion. How could she marry one of *them*? Layla remembered her brother's words, let them soothe her. Grant knew something she didn't…Layla had to trust that, though her neck muscles refused to unclench.

The king sighed, a deep, troubled sound. "We are all bound by the Prophecy of the First Ones, Elder Werrick. If she is the Fulfillment as you claim, I release her into your custody to be transported immediately to Etherea."

With a scowl of distaste upon his face, the Elder managed a small bow. "Thank you, King Rex."

Before another word could be spoken, the door to the audience chamber flew open. A young man strode into the room, his lips tight with anger. Behind him, a woman wearing the gaudiest dress Layla had ever seen hurried to catch up. They each had dark brown hair, but the shrewdness in their eyes most clearly marked them as kin. Though she'd never seen them before, Layla assumed them to be Queen Montessa and Prince Vance. Looking at them, she sensed a deep foreboding.

"Father, you can't be serious," the young man exclaimed. Layla held back the absurd sensation to laugh as his high-pitched, petulant whine struck her. "We cannot allow a Vanguard citizen to be transported to Etherea, much less marry their so-called prince."

King Rex's face deepened into a menacing scowl. Layla could see why Ethereals often ran from this man in battle. He looked imposing, but the prince did not appear to be at all phased by his father's displeasure.

"Vance, that is enough." The king's deep growl rattled through Layla, yet the prince continued his advance.

The queen cleared her throat. "Perhaps the Elder is mistaken, Rex. Shouldn't we at least wait until the girl has been tested?" Layla caught the false sweetness in the queen's tone and wondered if the king did too. How could a great man miss such obvious clues?

"That's enough from both of you." The king's face turned bright red with fury. "Guards, escort Prince Vance and Queen Montessa out of my sight."

Several guards stepped forward, working hard to subdue the struggling prince and queen. As the soldiers hauled a flailing Vance away, Layla watched his face turn purple with indignation. The prince focused his malicious, unrelenting gaze upon his father.

"A true Vanguard wouldn't make peace with Ethereals. A true Vanguard slaughters his enemies without mercy. You want peace? We'll only have peace when we erase the Ethereal plague from this world!" Vance's maniacal screams followed him down the corridor.

Before the doors closed, Queen Montessa joined her son's cries, "You've made the wrong choice, Rex. Mark my words, you will rue this day!"

Layla

For a trained horsewoman like Layla, traveling by carriage seemed odd, foreign. From the moment she could walk, her adopted parents placed her on horseback, per Vanguard custom. She knew both the gentle gait and the full-out sprint of her filly but not the bouncing wobble of a carriage. The constant jostle added to her unease while thoughts of her family increased her sorrow.

Across from her, Elder Werrick made a show of pretending she wasn't there, so she took the opportunity to assess him. What motivated a man like him? She knew so little about those who lived outside of Vanguard. She eyed him, hoping to gain miraculous insight, but she only saw a squat, grim man. Squished together in the confines of the small rolling cabin, he didn't seem nearly as imposing as he had earlier.

"Do you believe in the Prophecy, my child?" Elder Werrick broke the silence.

Did she believe in the Prophecy? What kind of question was that? She'd heard it preached her whole life. Of course, she believed the Prophecy. Didn't everyone? Even the Ethereals, who disagreed with the Vanguards on everything, believed in the Prophecy. He should have asked whether or not she believed she was the Fulfillment. For that, she would have had an entirely different answer.

"Of course." She held her face tight, revealing nothing.

"Then you must know what a glorious day it is. Most Elders search their whole lives for the Fulfillment without finding her. Whole generations of Ecclesiastics have lived and died never witnessing the promised peace, but today, everything changes. Peace will finally reign between the Vanguards and Ethereals."

He waited for her to respond. When she didn't, he continued, "You are the deliverer. Do you realize how important your role is?"

Layla narrowed her eyes. The more the Elder spoke, the more she discerned his true motivation. Deliverer— so that's what fueled him. If Layla somehow miraculously managed to bring about the long-awaited peace, Elder Werrick would be forever known as the savior who found her. But she couldn't even comprehend how this peace could possibly be engineered. Simply marrying the Ethereal prince—a thought that made her cringe—wouldn't magically bring it about, assuming the Ethereals didn't kill her or drive her mad with their mind games first. She willed herself to calm down. Grant promised her the

Ethereals were not monsters, contrary to what she had always been told. Choosing to believe her brother, Layla took a deep breath to still her anxious mind.

"Elder Werrick, I believe there has been some sort of mistake. As I told you in Medlin, I am no one special. The Prophecy mentions a special blessing from the First Ones. I do not have a gift, so I cannot be the Fulfillment."

Werrick smiled, though his face showed no joy. "Girl, I have spent years studying the Prophecy and the First Ones. Potential candidates have come and gone, seeping like sand through my hands. I would not have chosen you myself, but your mark from the First Ones cannot be denied."

"What mark? I bear no mark." She gestured to her body, emphasizing her point.

The Elder rearranged himself with great care, forcing her to wait for an explanation. "The First Ones have chosen you, and you must walk the path they laid out centuries ago. The answer to peace is somewhere within you. That is all we know and all we need to know…for now."

Did all Ecclesiastics speak in riddles? If Elder Werrick thought she had some great answer to peace within her, he had a terrible disappointment coming. How could she be expected to make decisions to bring about peace between two kingdoms whose inhabitants had hated one another since the time of the First Ones? People, older and smarter than she, had tried and failed for centuries. Did the Elder really believe she possessed some magical power? If he did, she questioned his sanity.

Elder Werrick pulled a small locket from his pocket and held it up with great reverence. Layla twisted her hands together in her lap, understanding this piece of jewelry somehow fit into Werrick's plans.

"This is a binding locket. Do you know what that is?" She shook her head. "This locket will bind you to the Ethereal prince, and he to you. The Prophecy did not explain how your marriage will serve both realms, but we have to have faith that it will. Blessed be the First Ones."

"Blessed be the First Ones." She spoke the words from memory, realizing with a start she'd never even stopped to consider them before today. Who were the First Ones really? She knew so little about them. And right now, exalting them felt false since thousands of years ago, they decreed her marriage to her greatest enemy.

Leaning forward, she took the locket to examine it. The outside of the plain gold heart revealed no secrets while the inside remained empty, nothing special. How could such a small, insignificant piece of jewelry bind her to the Ethereal prince?

Layla took a deep breath. "And if I refuse?"

Elder Werrick's bushy gray eyebrows crinkled. He stared at her with a mix of agitation and condescending amusement. The urge to attack him—a Vanguard instinct—almost overwhelmed her, but she held back. While this man repulsed her, he still had Samson, for the time being at least. She would continue to play along, as Grant had advised, and wait for her moment to seek revenge.

"Refuse? Girl, do you not see the First Ones have chosen you for a duty that no one else can carry out? You are special, blessed beyond measure."

Layla bit her lip to keep from laughing. Her only value lay in her ability to play along with the Elder's ambitions. Didn't he see this charade would only serve to endanger them all?

"What if I don't want to be bound?"

"You have no choice." His clipped tone revealed no compassion.

"It's my life." She would not be forced into a marriage she didn't want nor would she be forced to bear a burden as huge as peace between the Vanguards and Ethereals.

"No, Layla, you are the Fulfillment. Your life is no longer your own. You belong to the First Ones, to the Ethereal prince, but most importantly, to peace." He snatched the locket from her hands.

"I belong to no one."

"We'll see about that." He smirked, further enflaming her anger. "First Ones," Elder Werrick raised his hands above his head, the locket in his right hand. "Thank you for the Fulfillment. We have waited a long time to find her and for the promised peace."

"Wait. Stop. What are you doing?"

Violent opposition bubbled up from within her core. She jumped up to stop him, but the carriage's lurch threw her backward. With a grunt of frustration, she pushed herself back up. The Elder's foot shot out and knocked her down again. Fury coursed through her. Layla summoned up her Vanguard strength. As she went to rise again, heaviness fell upon her. She whipped her head around to locate the source but nothing held her down. The Elder must be the cause, though she didn't understand how.

"With this locket, I bind Layla Givens, the Fulfillment, to the Prince of the Ethereals, and I bind the Prince of the Ethereals to Layla Givens, the Fulfillment."

"No." Layla shrieked. "You can't do this."

The heaviness suddenly lifted. Despite the bouncing carriage, she found her footing and lunged toward him, knocking the locket onto the floor. She retrieved it, hoping to throw the accursed jewelry out the window, but Elder Werrick grabbed her wrist. The mysterious weight crashed upon her again, and Layla dropped to her knees. With a surprised yelp, she loosened her grip. The locket again fell to the carriage floor.

"It's no use, girl." Elder Werrick breathed heavily as he stooped to pick up the golden heart before she could make another attempt. "Even without the locket, the binding would hold." She looked at him skeptically. If the piece of jewelry weren't important, why had he fought so hard for it?

He tucked it inside his tunic with a self-satisfied sneer. "But since you seem to have no reverence for the First Ones or the locket, I will keep it for the time being."

Layla flopped back down into her seat, flustered and angry. Now, on top of everything else, he'd bound her to her mortal enemy. She huffed with indignation at the thought.

"So what does it mean to be bound? Will I fall head over heels in love with this prince the moment I lay eyes on him?" She didn't bother to hide her sarcasm.

A cold, heartless laugh shot out of Elder Werrick. The obnoxious sound rattled around the carriage, hurting her ears and making her even more furious. Once she knew Grant had taken Samson and her parents to a place of safety, Layla prayed she'd get the chance to exact vengeance upon the Elder before she escaped. The idea of his imminent demise almost teased a smile from her lips.

"I do not know for sure. I do know that for now your hearts are joined. You will love one another, maybe not immediately, but definitely in time."

"I should choose whom I love, not be forced. I didn't realize the Ecclesiastics played mind games like the Ethereals. I thought you were neutral."

"If you weren't the Fulfillment, I would slap you, girl."

"And if you didn't have my brother, I would rip this carriage apart and hurl your body all the way to the Outlands." The idea almost made her laugh...almost.

He eyed her, contempt distorting his already ugly face. "You show no regard or respect for my people or the First Ones. I have spent my whole life looking for you, girl. You should be in awe to be chosen."

Crossing her arms, Layla glared at him. She certainly didn't feel awed to be a pawn in the Elder's twisted games. He could continue to delude himself and others, but she wasn't fooled. Werrick cared about himself far more than he cared about the Prophecy or the First Ones.

The carriage jerked to a halt. Layla found herself in Elder Werrick's lap, much to her dismay and his. Elder Werrick threw her off unceremoniously and yanked back the carriage's curtain.

He stuck his head out the window and called out to the driver. "What's happening, Sims?"

Layla pushed back the curtain in front of her window and also looked out. A sea of black robes surrounded them, along with a few escorting Vanguard soldiers given by King Rex. She wished to see Grant's face among them. Though she knew their family needed him more than she did, Layla longed for the comfort of one friendly face.

As a rider approached, the black robes parted. Layla's gaze settled upon the cause—Prince Vance. He rode forward atop his midnight black horse, knocking aside Ecclesiastics blocking his path. She hadn't liked him back at the palace, and she still didn't care for him now. With a sigh, Elder Werrick opened the carriage door and stepped down. He bowed stiffly to Prince Vance and then straightened.

"My prince, to what do we owe the honor of your visit?" Though Layla had only known the Elder for a little while, even she could detect his false homage. Did anyone else notice his insincerity?

"Give me the Fulfillment." Vance spoke with a new air of authority. His haughty demeanor exuded a desperate need for respect and adoration. Layla's lip curled in response.

"But she is meant for Prince Wilhelm. She is to be his bride and usher in peace. I have already completed the binding ceremony…with your father's approval."

"My father is no longer king." Vance's hazel eyes sparkled with a haughty pride.

Layla's mouth flopped open, but she quickly snapped it closed. What did Prince Vance mean? What had happened to King Rex? And selfishly, what did that mean for her?

"My prince?" Elder Werrick appeared as confused as Layla.

"You will address me as King." Vance raised his eyebrows and lowered his chin, almost daring Werrick to challenge him.

"Of course…King Vance." The Elder stumbled over his words. "Please understand that I cannot give you the girl. The Fulfillment is in the care of the Ecclesiastics until she reaches the Ethereal prince. She is promised and bound. We must deliver her."

"She is a Vanguard, and I will not let a Vanguard be given to the Ethereals. Never!" He raised his sword high above his head. Reality squashed Layla's momentary excitement. Part of her would gladly follow the prince— the king, whatever he called himself—back to Vanguard and away from this nightmare, but the other part refused to jeopardize Samson's life. Until she heard from Grant, she needed to play Werrick's game.

The Elder teetered, unsure in a way Layla had not seen. "My king, she is the Fulfillment. It is her destiny, predetermined by the First Ones."

"Save your religious drivel for someone who cares. You will hand over Layla Givens, or I will slaughter every last man here. I brought the full force of the Vanguard army with me, Elder. Your men don't stand a chance against mine and you know it."

Elder Werrick looked pained. Her momentary pleasure, watching the Elder squirm under Vance's unrelenting glare, vanished. Crippling fear took its place. If Vance forced her to return to Vanguard, what would become of her family?

"Stand aside, old man." The prince flicked his wrist while Werrick remained in place, his jaw set. Vance dismounted and shoved the Elder out of the way. In one swift motion, he ripped the carriage door completely off the hinges, and jerked Layla out. She screeched in surprise. Without another word, Vance planted her on the back of his horse, swung up in front, and tore off toward his palace.

"My prince—" Layla gripped him tightly around the waist to keep from falling off the horse.

"King, I'm king now." He hurled the words over his right shoulder.

"My king..." She amended the title, though the words stumbled from her mouth. "Please, the Ecclesiastics have my brother. If I don't cooperate, they will kill him. I have to go back."

Vance laughed—an unpleasant, feminine sound. "You won't have to worry about that for too long." His ominous implication unsettled her.

"Why not?"

Vance glanced back at her, a smirk on his otherwise handsome face. "I plan to kill you."

Layla blinked. Her mind fumbled to comprehend. "Kill me?"

"Pity too because you're an attractive girl, but yes, Layla, I have to kill you."

She wanted to scream or argue, to beg for her life, yet only one word slipped from her mouth. "Why?"

"The Ecclesiastics will rally around you, calling for peace with those immoral Ethereals. I will never make peace with them—never. As long as you are alive, that Elder and his insane Ecclesiastics will push for it, but if I kill you, their cause dies right along with you."

Without taking time to formulate a plan or contemplate her actions, driven solely by all-encompassing terror, Layla released her grip on Vance's waist and rolled off the horse. The ground's jarring impact knocked the breath out of her. Her teeth bit into her tongue so hard she tasted blood. At the same time, excruciating pain shot up her arm. Layla gasped, but she forced her brain to ignore the pain, willing herself to stand.

Using all the strength she could muster, Layla jumped up and took off toward the forest, hoping to find cover amongst the trees and bushes. Blinding pain coursed through her arm, but the thought of stopping and allowing Vance the opportunity to kill her propelled Layla forward. She used her good arm to support the injured one, to stop the terrible jarring sensation that occurred with each step. Hurt and alone, Layla knew she would not be able to outrun Vance and his men. She needed to find a place to hide.

To her relief, she spotted a tangled web of bushes just ahead on her right. Layla gathered all her strength. Just a few more steps...

Without warning, an arm shot out and grabbed her, forcing her to the ground inside a large pile of under-brush. A large hand clapped down on her mouth and prevented her from releasing the scream forming in her throat.

"Be quiet if you want to live," a rough voice murmured.

Unwilling to let another stranger take hold of her fate, Layla used all of her Vanguard strength to lift upward. She believed she could knock off the unsuspecting man despite the use of one arm. To her surprise, he pushed her back down like she weighed nothing, as if her strength meant nothing. Layla's sore arm lay pinned beneath the weight of her body. She whimpered from the sheer agony, tears springing to her eyes.

He must be another Vanguard, she thought. Perhaps he fought on the behalf of King Rex—against Vance. Layla let her body go limp, signaling her surrender. Her imprisoner's arms loosened.

"If I let you go, will you promise not to run or scream?"

His breath, a wave of hot air, tickled her ear. She nodded. He rolled to the side, crouching so he could see, yet not be seen. Layla turned, curious to look upon the face of her captor—or was he her rescuer?

Before she caught a glimpse, he leapt up, sword in hand. She peeked over the nearby bushes to see four Vanguard soldiers look over in surprise. They appeared just as startled by this stranger's presence as Layla had been.

From the back, she saw his dark hair, almost as dark as her own. He stood tall with a surprisingly muscular physique, though not as bulky as most Vanguard men. Her pulse rose.

"Who are you?" a soldier demanded.

"Who am I? Who are you?" His rich, deep cadence pleased her.

"We serve King Vance. Step aside! We are in pursuit of a criminal."

"King Vance? I've never heard of King Vance. I know of Prince Vance and King Rex, but no King Vance."

"Stand aside, sir, or you will be sorry."

"I doubt that," the stranger quipped, "but I do love a good challenge."

Layla watched as her rescuer swung his sword and cut down the two soldiers closest to him. He moved with a speed and grace that most Vanguard soldiers did not possess. Who was he?

The other two soldiers, shocked by his sudden attack, drew their swords and lunged. Despite her hurt arm, Layla leapt up to assist. She kicked the closest soldier with all her might. The force sent him sprawling backward into a massive oak. Layla stumbled as well, using her good arm to break her fall to the ground.

In her periphery, the mysterious stranger averted the third soldier's charge. He stabbed the man straight through the chest with remarkable speed. The final, lone soldier let out a shocked cry. Seeing his comrades dead around him, the final soldier threw down his sword and fled.

"He's no true Vanguard." Layla didn't bother to hide her disdain. "A true Vanguard never runs from a battle."

Her rescuer wiped his forehead and let out a chuckle, though he kept his gaze trained on the other man's retreating form. "And here I thought you actually needed my help."

"I would have fared just fine on my own." She spoke the words with confidence, though only half serious. In truth, Layla needed his help. Her wounded arm made single combat much more difficult.

"I can see that." She noted the half serious, half teasing nature of his remark. "Are you okay? I noticed you holding your arm."

He turned all the way around to face her. Layla raised her eyes to meet his, startled by his handsome features. His piercing green eyes flashed with adrenaline from the fight. To her surprise, his mouth, which had been smirking when he first turned, dropped open. Heat, unfamiliar though not unpleasant, shot through her, warming her cheeks.

"Are you alright?" He asked the question with a newfound tenderness.

She nodded, her sore arm forgotten. "I'll be fine."

"Spoken like a true Vanguard." He laughed. "I think your pursuers are gone for now. Shall we leave before they come looking for you again?"

She nodded a second time. Grinning, he offered his hand, pulling her up off the ground in one swift motion. At his touch, a shock traveled through her fingers, up her arm, and all the way through her whole body. Surprised, they both jerked back. He stared down at his own hand, looking perplexed. He cleared his throat and stared her straight in the eyes.

"I'm Nash."

CHAPTER FOUR

Layla

S he paused, unsure if she should reveal her name. Deciding to trust him—at least with this information—she said, "I'm Layla."

"Well, Layla," Nash drew out the syllables in her name, a grin upon his face, "we'd better hurry."

He placed his hand on the small of Layla's back, guiding her toward his horse. The point of contact tingled, but neither of them moved away this time. Despite his tenderness, he jostled her sore arm, jolting her back into reality. She bit her lip, but a soft cry still escaped.

"I don't think you revealed the true nature of your injury. Let me take a look."

She eyed him, deciding whether or not to trust this stranger who stirred up such unfamiliar feelings inside her. Reluctantly, Layla nodded. Nash touched her arm, sending both pain and pleasure sensations up and down it. His fingers expertly examined the bones from her fingers to her elbow.

In an attempt to distract herself, she studied his face. His green eyes focused on her injury, maybe to catch anything his hands might have missed. His dark brown eyebrows knit together in concentration, much like they had been a moment ago when he helped her up. She responded, on an instinctual level, to his intensity and decided he must be a Vanguard. Since he fought against Vance's men, she concluded he must not be a member of Vance's guard, so who was he? Why did she instinctively trust him when her mind screamed for her to have caution?

"I don't think it's broken. Can you ride?"

"Ye…yes." So caught up in her own thoughts, she barely registered his question.

"Do you need help getting on the horse?" His gaze bounced back and forth between her face and her arm.

"Of course not. I've been riding horses since I was a child."

She shuffled over to the animal and hoisted herself toward the saddle. Without the use of both arms, Layla lost her footing, falling backwards. Nash, who seemed to know she'd fall, caught her in his awaiting arms. She stared intently at her shoes, determined not to meet his gaze and the mirth that most likely resided there.

"Do you need help?" A cough failed to cover his laughter.

Layla flushed. Without a word, she allowed him to lift her into the saddle. He swung up behind her and grabbed the reins. Nash wrapped his free hand tightly around her waist, urging the horse on. She focused on the landscape as it flashed by and ignored the electric undercurrents rolling between them.

"Those men said you were a criminal. What did you do—use that side kick of yours to hurl someone important into a tree?" He laughed at his own joke, his breath tickling her ear.

She ground her teeth. "I'm not a criminal."

"If you say so."

After a moment of silence, she realized he didn't intend to press the issue, though a small part of her wished he would. Layla longed for the ease she had with her brothers, a familiarity that allowed her to explain her situation and receive advice, but Nash wasn't her brother. He was a complete stranger whom she may or may not be able to trust. For all she knew, he could be a criminal himself.

"Are you a criminal?" She smiled even though he could not see her.

"No, I'm not." While she worked to hide her truths, he seemed more than willing to share his.

"Are you a Vanguard?"

With that question, he tensed. "I have no allegiance." The same hard bark he'd used with Vance's soldiers returned. Perhaps she'd been wrong about his openness.

"So, you are an Outlander?" She pressed the point, unwilling to let his vague answer suffice.

If he had no allegiance to Etherea or Vanguard, and did not wear the robes of an Ecclesiastic or Volton, he had to be an Outlander. Only they, who lived well past the Borderlands, held no allegiance to either realm. She frowned. That explanation didn't make sense though. Nash possessed the strength and build of a Vanguard. Not that she knew a great deal about the Outlanders…

"I am no one."

His words eerily mirrored the ones she'd spoken to Elder Werrick earlier. Layla wanted to push him further, but his icy dismissal clearly conveyed his refusal to continue their conversation. They rode for a long time in silence. Layla had no idea where they were. He'd taken her deeper into the forest, far away from the main road. For all she knew, Nash could be kidnapping her, yet she felt safe.

"Where are you taking me?" She turned slightly, keeping her balance on the saddle, to catch a glimpse of his face.

"Where you seemed to be headed before Prince Vance attacked you…to the river that borders Vanguard and Etherea." His green eyes radiated truth.

Relief flooded through her as she turned back toward the front. Even though she'd rather pluck her eyes out than meet her mortal enemy turned betrothed, Layla had to protect Samson. She had to go to Etherea and play the role of the Fulfillment for just a little bit longer.

"So you know who I am then." She said it as a statement, rather than a question.

"Should I?"

"I am no one." Risking his wrath, she imitated his earlier inflection.

To her surprise, his laughter rang out heartily. She found herself smiling in response.

"I think we're far enough away now." Nash yanked back on the reins to slow his horse. "We'll stop for a bite to eat."

Without giving her a chance to protest, he helped her off the horse and settled her against a tree. He pulled two apples from his saddlebag and handed one to Layla. She devoured it.

"Slow down." Nash chuckled softly. "You'll get a stomachache. I have more food if you need it."

She grasped for an explanation, juice running down her chin. "It's just that I haven't eaten in a while."

He rummaged around in his bag again and came up with a large chunk of bread and wedge of cheese. She accepted them with a sheepish but grateful grin. Halfway through the bread, she stopped and, remembering her manners, offered him a piece.

"Thank you, but you can have it. You seem to need it more than I do." He finished off his apple, stood, and wiped his hands on his pants. "I'm going to go find some sticks to make a splint for your arm."

"But…" Layla hesitated. If he left, she would be alone, in an unfamiliar part of the world with Prince Vance and his men in pursuit.

"I promise not to go far." Her face grew warm at his attempt to reassure her. She hated to seem weak or helpless. "If anyone comes, kick them in that direction." He pointed to a more densely wooded area, stifling a smile. She stuck out her tongue, but her lips turned up into a wide grin.

Nash returned just as Layla finished the wedge of cheese. Careful not to further injure her arm, Nash guided it, with exquisite care, to rest on his leg. The buzz between them rattled her sore bone painfully, but she held still to avoid interfering with his work.

"I need something to hold the sticks in place." He looked around but shook his head, indicating that nothing around them would suffice.

Shrugging, Nash ripped off the sleeve of his shirt to reveal his taut biceps. Layla's eyes widened, but she looked away before he could see her expression. Nash, seemingly oblivious, placed the sticks underneath her arm and lightly wrapped them. He worked with great efficiency. She watched with fascination.

"There." He grinned. "That should hold for now."

"Thank you."

He laughed, soft and quiet, different from his loud, boisterous one. "You have leaves in your hair."

Nash leaned forward to brush them out. At this distance, she could smell him, apple combined with woods. A strange hitch emanated from her throat.

Time froze. Her purple eyes locked with his green ones. Nash lifted his shaking hand to touch a strand of her hair while his other one rose to softly cup the side of her face. With a start, Layla realized she actually wanted him to kiss her. He leaned in, and for a moment, she let herself believe they were the only two people in the world.

Just before their lips met, a high-pitched wailing pierced the air. Nash jumped back, grabbing his ears.

Layla slammed her hands over her own ears, sending pain ricocheting through her arm, but nothing blocked out the horrible sound.

"What is that?" she screamed in agony.

"Ethereal defenses!" Nash yelled back to her, no more than a whisper compared to the penetrating blast.

Layla fell on her side, desperate to stop the invasive noise. Not very far away, Nash writhed in pain. She reached out her uninjured arm to grab onto his hand.

"Nash."

He turned toward her, anguish in his eyes, and extended his own hand. Just as the tips of his fingers made contact with hers, she lost consciousness.

CHAPTER FIVE

Layla

Layla bolted up. Bewildered, she looked around, trying to assess her surroundings as quickly as possible. She sat in a massive bed, surrounded by opulent yellow coverings inside one of the biggest rooms she'd ever seen. Ornate curtains, a charming combination of red and yellow, lined a whole wall of windows, which had been drawn to block the light as she slept. Braided Day of Dawning ribbons hung around the room. Braided? Vanguards didn't braid their ribbons. Where was she?

Layla racked her brain, remembering Nash and the earsplitting pain. Nash. Where was he? She hoped that he'd managed to escape somehow, though she couldn't imagine how anyone could move with that horrible sound invading every crevice of the body.

As she pushed off the covers, pain shot through her arm. Layla glanced down and noticed that Nash's carefully made splint had been replaced by a real bandage, tightly wrapped. Further inspection of her body revealed she'd been washed and redressed. Layla flushed wondering who had been the one to clean and clothe her. Upon finishing the scan of her physical condition, her gaze landed on a young woman sleeping on a chair in the farthest corner of the room.

Layla cleared her throat. The startled young woman jumped up and then fell back into the chair, dazed. She stood again, regained her footing, and shuffled toward the bed. Layla's mind, still a bit foggy, began slowly putting the pieces together. The alarm—Nash called it "the Ethereal defense system." She must be in Etherea.

On Vanguard instinct, Layla's good arm shot out and caught the other girl, who'd dared to approach the bed, around the throat. The Ethereal's brown eyes widened, distorting her attractive face. She grabbed at Layla's hands but proved to be no match for the much stronger Vanguard.

"Please, stop," the girl choked out the words, rasping.

"Where am I?" Layla squeezed tighter. "Where is Elder Werrick?"

While the thought of seeing that man again repulsed her, Werrick still had Samson. Until she heard from Grant, Layla planned to stick with the Elder for better or worse. The Ethereal flailed around as her breath slowly seeped out of her body. Deep inside, Layla knew she should let the girl go, yet the Vanguard drive to eliminate all Ethereals proved quite consuming.

Just as the other girl's eyes started to close, she wheezed, "Please, I know Grant…"

Layla jerked back her hand. The Ethereal fell to the ground, clawing at her throat and gasping for air. Layla jumped up, lording over the fallen girl. She hauled her up, placing the blonde in a seated position on the bed.

"What did you just say?" Layla searched the other girl's face, hunting for signs of dishonesty. "Is this some Ethereal mind trick?"

"No trick." The words sounded strained.

"How do you know about Grant?"

The girl looked up at Layla with soulful brown eyes. In them, Layla saw the same expression she'd seen in Grant's at the Day of Dawning festival. His secret love… an Ethereal. No wonder he'd never brought her home. It all made sense and also explained why he'd been so adamant that the Ethereals were not as Layla had always believed.

"You're his girlfriend." Layla slumped in shock. A good Vanguard always maintained alertness, but in the face of such shocking information, she dropped her guard.

"I'm Vespa. And yes, I love your brother."

"First Ones." Layla cursed her ancient forbearers for their twisted humor.

She eyed Vespa critically. With her long flowing blond hair and friendly brown eyes, Vespa appeared both beautiful and innocent. Her fancy gown spoke of high birth, perhaps even royalty. Had she been the one to care for Layla at the behest of the royal family, or had she volunteered out of love for Grant? Though the girl seemed kind enough, Layla still couldn't understand how her brother met and fell in love with the enemy.

"I'm sorry I startled you earlier." Vespa's hand touched her throat, her fingers fluttering along the angry, red spot Layla left there. "We thought you would be arriving with the Ecclesiastics. Otherwise, we never would have sounded the alarm."

"Where is the Elder?" Layla asked.

"He arrived late last night."

"Does he know I'm here?"

"Yes." Vespa nodded. "He seemed relieved."

Layla returned the nod, relieved herself. For now at least, Samson wouldn't be harmed by the Ecclesiastics. She just hoped he would escape before she actually had to marry the Ethereal prince.

As she stared at Vespa, Layla again wondered if the girl had used a mind trick to make her believe the wild claims about Grant. She couldn't wrap her brain around the idea of a Vanguard soldier falling in love with an Ethereal highborn. Perhaps just the close proximity to Ethereals drove people insane. Not knowing which thoughts belonged to her and which Vespa had planted made Layla's head spin. She ground her teeth and squeezed her eyes shut against the onslaught.

"I'm not Altering your mind if that's what you're wondering." Layla's eyes flew open, thrown off by Vespa's intuitive statement.

"How did you know I was thinking that?" The question flew out with more harshness than Layla intended. "Are Ethereals mind readers too?"

Vespa, despite their unease with one another, laughed. "No. I can tell by the look on your face, Layla. You look like you can't decide whether you want to believe me or kill me."

The corner of Layla's mouth turned up in amusement, though she quickly rearranged her face to hide it. She still didn't know Vespa or trust her. A good Vanguard remained alert at all times, especially in the lair of the enemy.

"So, you don't believe me about Grant." Her brown eyes regarded Layla with curiosity and weariness.

"No, I don't."

"Well, whether or not you believe me, I ask that you keep this information to yourself, if not for my sake then your brother's. I only told you because I thought you were going to kill me. I wanted to Alter your mind to make you stop, but I promised Grant I wouldn't use my powers against you."

"You spoke to my brother recently?" Vespa's assentation drew in Layla despite herself.

"I saw him briefly. He asked me to look after you."

Layla sorted through the information to catch any hint of deception. While Vespa kept her tale cryptic, Layla heard Grant's personality in the retelling. He would ask Vespa to take care of Layla, and he would insist she refrain from using Alterations.

"What about our parents? Did he mention them?"

"He said they are being taken to a safe place, where the Ecclesiastics cannot reach them. When he left, Grant said he planned to head toward the Ecclesiastical compound to intercept the carriage holding your other brother. I'm sorry, but that's all I know."

Layla swallowed hard, making a noise. Vespa knew a great deal about their family and about the dangers they faced. Perhaps she did know Grant and had secured his affections. After all, this scenario lined up with his unusual behavior. She had never known her brother to be imprudent, but his attraction could have overwhelmed his better senses. Nash's face flashed across her mind. She flushed, recalling how she'd almost let a complete stranger kiss her.

"So, you really are the Fulfillment? Grant told me the measures your family took to keep you hidden from the Ecclesiastics." When Layla didn't reply, Vespa continued, "And you're here to marry our Prince Wilhelm."

"Forgive me, but I can't say I'm thrilled to marry my enemy."

"I'd forgotten how much you Vanguards loathe us." Vespa stood, her back straight and proud.

Layla grinned, appreciating Vespa's moxie. In the face of an enemy with superior strength, without the ability to defend herself using Alterations, the Ethereal still stood her ground. Layla respected that.

"How did you hurt your arm?" Vespa tried again.

"I jumped off the back of Prince Vance's horse."

"You did what?" Vespa's brown eyes widened in amazement and a grin of surprise lit up her face. Though she tried not to, Layla smiled in return, understanding how this girl managed to bewitch her brother.

"He said he'd kill me, so I just jumped."

"He said what?" The smile disappeared off Vespa's face. "That's a personal affront to Prince Wilhelm, Layla. You are to be his bride. You are bound to him. For Prince Vance to threaten you is an act of war." Vespa stood and shook her small fists. "No one threatens my family."

Layla raised her eyebrow, confused. "Your family?"

"Of course, I'm Princess Vespa, Wil's sister."

"You're who?" Layla's brain spun to process how her brother, a lowly Vanguard solider, had secured the affections of the Ethereal princess. This whole time, she'd assumed Vespa came from good breeding but would never have guessed her true station.

Her emotions swirled. Anger—Vance's actions were an affront to Prince Wilhelm, what about the affront to Layla herself? Dismay—Wilhelm's bride, bound to an Ethereal. Kinship—like Layla, Vespa appeared fiercely protective of her family. Worry—how would Vance's choices impact her brothers? Bewilderment—her first conversation with an Ethereal and she'd already managed to stir up more trouble between the two sides... some Fulfillment she was turning out to be.

A soft knock on the door pulled Layla from her thoughts. She glanced at Vespa, who regally called for the person to enter.

A small mousy woman spoke from the doorway. "My lady Vespa, the king bid me to check upon the Fulfillment."

"She is awake." Vespa gestured toward Layla.

"Very good. The king and prince wish to see her." The servant backed out of the doorway, her wide eyes never leaving Layla.

"Tell my father and brother we won't be long."

Layla clenched her fists; an instinctive desire to protect herself coursed through her veins. The king? The prince? What if they didn't believe in the Prophecy? Would they kill her, or would they return her to Prince Vance, who would most certainly kill her? Or, equally as dismal, what if they forced her to fulfill her duties and go through with marriage to Wilhelm?

Chapter Six

Wil

Prince Wilhelm paced back and forth in the audience chamber, unable to reign in his anxiety. He glanced at his father, King Jesper, who sighed audibly. The prince knew his father hated when Wil paced, but today he couldn't sit still. Today, he would meet her...his bride. Of course, he'd already seen her briefly—when he and his soldiers came across her unconscious body—but he would officially meet her in just a few moments.

Since he was a child, Wil had been taught all about the Vanguards' barbaric, war-mongering ways. He had expected to find a feral, half-crazed warrior woman outside his gates, yet Layla had looked so small and fragile lying there on the forest floor...

Wil pivoted and strode in the other direction, a prisoner to his thoughts. Everything had happened so suddenly and he hadn't had a chance to process it all. The Prophecy required him to marry a Vanguard...a Vanguard.

Wil shook his head, glancing toward the door. He half expected his bride to come barreling through it, slicing up guards along the way. Now that Layla had rested and received medical attention, he worried her true savage nature would emerge. The Elder insisted she fulfilled the requirements of the Prophecy, but Wil remained skeptical. He sighed in frustration. How could he be expected to marry a Vanguard? And if he did, how would that usher in any sort of peace? Wil swallowed with great difficulty—the pressure of their union and what it could mean for their two nations choked his throat like a hangman's noose.

According to Elder Werrick, Prince Vance disposed of his own father over the ordeal. Wil had heard the stories of how rash and brazen Vance could be. In fact, his own father often worried about the day King Rex died, leaving Vance in control of Vanguard. Without his father to control him, the new King Vance surely planned to wage a relentless war against the Ethereals. Peace had never seemed less likely.

When his father rose, Wil dragged his attention away from his brooding thoughts and directed them to the audience chamber door. He sucked in a breath and let it back out slowly as he moved toward the throne to take his expected place at his father's left hand. Elder Werrick led the procession, followed by Wil's sister, Vespa. With so many people standing in front of her, he couldn't even catch a glimpse of his future bride.

Elder Werrick introduced the girl with great pomp, unexpected since the girl's blood contained no royal heritage. "King Jesper, I am pleased to announce I found the long awaited Fulfillment."

The Ecclesiastic bowed, not quite low enough for proper respect. Jesper glanced at Wil and shook his head. Wil knew his father believed in the Prophecy and the work of the Ecclesiastics, to a point, but the king barely tolerated Elder Werrick. In Wil's estimation, his father showed good judgment being wary of the man. There *was* something strange about him.

Wil sat up a little straighter in his seat, hoping to catch sight of Layla, but she too bowed before the throne—down to her knees in a gesture of full respect. Her dark hair swirled from the top of her head all the way to the floor, obscuring her face. Wil drew in a surprised breath. She had approached the throne without incident and bowed low before the king. Already she surprised him.

The Elder continued speaking, "My king, allow me to present, Layla Givens, the Fulfillment."

Werrick gestured grandly behind him. Vespa stepped aside. From his seat, Wil peered down with great interest.

"My king." Her whisper carried an intriguing melody. "My prince."

The young woman lowered herself again. When she rose, her purple gaze landed on Wil. He sucked in a sharp breath. Her exquisite beauty, combined with her calm demeanor, shocked him to the core of his being. She'd only been here for moments yet had already managed to astonish him.

Wil stood abruptly, alarmed by the force of his re-action to Layla. He walked toward her, entranced. Her purple eyes studied him. Never before had he seen eyes that color. And her long, silky black hair…he had to clasp his hands behind his back just to keep from reaching out to touch it. He knew better than to underestimate her strength—for all Vanguards possessed impressive might—yet his tall frame dwarfed her tiny build. She barely came up to his shoulder.

"My prince." She lowered her gaze as he approached.

"Call me Wil." He longed to place a finger under her chin, to lift her head until he could again stare into those unusual eyes.

"Wil." She repeated the word, trying it out. He smiled, liking the sound of his name upon her lips. "I am Layla."

"Layla." He spoke her name out loud for the first time. An unexpected bolt of pleasure coursed through his body.

Elder Werrick bustled toward them. He placed one hand on Wil's shoulder and the other on Layla's to move them closer together. A strange buzzing emanated from the Elder, sending a shock wave down Wil's arm. He stepped to the side, just out of Elder Werrick's reach, as the older man spoke. "King Jesper, they appear to get along beautifully. When shall we have the wedding? Tomorrow?"

Wil whirled around to face his father. While he found Layla alluring, Wil wasn't prepared to connect his life, his future, and his kingdom to a stranger. He may not be king yet, but he still had to consider his people when making major decisions. His father's steely blue gaze briefly brushed over Wil and Layla before landing upon the Elder.

"Let's not be hasty, Elder. There is time. Peace has waited centuries...what's a little longer?" Wil detected the simmering anger behind Jesper's words. He knew his father did not agree with this marriage, despite the king's touted belief in the Prophecy, and hoped to delay it long enough to figure out a way to extract them all from the arrangement.

"With all due respect to your position as king, I must insist they marry immediately." Werrick's sneer contradicted his words.

Wil noticed a side door open. Relief flowed through him when Volton Mars, his longtime tutor and friend, joined them. At the sight of the Volton, Elder Werrick recoiled. Bad blood ran between the men, though Mars had never told Wil the reason.

"Werrick, still forcing your will on others, I see." Volton Mars moved a few steps closer to Wil, his gaze trained upon the Elder.

"Mars, still injecting yourself where you aren't needed, I see." Werrick regarded the other man with clear loathing.

Though the two men stood apart, their mutual tension and disgust permeated the whole room. Wil made a mental note to get the full story from Mars in the future. From the corner of his eye, the prince saw Layla observing the men with similar fascination. Her purple eyes glittered.

"King Jesper is right. There is no need to push these two into marriage just yet. If they are to bring about your supposed peace, let them do so as friends as well as spouses." Mars walked to Wil's side in a show of solidarity.

The Elder's face turned bright red. "For centuries, we have been waiting upon the Fulfillment. Now that she has been found, you would prevent the Prophecy from finally coming true? That's blasphemous."

"And speaking against the king is treasonous." Jesper stood, his posture full of warning. "I do not take treason lightly, Elder Werrick. You will obey my order, or you will leave Etherea and take your Vanguard girl with you. If you expect me to marry off my heir to one of Rex's subjects just because you say so, then you're more obtuse than I thought."

"Obtuse." Elder Werrick huffed. "I'm the Elder of the Ecclesiastics, practically a king in my own right."

"Then go back to the Borderlands." Jesper pointed to the door, his face red with rage. "But if you plan to stay in my kingdom to ensure the Prophecy, you will do so in obedience to me."

Beside Wil, Layla let out a small snort of laughter. His own lips turned up in response. Elder Werrick looked around the room, making eye contact with each person. Sighing, the portly man turned back to the king.

"I need to stay in Etherea and oversee the marriage of Wilhelm and the Fulfillment."

"Layla," Wil interjected. "Her name is Layla." He glimpsed her smile.

Werrick pursed his lips together, displeasure written all over his face. "I will obey your commands, King Jesper. Please let me know when you wish to proceed with the wedding."

The Elder turned and walked out the door, his robes flapping wildly behind him.

Vespa piped in, "Father, shouldn't we retire to the dining area? Mother has been ordering the servants around all day in preparation for our first dinner with the Fulfill…" She glanced at Wil. "Layla."

"We should." Jesper rose.

Wil stood close enough to touch Layla yet kept his hands down. "May I escort you to dinner?"

She lowered her eyes again, a faint flush tinting her cheeks. "Yes, thank you."

He started to offer his arm, an Ethereal custom, but decided against it. While he knew a great deal about the Vanguard leadership and military, he knew little of Vanguard courtesy customs. He fell in step beside Layla rather than risk offending, frightening, or enraging her. If his future bride noticed his internal deliberation, she acted like she didn't. They strolled toward the dining room in companionable silence.

Vespa hurried ahead to walk with her father, giving Wil and Layla their privacy. Suddenly alone with her, his tongue ensnared his speech, yet at the same time, he wanted to impress her. Surely she had preconceived notions about him and his people, just as he had of her. If they did marry and had to work together to bring about peace, those prejudices would have to be addressed, the myths dispelled, but Wil was at a loss for how to make that happen.

He started with a safe topic. "I'm sorry your journey was so arduous."

"Thank you."

He wanted her to say more. Despite her short reply, Wil pressed forward, attempting to draw her out. "I hope you will be happy here. I know our two sides have been at odds for...well, forever." He laughed, a strangled, nervous sound. "But maybe we can come to know one another and work toward peace."

She gazed up at him, her face curious. His pulse quickened. Though he'd seen his share of beautiful women, none struck him as Layla did. She had the Vanguard fierceness—he saw it blazing in her eyes and in the way she set her chin—yet he did not see the volatility he'd been told resided in her people.

"So, do you mean to play tricks with my mind?" Whether she was joking or serious, her face gave no indication.

He stifled a laugh, reminding himself that she did not understand their laws or customs, which forbade unprovoked Alterations. "No, I will not enter your mind without your permission nor will any member of my family or realm. Serious harm will come to anyone who tries. You have my word."

Her shoulders relaxed, and they shared a tentative smile. Could some bond actually be forged between them that just might save both of their kingdoms? Her presence encouraged him to envision it.

"So, are you planning to beat me up?" Wil grinned to show his jest, hoping his teasing did not offend her.

"I thought about it." She paused and cocked her head, her purple eyes sparkling. "But I decided to spare you for now."

His laughter echoed down the hallway reaching far enough to garner the attention of his father and sister, who turned back. After a moment's hesitation, Layla joined him. His heart lightened.

CHAPTER SEVEN

Layla

Once they reached the dining room, Vespa guided Layla to a seat right beside Prince Wilhelm. *Wil*, Layla reminded herself, testing it out. Like his sister, Wil wasn't at all as she expected. Of course, she still didn't know if she could trust her own mind's interpretation of events. She hadn't yet ruled out the possibility that Wil, Vespa, or King Jesper somehow altered her perception.

Wil took his place beside her. Their eyes met, and he smiled. She returned it, their moment in the hallway still lingering between them.

His features pleased her eye far more than she expected. Like Vespa, he had dazzlingly blond hair, but unlike his sister, Wil's eyes blazed a shockingly deep, yet bright, shade of blue. When he looked away, she took the opportunity to study his profile. He had a strong, chiseled jaw, and lips that appeared ready to smile at any moment. He turned and caught her staring—at his lips no less. Her face grew warm. She knew her cheeks flamed a mortifying shade of pink.

The king took his seat. Layla noticed two open spots: one across from her, near Vespa, and the other beside King Jesper. Layla assumed one belonged to the queen, but who would sit in the final chair? Elder Werrick? If so, Layla would most certainly lose her appetite. She'd seen more than enough of the pushy Ecclesiastic and looked forward to a long reprieve from him.

On cue, the queen bustled into the room. She, too, sported bright blond hair, though she kept hers swept up in a tight bun on the top of her head. Her observant brown eyes fell immediately upon Layla. The Vanguard sat still, bearing the other woman's intense scrutiny without flinching. They faced off silently, each assessing the other. Though the queen had a large smile on her lovely face, her eyes conveyed suspicion. Layla swallowed hard. Maybe Vespa and Wil didn't plan to rearrange Layla's mind, but she believed the queen would be perfectly willing.

Wil cleared his throat. "Mother, you've created a lovely meal for our new guest. Allow me to introduce Layla Givens. Layla, this is my mother, Queen Sansolena."

Layla broke gaze with the queen. When Wil winked, she realized he'd sensed her discomfort and sought to alleviate it. She nodded at him to convey her gratitude. The queen's eyes narrowed, but she quickly recovered.

"Welcome, Layla. I apologize for not being in the audience room to greet you, but my presence was required elsewhere."

Layla met the queen's eyes again. She wanted the Ethereal to know she would not back down. "My queen, I am honored to meet you."

"Where is that no good son of ours?" King Jesper interrupted. "I'm hungry, and I know you," he looked pointedly at the queen, "won't let us eat without him."

"He'll be here any moment." The queen's cheek twitched, but her smile remained plastered to her face.

Layla believed the queen hid exasperation behind that mask, though with the king or with this other son, she couldn't determine. As a Vanguard from a remote, small town, she knew very little about the Ethereal royal family, so the revelation of a second brother surprised her. She leaned in closer to Wil.

"You have a brother?" Layla hoped only Wil could hear her.

"Yes, he's eleven months older than me."

"Older? Forgive me, Prince Wilhelm…"

"Wil, please call me Wil."

"Forgive me, Wil, but I thought the eldest son became king."

Wil glanced toward her and then looked down at the table, but not before she caught the reluctance in his blue eyes. Layla's interest piqued. Perhaps she could use any discord in the royal family to her advantage when the time came to make her escape. Guilt rocked her for plotting against Wil, who seemed nice enough, but her loyalty lay with her family, not him.

"My brother abdicated, released his birthright. He told my father he had no desire to be king, so I will take the throne one day."

King Jesper, who previously gave no indication he'd been listening, leaned forward, his mouth twisted in anger. "And we're all the better for it." The queen shot her husband a reproachful look. He grinned at her, shrugging his shoulders. "It's true, Sansolena. We all know it."

The dining room door flung open, and a young man hauled himself in boorishly. Despite his dramatic entrance, he made a leisurely approach to the table, which left King Jesper seething in his seat. Layla studied the king's reaction with great interest before turning back to the newcomer. While he remained too far in the shadows for Layla to clearly see his face, she guessed he must be the eldest son. The firstborn prince tossed an object into the sky and caught it. His lackadaisical attitude continued to hold up dinner, but he did not increase his pace. Something about the way he walked caught Layla's attention. It seemed vaguely familiar…

"Finally." The king spoke with great agitation. "Sit down so we can eat."

"I can't believe you used the alarms on me today, Father."

That voice! Layla froze. She became so still Wil looked over at her, his eyes wide with concern, but she couldn't make herself move. She knew that voice.

Will smiled. "Layla, I'd like to introduce my brother."

The newcomer stepped into the light, his whole face illuminated. Layla sucked in a sharp breath. That dark hair, those piercing green eyes…she knew that face.

"Nash," Wil finished.

Layla pushed the food around on her plate, unable to imagine forcing the meal into her tangled stomach. Nash—an Ethereal? Nash—Wil's brother? She could hardly come to grips with the idea. How could this be? Nash told her he had no allegiance, yet he was the son of King Jesper. Father and son did not seem to be on friendly terms, and according to Wil, Nash abdicated the throne. Still, Layla couldn't shake the notion that he'd lied to her in the forest—maybe not directly but by not revealing this pertinent information.

She tried not to glare at him from across the table, yet found her gaze wandering his way. For his part, Nash stared at his plate. He never once lifted his head. She wondered what he thought as he studied the peas in front of him with such intensity. Despite the revelation of his parentage and her anger over his purposeful omission, Layla still felt drawn to him in ways that angered, annoyed, and intrigued her.

Wil leaned over, his blue eyes searching. "Are you not hungry?"

Guilt pricked her. Wil did seem kind, yet she couldn't allow herself to become emotionally connected to him… or his brother. Remaining detached and waiting for Grant's signal took priority over any other feelings she may have. Sneaking a peek at Nash, Layla found him studying her interaction with Wil, an unidentifiable expression on his face. Why had he chosen this moment to finally look up from his food? She flushed and turned her head away, feeling her resolve slip. *Samson, Samson,* she repeated her imprisoned brother's name over and over to center herself.

"I…" Layla fumbled. Wil still awaited an answer beside her. "I need to be excused."

She jumped up from the table. If she stayed in that room with Nash for one second more, Layla might be tempted to call him out for his deception…either that or throttle him. Each choice held its own appeal. No one at the table spoke to grant her permission to leave, so she pushed open the dining room door and walked out.

"…typical Vanguard impulsiveness." She heard the king disparage her just as the door closed.

Further enraged, Layla raced down the hallways, veering left and right, completely lost. Hurt, angry, and confused, she pressed herself against a wall and slid down until her bottom touched the floor. She buried her head in her hands. The Elder ruined her life with his ridiculous proclamation. She was not the Fulfillment.

At the sound of footsteps, Layla jerked her head up. She jumped to her feet, crouching in a defensive pose. A Vanguard should always be alert, never found in a compromising position. To her surprise, Nash barreled around the corner, nearly crashing into her.

"What are you doing here?" His inquiry, a mix between question and accusation, carried down the hallway.

"What am I doing here? What are *you* doing here?" Layla spoke louder to match his pitch.

"I live here." He gestured to the floor with one hand and the ceiling with the other. His blasé demeanor infuriated her. Last time they spoke, he conveniently left out his paternity, so how could she have known he lived here—in the castle, as a *prince*?

Her ire rose. "I thought you had no allegiance."

Nash turned away. He dug his hands in his hair. "It's complicated."

"Yeah, well it's complicated for me too."

They stood in awkward silence for a while. "What happened in the forest, Nash? How did you get away?"

"The Ethereal defense horns sounded when we came into range. It's my fault. I let myself get distracted, and I didn't realize we'd gotten close enough to be spotted by the Ethereal lookout." His green eyes held an apology. "I'm sorry, Layla. The horns aren't lethal, but they certainly make you feel like you're dying."

She recalled the horrible sound permeating the air, surrounding and engulfing her with its deafening noise. "Yes, they do, but you still didn't tell me how you got away." In the forest, she had refrained from pushing him about his fealty, but she wouldn't let him get away without answering her questions now.

"I crawled far enough away from you before my brother and his soldiers came. That's no small feat, I assure you." He looked pleased with himself. "No one knows we were together in the forest." She breathed a sigh of relief. "Your turn, Layla. Tell me why my family is treating a Vanguard like an honored guest."

"You don't know?"

"I wouldn't ask you if I did."

Nash caught one of her locks in his finger and twirled it. The same magnetic trill that electrified them in the woods flowed from her hair into his fingers and back again. He moved toward her slowly. She backed up against the wall. As she had earlier, Layla focused on her reason for being in Etherea, to remain detached, but she struggled in the face of their mutual attraction. When Nash lowered his mouth toward hers, she reached deep inside to find the strength to stop him when she wanted nothing more than to connect.

"Stop." She pushed the word out with great effort though it sounded as soft as a whisper. "I can't."

"Why not? You didn't seem resistant to kissing me in the woods." Confusion on his face altered, but did not detract from, his handsome features. To emphasize his point, Nash pressed his lips lightly against her cheek. She almost faltered.

"I know, Nash, but that was before."

"Before what?" His questioning gaze searched her face and then realization dawned on him. "I see. You mean before Wil."

Nash pushed off the wall. His green eyes, which had been so soft and caring in the forest, now shined brightly with warring emotions. She cringed, an uncommon Vanguard reaction.

"Elder Werrick believes I am the Fulfillment." The words rushed out of her. "He bound me to your brother. I am to be his bride."

Nash backed away, horrified. Before she could stay her hand, Layla reached out to touch him, but he deftly avoided the contact. He jerked his head in a curt nod, though she couldn't read his expression.

Layla shoved down the sadness flooding through her. She needed to keep him at bay. The more she pushed everyone away, the easier it would be to leave. Her focus must remain on her family, not on the Prophecy or these Ethereals.

Layla turned and prepared to run even though she didn't know the way back to her room. She would rather spend the night lost in the hallways of the castle, taking her chances with random Ethereals and their powers of Alteration, than stand here with Nash for one more agonizing moment. Anger—at herself, at him, at the whole situation—welled up inside of her.

As she turned to go, he grabbed her arm, and despite everything, her body responded. She yearned for his kiss, could almost taste it. Nash's strength, his intensity, appealed to her Vanguard nature, adding potency to their already inexplicable chemistry. Guilt stabbed her, surprising in its ferocity. *Samson...*

Layla yanked herself away before he had the chance to speak. She didn't dare meet Nash's eye but turned instead on her heels. Running like her life depended on it, she fled until her feet could carry her no more. Layla threw open the first door she came to, slammed it shut, and collapsed onto the floor.

Wil

T hough Wil wanted to follow Layla out the door the moment she leapt up, he stayed in place. She clearly desired privacy, and if he were honest, he couldn't imagine how hard it must be for her here. If the Elder had dragged him from his home, placing him at the table with his mortal enemy, Wil had no idea how he would react. He knew for sure he would miss his family, particularly his siblings. Did Layla even have siblings? He knew so little about her…

King Jesper droned on, reiterating his opposition to Wil's potential marriage and hashing out different scenarios to avoid it. The prince remained rooted to his chair, even after Vespa and Nash left, but he couldn't stand it a moment longer.

Wil stood. "Father, I must retire."

"We have important business to discuss, Wil." Jesper's blond eyebrows shot up, his surprise over being interrupted evident.

"Yes, son, you are the future king. Stay and listen to your father." His mother gave him a look he couldn't quite decipher.

Exasperated, Wil simply walked out. His father's angry tirade stalked him down the hall. He'd shocked himself by leaving the room, his father in mid-sentence. He almost never disobeyed his parents. In their eyes, he and his siblings had clearly established roles—Nash the hellion, Vespa the angel, and Wil the honorable—but tonight, he'd challenged that position. What had overcome him?

At the end of a long hall, Wil spotted Nash staring forlornly down a different corridor. None of the rooms on that wing—their father's office, the library, and the schoolroom—typically held Nash's attention. Yet, his brother's eyes remained fixed.

"Brother?" Wil's mind spun as he attempted to understand Nash's odd behavior. His older brother had walked out on dinner, not long after Layla, but Nash often shunned time with their father. Why then had he come here, to this particular part of the castle, when his bedroom sat a good three halls to the right?

Nash turned to face Wil with wild eyes. "Wil." He sounded nonchalant, but his face betrayed the veneer.

"Is something the matter?" Wil frowned.

"I hear congratulations are in order. You are to be married."

Wil arched an eyebrow. "Not if Father has his way."

Nash snorted. "Father always thinks he knows best. Maybe in this case he does, brother. A Vanguard on the Ethereal throne...it would never work."

Nash's troubled eyes betrayed his light tone. Wil could not understand what would be bothering his brother. Though they would lay down their lives for one another without a second thought, they often had trouble relating—thanks to their father, their personality differences, or a combination of both.

Was it the throne? Did Nash regret his abdication? If so, Wil didn't understand. Nash had never shown any interest in succeeding their father.

"You chose to give up the throne." Wil heard the strain in his own intonation. They never talked about this topic.

Nash nodded. "And I'd choose it again. If you're looking for Layla, she went down that corridor toward the library." He pointed to the left.

Wil hesitated, wanting to say more, but gave up. "Thanks, Nash." He took off down the hall, leaving his brother sulking behind him.

▽▽▽▽

Wil pushed open the library door. In the corner of the room, Layla sat against a bookcase, periodically banging the back of her head on it while muttering to herself. Though he found the behavior odd, Wil headed toward her, undeterred.

"Layla?" His heart pounded so hard he could feel it like a drum in his throat. "Are you okay?"

"Do I look okay?"

The heat of her anger washed over him. Surprised, he backed up. She'd held herself together well in the throne room and dining room, but now Wil wondered if he would finally see her wild Vanguard nature. He turned to leave.

"I'm sorry."

She sounded so vulnerable. He stopped in his tracks. Standing rigidly, with one ear cocked just in case she planned to attack, he waited to see if she'd say anything else.

"I don't know what I'm doing, Wil."

He pivoted to find Layla with her head in her hands. Moved, Wil sat beside her, careful not to touch her and potentially damage their fragile truce. Layla ran her hands aggressively through her hair. He didn't under-stand the behavior. Did she hope the act could dislodge whatever unpleasantness lived in her head?

"I don't know what I'm doing either." The words tumbled out. She smiled. Encouraged, Wil decided to divulge more. "To tell the truth, I'm stuck between the Prophecy and my father."

"What do you mean?"

He adjusted himself so he could see her eyes and gauge her reaction. "With the Prophecy, do you feel a certain re-sponsibility?"

She raised an eyebrow, though her eyes revealed little. "I am not the Fulfillment."

"But what if you are?"

"I'm not." Her purple eyes sparkled with resolve. "I understand your dilemma. You would feel a responsibility to bring about the will of the First Ones…if I were the Fulfillment, which I'm not."

He smiled with relief. She had somehow managed to find understanding amidst his ramblings. "Yes, but my father is doing everything he can to thwart this marriage."

"He is?" This time, Layla looked shocked but pleased. A brief pang of disappointment jolted Wil. He shouldn't care, yet he did. "Do you think your father will succeed?"

"I've never known him to back down when he really wants something."

A dreamy look crossed her face. "If he does succeed, I could go home."

Wil shifted, moving just a little closer to her. "Did you leave someone special behind?" He almost didn't ask, but his curiosity overrode his better judgment.

For a long time, Layla didn't answer. She stared at the bookcase across from them for so long Wil thought she might not answer. "No. I just miss my family."

He nodded, identifying with that notion. "I would miss my family too. Do you have siblings?"

"Yes, two adopted brothers—Grant and Samson." Her voice hitched when she said Samson's name. Wil wondered why but feared alienating her by asking.

"Will you tell me about your family, about your people?" He'd always been interested in the Vanguards and the Outlanders. Despite Volton Mars' lessons, he understood little about them.

"No."

The slightly hostile and extremely resolute expression on her face struck a humorous nerve within Wil, and he burst out laughing. Layla whipped her head around, glaring at him, but after a moment, she joined in his laughter. He liked the pleasant nature of her laughter.

"Do you want to tell me about Etherea?" She raised an eyebrow, her eyes challenging him.

"Sure." He shrugged. "I have nothing to hide."

"Really? You'd tell me just like that? I could be a Vanguard spy for all you know."

Wil nodded his assent. "You could be." He grinned. She returned it.

"Okay, Wil, tell me about the Ethereal people."

"What do you want know?"

"Everything."

He laughed. "Could you be a little more specific?"

The teasing look melted off her face, replaced with seriousness. "You and your bro..." Her hesitation piqued Wil's curiosity. "You and your family seem to have heard of a binding, yet I never had until Elder Werrick told me today in the carriage. Why is that?"

Wil started to press her, to ask why she'd almost said the word "brother," but he decided against it. He returned his thoughts to her question instead. "Volton Mars told us all about the Prophecy, the Ecclesiastics, and the binding. As sons of the king, Nash and I knew we could potentially be called upon to marry the Fulfillment."

"But what is the binding? It's not mentioned in the Prophecy, so why did Werrick perform it?"

Wil settled against the bookshelf. "According to legend, Ecclesiastics used to bind all couples before marriage in an elaborate pre-wedding ceremony. Over time though, more and more people elected to not be bound, and the practice faded into near oblivion. I'm not sure why the Elder bound us."

He watched her turn the information over in her mind. Dawning briefly crossed her face, but she elected not to share. Wil continued to study her with fascination.

"Can the binding be undone?"

"I don't know. I'm not sure it's ever been attempted, but if there is a way, my father will find it."

She bit her lip in concentration. "Tell me about the mind control. Vanguards believe Ethereals drive people mad with their mind games."

He wrinkled his brow, disturbed that she believed his people capable of such atrocities. "We do have the ability to influence thoughts and memories, called Alterations, but we have many laws governing it. In Etherea, a person can only perform an Alteration with permission. There are a few exceptions, though. Alterations can be performed by a parent on a child or by a king on his subjects without permission."

"So parents can Alter their children's minds for any reason."

"Technically yes, but Alterations are rarely performed under any circumstances."

"You do use them to fight." He detected no hostility in her statement.

"Yes, we use them in battle against your people. Since you Vanguards have superior strength, we have to take advantage of our unique abilities in order to compensate."

"Have you performed Alterations?" She sounded curious, but he caught a hint of apprehension.

He hesitated for a moment. "Yes, I practiced them as a child for training, and now I use my abilities, when necessary, in battle."

Layla nodded. The look on her face told him she accepted his part in their war without judgment. If she had his ability and could use it to protect her family, Wil instinctively knew she would.

"I struggle with it sometimes." He surprised himself by admitting to her this shame he'd never revealed out loud.

Layla's eyes widened. "You do? In Vanguard, we pretty much believe Ethereals are soulless."

"Soulless." He repeated the word, turning it over and over in his mind. "I can assure you, Alterations present a moral dilemma for the Ethereal people, which is why we have so many laws governing them."

"I didn't mean *you* were soulless." She pushed a section of hair from her face, revealing a slightly pink flush on her cheeks.

"I know." He knew, but it still stung. "I think entering people's minds without their permission constitutes a violation of dignity. A person's thoughts and ideas should remain his own, yet I am charged with defending my family and my kingdom. I will do whatever I have to do to protect them."

"As you should." She paused for a moment, biting her bottom lip. "How does it work in war? I've heard stories in Vanguard, but as we've both discovered, our respective groups hold many misconceptions about one another."

"True. Well, the best way I can explain it is that we make your soldiers see things that aren't there. Terrible things, truly awful things. Listen, Layla, I'm not proud of it, but it's the only weapon we have. Your people are superior in every other way. We would be slaughtered if we didn't use our abilities."

"How do you make sure your own soldiers aren't affected?"

"We try to concentrate on specific minds, but that doesn't always work. So, all Ethereals are taught at a very young age how to protect their minds against Alterations. Only parents and the king can override a personal mind guard."

"The king." She repeated, though it sounded more ominous coming out of her mouth.

"Yes."

"So, when you are king, you will have the power to override anyone's mind whether or not they guard it?"

"I could but hope I never have to."

CHAPTER NINE

Nash

Nash leapt out of the bed, unable to spend any more time staring into the darkness. Restlessness, not an uncommon mood for him, consumed him, but for a different reason than usual. Tonight, he couldn't stop thinking about Layla. He'd met her only the day before yet experienced a strong, unexplainable pull toward her. It didn't even make sense then, and it especially didn't make sense now that he knew Elder Werrick had bound her to Wil.

Bound to Wil…he banged his fist against the wall in frustration. Everything always came down to Wil. As much as he loved his brother, Nash's jealousy tainted their relationship. Wil had the one thing Nash had always wanted but could never get: their father's approval. And now, he wanted something else—no, someone else—that also belonged to his brother.

With a sigh, he headed out into the hallway. His feet carried him straight to Layla's door, lured there by the possibility of interacting with her again. He knocked softly.

"Layla?" Nash kept his pitch low but called with enough volume for her to hear.

No reply. He knocked again and said her name a little louder. Still nothing. Against his better judgment, he cracked open the door. Her made bed told him she wasn't in it and hadn't been at all tonight.

The library—the place he'd last seen her go. He would start there. Nash tore off down the hallway, already anticipating another delicious verbal assault from the alluring Vanguard. He wondered again how this girl, one he barely knew, enchanted him so.

His hand trembling from the excitement of the chase, Nash reached for the doorknob to the library. Laughter from inside stopped him cold. He recognized the male voice. Wil. Nash tasted the bitter but familiar flavor of disappointment on his tongue.

Unable to resist, Nash eased open the door, just wide enough to see inside. A knot of anger and jealousy twisted up inside him. Layla, as beautiful as the first moment he saw her, sat on the floor beside his brother, so close they almost touched. Their former unease appeared to be waning in favor of a tentative friendship.

Nash knew he should let it go. If his father somehow failed to block the marriage, Layla would become his brother's wife, and truth be told, she would be better off with him. Destiny, and their father, had chosen Wil as

king—a great king at that. He held the love and adoration of the whole kingdom, and Layla also would as his
queen. If Nash really cared about her, which he oddly
did, and if he really cared about Wil, which he always
had, he would just let it go. And yet...

"Nash." A whisper from down the hall sent him reeling back.

He nearly lost his footing, mortified to be caught spy-
ing. If anyone asked about his unusual interest in Layla,
Nash's answers could land them both in trouble. Besides,
he couldn't explain something he didn't even understand.

His brain registered the singsong vocal quality, and he
relaxed. "Vespa?" Nash squinted in the dimly lit hallway.
Almost all of the candles in the corridor had been left to
burn down to paltry stumps. Where were the servants
who kept the lights going?

"Shhh." His sister pointed a finger toward the library.
"Wil is in there...with her."

"I know, but what are you doing here?"

"I could ask you the same thing." She yanked a strand
of blond hair over her ear, her brown eyes challenging
him to a verbal spar.

He chose to lie instead of engage her. "I'm looking for
Wil."

Thankfully, the darkness kept his face hidden because
Vespa always seemed to catch him in his lies. He'd have
to be especially careful around Layla with his observant
sister watching. She looked sweet and innocent—and in
many ways, she was—but Vespa also knew how to ferret
out even the most obscure information.

"He's in there with Layla. Don't disturb them now, brother. They both seem to be getting used to one another and this crazy notion that they will bring about peace together."

"Oh come on, Vespa. We both know Father will never let that happen." His bitterness rang clear, and he clamped his mouth shut in frustration.

Vespa narrowed her eyes, studying him with renewed interest. Nash tried not to move his facial features, and after a moment, she dropped her gaze.

"I'm not sure if Father will be able to stop this marriage, Nash."

"Why? What do you know?"

Vespa looked away, tucking her golden strands behind her ear for the second time—a nervous habit. Why would she be nervous? Nash, now even more curious, discerned information from her face despite the darkened hall, but something in her hair caught his attention.

"Wait, why do you have leaves in your hair, Vespa?"

She blushed so brightly that he could see it even in the diminished light. Her hands rose to push back her hair yet again, though it had not moved since the last time she touched it. It heightened his curiosity, and a hint of worry snaked up his spine.

"Please don't ask me that, Nash." She implored him, a hint of desperation in her plea.

"Are you in trouble?"

"No, nothing like that. I don't want to lie to you, though, so please just don't ask me."

As much as he wanted to push Vespa for an answer, Nash relented. They were all entitled to their secrets… he had his.

His mind wandered, remembering how Layla's purple eyes flashed at him in the hallway. Nash had never met anyone like her. He admired the fighter inside her—her fierceness, her passion.

"I'll walk you to your room." He placed a hand on the small of Vespa's back, guiding her forward. "A princess shouldn't be wandering the halls alone at night."

Vespa smiled gratefully and relaxed her shoulders. She removed his hand from her back, folded it across his chest, and tucked her arm in his. He stifled an exasperated big brother sigh. She had always loved to be paraded around, even as a toddler.

"Nash, why were you outside the gates in the forest today?" His stomach dropped, but he kept walking without breaking stride.

"You know I have to get away from this place sometimes. I go to the woods, to the Vanguard side, where no one knows me. It's peaceful there."

"Aren't you afraid the Vanguards will kill you?"

She sounded so concerned. He couldn't help but smile, pleased that someone worried about him. So many times he felt completely alone in this castle, in this family. Without Vespa and Wil, he would be.

"I look like a Vanguard with this dark hair." He gestured to his head with his free hand. "No one ever bothers me."

"I wish I could get away from here sometimes too." Vespa sighed. "I'd be spotted immediately with my bright blond hair though."

"In an instant." Nash laughed.

"Did you go to get away from Father?" She sounded sad. As her big brother, he hated to see her upset and, even worse, be the cause of it.

"Yes." At the mere thought of his father, Nash's good mood disappeared.

"Maybe if you tried harder..."

"Tried harder to what? Make him proud? Make him look upon me with anything but contempt? He never will, Vespa. I've tried and tried to please him until I'm just tired of trying anymore. He's hated me since the day I was born, and he always will. I just...I just wish I knew why."

Vespa patted his hand sweetly. "Well, I love you and am proud of you, big brother. What's Father's problem anyway?" She laughed, trying to lighten the mood. Nash smiled in spite of himself.

"Here we are." Nash stopped in front of his sister's room. "You'd better make sure you get all those leaves out of your hair before someone else sees you."

"Thank you, Nash." She smiled up at him with solemn brown eyes.

"Anytime."

"No, thank you for not pushing me to tell you where I've been."

"We all have our secrets, baby sister."

CHAPTER TEN

Layla

Layla rolled over and groaned, trying in vain to block out the bright sun streaming through her open curtain. Since she'd been up half the night talking with Wil, she'd gotten a woefully insufficient amount of sleep. Exasperated, she flung the covers over her head and buried herself deeper into the bed.

"You need to get up, sleepy head." Vespa's energetic melody implied cheeriness incongruent with Layla's level of fatigue.

She peeked out of the covers and sighed. "Did you open my window and wake me up?"

"Yes, I did."

"Go away." Though Layla conveyed annoyance, Vespa simply laughed.

"I think you'll want to hear what I have to say, Layla."

At that, Layla jumped up. Her head spun with the sudden motion, but she ignored the sensation and focused instead on the Ethereal princess. "What do you mean? Did you see—"

"Shhh."

Vespa leapt toward the door, taking an inordinate amount of care closing it and ensuring the lock. At the maddeningly slow pace, a scream welled up inside Layla, but she held it down. She understood the need for secrecy. They both needed to safeguard Vespa's rendezvous with Grant. If anyone ever found out, all three of them could be in serious trouble.

Layla waited for Vespa to perch herself on the other side of the bed. "Well? Did you see Grant?"

"Yes, last night."

The questions burst out. "What did he say? How are my parents? Is Samson safe? Is Prince Vance still in charge of the kingdom and bent on killing me?"

Vespa smoothed her dress, her calm annoying in the face of Layla's frenzy. "You aren't going to like what he had to say, Layla."

With that simple phrase, the blood rushed to the top of her head, threatening to erupt. Immediately she thought of Samson. Had he been killed in his escape attempt? Had the bash on her mother's head proven fatal?

"Tell me." The command escaped in a strangled squeak.

"I'll start with the good news. Your parents are in a safe place, and your brother has successfully escaped from the Ecclesiastics."

Relief flooded through Layla. "That's wonderful. I can leave and join them then. This nightmare might finally be over."

"Well, that's the bad news." Vespa sighed, fidgeting. "Grant says you have to stay here."

"What?" Layla could barely contain her outrage. "I can't stay here. The longer I'm here, the greater the chance Wil and I are forced to marry."

Vespa's brown eyes sparkled. "Would that be so bad?"

"Yes." Regretting her waspishness, Layla softened her voice. "Neither of us wants to marry."

The princess let out a strange cluck but said nothing. Layla scowled even deeper. Stay? Had Grant lost his mind? Or were he and Vespa so taken with one another that they believed in forcing relationships on others? Either way, now that she knew the Elders no longer held Samson hostage, Layla planned to escape—with or without Grant's help.

"Grant said you would be resistant, and I can see he was right. Listen, Layla, the Ecclesiastics have been busy proclaiming your name all over the three kingdoms and throughout the Borderlands. They've even forced artists to work around the clock drawing pictures of you for distribution."

"How? I haven't posed for any pictures."

"We all know the Elder has his mysterious ways. The point is Werrick has ensured you will be found should you try to run. And if you go back to Vanguard, Prince Vance will kill you in spectacular fashion, simply to make a point to us and the Ecclesiastics. You have to stay here to protect yourself and your family. If you go to them, you will put them at risk too. Think, Layla. You know what I'm saying makes sense."

Furious, Layla squeezed a fistful of bed sheets to prevent herself from lashing out. She wanted to tear this room apart, stone by stone, but it wouldn't change anything. Grant and Vespa were right. While he held Samson captive, the Elder worked hard to guarantee Layla remained a captive too. Perhaps he even knew Samson would escape. After all, Werrick had sent her brother off with no guards. The man always seemed to be two steps ahead. She growled in frustration.

The two young women sat in silence while Layla worked to calm the furious beating of her heart. Vespa fidgeted at the end of the bed, starting to speak then closing her mouth before anything escaped. Her eyes sorrowful, the princess placed her hand on top of Layla's in an unexpected gesture of friendship. Layla's grip on the bed sheets loosened.

"Would you like a tour of the castle and surrounding grounds?" Vespa's lips pulled up into a tentative smile.

Layla didn't bother to hide her bitterness. "If my brother is right, I suppose I should get to know my new home."

Vespa smiled broadly, ignoring Layla's peevishness. "Let's go."

Layla squinted in the sunlight. Vespa, with a mysterious air, marched purposefully forward while Layla languished behind. The distance between them gave her a brief reprieve to come to terms with her predicament. Since the moment she arrived, she believed her time in Etherea would be limited, but now her assumption appeared erroneous. Rage rose within her, directed mostly at Elder Werrick. She wished she could have just ten minutes to wipe the smug smile off his round face.

Vespa slowed, waiting while Layla caught up. "So, what do you think of my home?"

"I like it very much."

All morning they'd travelled around the castle, visiting many of the shops set up within the safety of the palace walls. Vespa promised to show Layla all of Etherea one day, once the threat from Vance diminished. Despite her initial reservations about living in her enemy's territory, Layla had to admit the Ethereal's beauty took her breath away. Whereas the Vanguard valued function over style, the Ethereals seemed to enjoy a little of both. Most buildings mixed operation with elegant design. She liked the aesthetics of Etherea even more than her own home country.

Though the Ethereals they encountered regarded her with interest, no one expressed any hostility. Their behavior surprised Layla. If an Ethereal like Vespa walked down a street in Vanguard, especially so close to the king's palace, the Vanguard people would respond. However, the Ethereals' reaction forced Layla to reevaluate her lifelong perception of these people. Had everything she'd been taught been wrong?

"So, where are we going now, Vespa?"

"I'm taking you to the legendary West Wall."

"The maze?" Layla stumbled a bit, surprised to be taken to such a secret location. Was Vespa even allowed to show her—a Vanguard—such a mysterious Ethereal landmark?

"You've heard of it then?" Vespa's eyes sparkled mischievously.

Layla wondered again if they should even be here. "All Vanguards know of the West Wall Maze. It's completely impenetrable."

Vespa nodded. "Three hundred years ago, the Ethereal king, Crazy Clovis, grew bored Altering minds the traditional way and decided to create the ultimate mind trick. He spent the next twenty-five years of his life overseeing the most complicated maze ever constructed. Oh, Volton Mars would be so proud if he could hear me right now. He always says I don't listen to his history lessons." She smiled broadly, lighting up her whole face.

"No Vanguard has ever successfully navigated the whole thing." Layla recalled her own history lessons.

"Correct. Early on, Vanguards attempted but got stuck inside the walls and were easily apprehended."

"If it's so difficult to get around, how did the Ethereal guards inside manage to get the Vanguards back out?"

"A soldier stands atop the wall." She pointed up. Layla placed a hand above her eyebrows to block out the sun and allowed her gaze to follow Vespa's finger. "One soldier directs the other using hand signals. *Supposedly* no one has the maze completely mapped—not even the guards in charge of its defense."

"Supposedly?" Layla echoed.

"I may know three people who can find their way in and out." Vespa smiled conspiratorially.

Layla ventured a guess. "You, Wil, and Nash?"

"We played in here all the time as children. Since this section of the castle is deemed secure, the guards only check it twice a day, and there are no defensive horns on this side of the wall. My brothers and I mapped out the whole maze, including the secondary maze of bushes at the end."

"Can you show me how?"

"You want to be the first Vanguard to traverse Clovis' maze? That crazy king might come back from the place of the First Ones and kill me where I stand if I show you his secrets."

"Is that a yes?" Layla laughed.

Sighing for emphasis with a self-satisfied smirk gracing her face, Vespa motioned Layla forward. The path, which had been cobblestone before, transformed into a white stone walkway yellowed with age. Around them, ecru walls emerged, tall and lurking, until they could see nothing else. Layla squinted. The light walls magnified the sun's strength.

Vespa weaved expertly through the complicated corridors. When they neared what Layla assumed to be the end of the maze, the princess changed course, dragging them backward almost to the very beginning. They twisted and turned until Layla's sense of direction and balance disappeared, leaving her lost and dizzy.

"Is this how you escape to meet my brother?"

Vespa looked back. "Yes."

"And it's how Nash moves between Etherea and Vanguard with ease."

"Mmmm-hmmm."

After a perplexing array of identical passageways, the girls finally emerged from the white walls into yet another set of winding walks, this one created out of tall hedges.

"I am beginning to see why no Vanguard has ever been able to make it through."

"It's not difficult once you know your way." Vespa tossed her golden hair over her shoulder just as flippantly as she dismissed Layla's remark.

Layla heard the sound of the River Lars, which separated the Ethereal and Vanguard borders. "We must be nearing the end."

"We are."

They emerged from the rows of bushes. After such a long journey, Layla expected some sort of magical oasis but found a long stretch of grass that led to the river instead. She frowned.

"That's it? I expected something more."

Vespa laughed. "This speck of land isn't the prize, Layla. It's the freedom—from our father, from our roles, from our regular lives."

Freedom. She longed for the illusive sentiment. If she could find a way to free herself, Layla knew she would take it without hesitation. Her baffling attraction to Nash and her budding friendships with Vespa and Wil were simply not enough to keep her here. But she also knew true freedom no longer existed for her anywhere. Her life lay before her, scripted by someone else—bound to the Ethereals, anointed by the Ecclesiastics, and hunted by her own kind. She had nowhere else to be but here, no true freedom within Etherea or Vanguard.

"Vespa?" a male called from across the river.

The princess squeaked in surprise while Layla reached instinctively for a sword but came up empty-handed. King Jesper didn't trust her enough to allow her a weapon, and, even if she did have one, the Ethereal dress she now wore wouldn't hold it.

"Wil?" The princess bent down low, keeping quiet as she peered into the foliage. "What are you doing here?"

Wil emerged from a tangle of bushes on the Vanguard side. After wading through the waist-high water, he crawled up the bank to stand with them. Layla studied her feet with sudden interest. Though she had spent a good portion of her night talking to the prince, his presence, now that she knew she had to stay and may have to marry him, unsettled her.

"I'm looking for Nash. What are you two doing here?"

"I showed Layla the maze." Layla heard the pout in Vespa's reply, a response to Wil's reprimand. As a younger sister herself, she understood the dynamic.

Her half-grin vanished when a chill spread through her body, leaving the hairs on her arms standing at attention. Layla's head snapped up. She scanned the shoreline; something felt wrong.

"You think Nash is out here?"

"I think so." His face drew up in concern. "Why?"

"All of King Jesper's children are currently outside the castle walls, beyond the reach of functioning defense horns, and without guards. It's a perfect ambush situation. We need to leave." Layla grabbed Vespa's arm and motion for Wil to follow.

"No Vanguards ever come here." Despite the disagreement written all over his face, he trotted behind her. "After numerous failed attempts, your people gave up."

"Something is wrong, Wil. Trust me."

Vespa clucked dismissively. "You Vanguards are always—"

The sound of beating hooves, approaching at breakneck speed, stopped the princess in midsentence. Wil and Layla's eyes met as they registered the situation. A group of Vanguard soldiers approached, swords drawn.

"Vanguards have not been seen on the west side of the wall in over a hundred years. What are they doing here?" Wil whispered the words mostly to himself. He yanked his head around to face his sister, dawning befalling his features. "Vespa, take Layla back through the maze. Hurry!"

"Come with us." Vespa blinked back her tears, quaking. "I don't want to leave you."

Wil shook his head. "We can't engage these Vanguards inside the maze. I'll fend them off while you two escape. Once you reach the castle, send help."

Vespa lifted her skirts and bolted toward the maze. "I'll get help, Wil."

Layla did not follow. "I'm not leaving. I can fight, Wil. I'm a trained fighter."

"But you're injured," He furrowed his brow. She watched his internal struggle play out across his face. "Please, go with Vespa."

"I am a capable fighter with or without injury."

"I know you are. It's just…"

"Just what?" Her pent up anxiety exploded.

Wil opened his mouth but closed it with a snap. Layla gritted her teeth. They didn't have time to continue this argument. If he would just give her the knife she knew he kept in his boot or the sword at his hip, she could help him fight.

"I'll have to perform an Alteration, Layla, and I don't want you to see that or be caught up in it." Remembering their conversation from the previous night, she softened. Layla knew how much he regretted being forced to use Alterations, and how much he wished to hide that part of himself from her. But if they were to be married, she needed to see every facet of his personality—especially the ability he both admired and loathed.

"Maybe they know we are here and maybe they don't, but those soldiers have obviously come to Etherea to kill people. Your people, Wil. As their prince, their future king, you must do what you have to do to protect them. Don't worry about me. I can take care of myself."

She nodded encouragingly. He smiled, though she still read concern on his face.

"You take my sword then." He sounded less like the Wil she had begun to know and more like the commander of an army. "Defend yourself until I have their minds under control. I'll try not to Alter yours, but I can't promise you won't be caught up in what I do. If you still have possession of your own mind once I've started the Alteration, run as far as you can from here." She nodded. "You're under my protection now. I can't let anything happen to you."

"Nothing will happen to me."

Wil glanced toward Layla once more. She gave him a confident nod. His eyes narrowed, centering on the approaching soldiers. An unexpected bolt of fear shot through Layla. She had never seen an Alteration before.

The first rider threw himself off his horse as soon as he crossed the river, landing right on top of Layla. She grunted angrily as the breath flew out of her lungs.

"Layla!" The splashing Vanguard horses muffled Wil's cry. She fought while noting how many soldiers made landfall.

"Focus on the Alteration. I'm fine!" She yelled back at him, hoping he heard her. Layla blocked her attacker's attempt to grab hold of her throat.

She struggled to get out from underneath the man's weight. Layla's injured arm hurt more than she cared to admit, but she refused to let it be the death of her. With all her might, she kicked out her legs. The man flew off of her. She jumped up, placing a sword through his stomach.

A second soldier on horseback grabbed her by the hair. She bellowed in pain. Careful not to drop the sword, she reached up to dislodge her hair from his grasp. Layla ran along beside the horse so she didn't dangle, but her feet barely touched the ground. Pain exploded from the tips of each individual strand of hair. Panicked, she wiggled violently and considered slicing off that portion of her hair with her sword. Only sheer vanity belayed her hand.

Layla heard another horse approaching. Terror ran through her. She could easily be gutted in this position, but lifting the sword proved challenging. She attempted to turn her head to see who charged her way, but it refused to budge. Panic seized her.

Suddenly, the soldier holding Layla released her. She fell to the ground, landing on top of her injured arm while her good arm flailed to the side to prevent the sword she held from stabbing her.

"Layla!"

"Nash?" She looked up to find him riding horseback, sword in hand. He'd just struck down her assailant, now lying in a bloody heap a few feet away.

"Swing up." Nash held out his hand.

She gripped the sword using the hand of her hurt arm. Ignoring the pain, she grabbed onto Nash with her good one. Those strange yet familiar vibrations passed from her body to his. Once settled, Layla clutched his waist to let him know she was ready, and he spurred the horse forward. As they passed by, she saw Wil, with Vespa beside him. When had Vespa entered the fray? Wil's ripped clothing and bloody face drew her attention, flooding her with fear.

"Wil's hurt." Layla called into Nash's ear. He didn't respond.

"Wilhelm?" Nash's question hung between the brothers despite the battle raging around them.

"Get Layla out of here! You know where to take her." Wil shouted as Nash's horse passed by. The future king's eyes never left the Vanguard soldiers.

"What about Wil and Vespa?" She squeezed Nash's waist, willing him to answer.

"They'll be fine," Nash added over his shoulder. "She can assist him with the Alteration; they're stronger together. If you worry about anyone, worry about your Vanguard soldiers. They don't know what horror is about to hit them with the combined minds of those two."

She shuddered. Fighting in hand-to- hand combat or with swords, she understood, but the mind games, she did not.

As Nash's horse leapt over the bushes, Layla heard ear-piercing screams. Her blood chilled with the terrified wails...the sounds of sheer horror. She pressed her face against Nash's back to shut out the distressing melody.

▽▽▽▽

Layla gripped Nash's waist even tighter as they galloped alongside the castle wall. Images of Wil, bloodied and torn, refused to leave her mind. The very idea of Vespa, so young and sweet, battling seasoned warriors turned her stomach.

"We have to go back."

"We can't," Nash said. "You don't know how to put up a mind guard, and you might accidently get caught up in the Alteration. Wil told me to get you to safety. He'd Alter *my* mind if I brought you back."

Layla recoiled at the thought of being trapped in the Alteration she'd just heard. Those men's screams continued to reverberate around in her mind. Wil had waited, fought off a superior power at his own risk, to avoid unintentionally involving her in the Alteration.

She choked back unexpected tears.

"They could die."

"They won't." Nash's body had remained alert and rigid the whole ride. Though he appeared confident, she knew he worried about Wil and Vespa too.

Anger, a much more suitable Vanguard emotion, forced its way to the surface, knocking the worry and tears back. "I'm a strong fighter. You didn't have to haul me away, Nash."

"I have no doubt you could have single-handedly fought off that Vanguard attack." She couldn't see his face to determine whether or not he meant those words. Was he teasing her or being serious? Layla gritted her teeth.

"I would have gotten free of the horseman without your help. I was just about to cut off my hair."

"Now that would have been a shame." She heard his grin. He took a deep breath and said, "Layla, I have no doubt you could have freed yourself." His hand covered hers, his thumb tracing the edges of hers. She knew he spoke the truth, and his sincerity touched her. "Look, whether we want to be or not, we're all caught up in this mess together. We have to work together, so you have to let me..." He hesitated. "Let us fight with you, for you."

Layla slumped back in shock, her grip loosening a bit around his waist, though their hands remained together. "Thank you, Nash."

Buzzing trailed up her arm. Dismissing this electricity between them grew harder and harder. After a moment, he dropped her hand. Her fingers still pulsed with phantom aftershocks.

Atop the wall, a group of soldiers shouted down at them. Layla's back stiffened. Did those soldiers mean to fight their own prince? A small whine split the air as they started the defensive horns. When Nash looked up, the soldiers reared back.

"Prince Nash?" One man leaned over the side, his face white. He whirled around to face his comrades. "Stop the horns!"

Nash waved his arm to again garner their attention. "Get to the West Wall. A group of Vanguards are attacking the prince and princess. One of you stay behind to open Holden's gate."

"Right away, Prince." The soldiers shuffled into action, bumping into one another in their haste.

Nash yanked on the reins and the horse skidded to a stop. A small gate opened. Spurring the horse forward, Nash propelled them on. Layla looked around. Though Vespa had taken her on a tour earlier, she didn't recognize this particular part of the castle.

"So, where are we going?"

"The palace has a series of underground tunnels. Wil, Vespa, and I discovered them when we were children. Several of the tunnels had been abandoned for decades, so we claimed them for ourselves. I'm taking you there. No one but Wil, Vespa, or Volton Mars will be able to find us."

"Do you trust the Volton?"

Nash didn't hesitate. "With my life."

A tingling started at her bellybutton, traveled up her chest, and spread to the top of her head, stinging her ears. They would be alone together in abandoned tunnels, hidden. The notion both terrified and elated her. A moment later, guilt, her constant companion, resurfaced and knocked the other two emotions away. Wil and Vespa fought out there, for her. Wil—her future husband if the Elder got his way.

"We're here." Nash pulled the horse to stop and jumped down. "Slide down quickly."

Once she rolled off into Nash's waiting arms, he slapped the back of his steed. The horse sped away. Nash grabbed Layla's uninjured arm and led her along. When they reached the castle wall, she saw no entrance. Nash groped along the stones. They appeared solid, yet when he touched the eighth one, the wall opened. Layla gasped in surprise.

Nash motioned toward the opening. "Get in."

She stepped inside while he pulled the heavy stone door closed, plunging them in darkness. He fumbled for her hand. When their fingers met, she saw an actual spark.

"Follow me."

He led her through a series of dizzying twists and turns. Layla clutched his hand tightly, afraid to be left behind. She would certainly never find her way out of this place alone. A few mind-boggling turns later, Nash stopped so abruptly that she bumped into him. When she pitched forward, Nash caught her. He sucked in a sharp breath as his lips brushed against her forehead. Her cheeks grew warm, and she suddenly appreciated the darkness. Nash cleared his throat and stepped back. His absence affected her just as profoundly as his presence.

"We're here. Stay put. I'll find some light."

The door creaked. He let out a curse as he stumbled over something on the floor. Layla suppressed a nervous laugh. She heard him strike a match and then brilliant light flooded out from the room. Squinting, she struggled to adjust to the sudden influx of light.

"Come in."

Layla shivered with an anticipation she couldn't pinpoint as she stepped through the doorway. She found an unexpectedly cozy little room hidden away in the underbelly of the castle. As she scanned the room, she noted a small table with four chairs, a large stash of food sitting on top of a drawer, and...a bed. Layla averted her gaze. A familiar burning started at her neck and rose all the way to the top of her head until warmth consumed her entire face.

She moved toward the table and sat in one of the chairs. Nash did the same. For a while, they avoided eye contact in awkward silence. Layla fought the urge to close the space between them, to complete the kiss they'd started in the forest. She didn't understand her unusual, almost unnatural, connection to Nash. As much as she wanted to surrender, she resisted.

Layla tried not to think about Wil and Vespa fighting down by the river, but the image invaded her mind anyway. She ground her teeth. Turning to Nash, Layla came up with something to take her mind off the fighting… and off his inviting lips.

"Why did you abdicate the throne?"

Nash shifted uncomfortably. "I didn't."

"But Wil said—"

"That's the official story. I'm not even sure Wil knows the truth, but I didn't give up the throne. My father took it from me. He said I had a choice: I could surrender the throne to Wil or be banished forever."

She gasped. "But why?"

"My father hates me. He always has." Pain flooded his eyes.

"Why?"

"I don't know for sure. I mean, I know he's disappointed that I'm not blond like most Ethereals. He hates that I can't perform an Alteration like Wil and Vespa, and he resents my unexplainable strength. My whole life, my father has been suspicious and uneasy around me. It's almost like he thinks my mother pulled me out of the River Lars and passed me off as their child." He laughed bitterly. "Who knows…maybe she did."

Without thinking, she reached across the table and placed her hand over his. Energy flowed between them, creating an audible hum in the air. Nash drew in a quick breath. Seeing the effect she'd had, Layla pulled back, but he closed his hand around hers. She stared at their clasped hands.

Her heart broke for him. "I'm sorry about your father. If he can't see how special you are, then he's a fool." Nash may have been a renegade, but she'd also seen how fierce, caring, and loyal he could be, no matter how hard he attempted to hide it. If she had noticed those traits in their short time together, how had his own father, who'd had a lifetime with Nash, missed it?

He lifted his eyes to hers, a smile playing on his lips. "Thank you." He dropped his gaze to the table as the smile slid off his face. "I fear my father has reason to doubt me."

"What do you mean?"

"I think I may have led those soldiers to the West Wall today. I put all of you in danger with my reckless behavior." His voice broke on the words. "I had to get away from the palace. They must have spotted me then followed me back. I'm usually so careful. I'm not sure how I missed them—"

"Stop." He lifted his head at her sharp command. When their eyes connected, she let her gaze drop to the table, embarrassed by the strong emotion permeating from within her. "There must be another reason. Don't blame yourself, Nash." She spoke to him, though her words hit the table.

"Why do you see the good in me when I've given you no reason to do so?"

Layla looked up to find him examining her. His imploring green gaze bore into her, almost like he could see straight into her core if she let him. When he stood, the breath rushed out of her lungs. Nash came around the table and lifted her gently out of her seat. She didn't fight him. Layla looked down, conflicted, but he lifted her chin. Without breaking eye contact, he lowered his lips to hers.

Instantly, her body reacted. She melded into him, pulling him closer. When he moaned, her whole body blazed to life in a way it never had. She couldn't seem to get close enough to him. He must have felt the same way because he wrapped his arms around her and pressed their bodies together, as close as they could get. All thoughts left her mind, leaving only Nash, all-consuming.

Abruptly, he stepped back, creating distance between them, until he stood a full arm's length away. He focused on the ground for a heartbeat. When he finally looked up, his green eyes burned with regret.

"I'm sorry, Layla." His words sounded strangled.

She stared at him, too dazed to respond. He clawed his fingers through his hair in agitation.

"I never should have kissed you. When I tried earlier, in the woods, I didn't know who you were, but now I do. It's inexcusable. I won't do it again."

Nash's face swirled with a mixture of desire, self-loathing, and frustration. Layla wanted to reach out to him, but she didn't, afraid of what might happen between them if she did. Though their attraction made no sense, she couldn't deny its power. She stepped back to create even more space between them. Behind her, the door flew open. Vespa fell through the entrance, an injured Wil weighing her down.

CHAPTER ELEVEN

Layla

After ushering Nash and Vespa out at Wil's behest, Layla closed the door. The hustle and bustle of moving Wil from the tunnels to his bedroom had left her little time to dwell on what happened with Nash, but now, those stolen moments flooded back with vividness. Layla turned to face her betrothed, pressing the palms of her hands against her warm cheeks. Was her indiscretion written upon her face? The truth burned like a brand within her.

The whole way to Wil's room, Nash wouldn't even meet her eyes. Did he feel as bad as she did? While they sat protected in the tunnels, giving into their passions, Wil fought to protect them, performing an Alteration despite the huge stab wound in his side. Shame reared up inside her. She had to quit thinking about Nash. He'd been right in the tunnels; they had to stop regardless of their feelings.

"How are you?" She pushed Nash from her mind with great difficulty, focusing instead on her duty, on Wil.

"I wish everyone would stop coddling me." Her eyes widened. Wil grinned sheepishly. "I'm fine. Really, Layla, it's just a scratch."

"A scratch." She gestured to the open wound under his right rib. "You have a huge gash in your side. I can't believe we left you and Vespa there to fight alone."

"I told Nash to take you away."

"I know you worried I would succumb to the Alteration, but you never should have left yourself that vulnerable. I could have helped you."

Wil searched her face, though she couldn't be sure just what he sought. "I know you could have, Layla. You should know that I think you are a very competent and capable warrior, but I sent you away for two reasons. The first reason, of course, had to do with the Alterations. What I made those men see…" Wil faltered, taking a deep shuddering breath. "I would never wish that on anyone—least of all you. But the second reason…" A pink flush tinted his cheeks. "The second reason has to do with my own weakness, Layla. Watching you out there compromised me. I couldn't focus for fear that someone would hurt you, and when I saw that soldier grab you by the hair and drag you toward the river, my heart stopped. I tried to reach you, but I couldn't."

"Wil, I…" Layla backed up a few steps, shaking her head.

"Please let me finish, or I might never have the courage to get it all out." He took a deep breath. "I've felt like such a failure, watching you dangle there by your hair while I remained helpless to stop it. You're supposed to be under my protection." He paused, staring directly into her eyes. "More than that though, I've come to care about you and don't want to see you hurt."

She smiled at him. Their new bond of friendship, forged last night in the library, coursed within her. While she and Wil did not have the same charged connection Layla experienced with Nash, she cared about the prince and would never want to see him hurt.

"You risked your life for me today. I won't forget it."

Clearly embarrassed by her praise, Wil broke eye contact. "Would you mind sending Nash in to see me? I'd get him myself, but…" He gestured to the wound at his side.

"Of course." Layla stood. "Aren't you going to get that checked?"

"I'm sure Vespa ran off to find Volton Mars the moment she left. Mars has tended to far more dramatic injuries than this one. I'll be fine."

They stared at one another for a moment longer. As she stood to leave, the door swung open, and King Jesper stormed in. His blue eyes flared with pure rage.

"You did this to my son." The king shoved Layla backward with such force that she fell back onto the bed beside Wil.

"Father!" Wil roared. He struggled to sit up but slumped against the pillow with a cry of agony. When Layla reached out to help Wil, Jesper smacked her hand away. Her Vanguard instincts kicked in, but she willed herself to be calm. Striking the king, no matter how horrible his behavior, meant certain death by the hangman's noose.

"You lured my sons and daughter to the West Wall to be slaughtered." Jesper loomed over her, his hand raised to strike.

Nash, Vespa, and Volton Mars stumbled through the door, their mouths slack from shock. Vespa ran over and touched her father gently on the shoulder. He shook her off, throwing her into Nash's waiting arms.

"Father, I took Layla to the West Wall." Vespa cried, righting herself. "She had no idea we would go there."

"Lies!" Jesper spun around to face his daughter. "Why are you lying for this traitor?"

He turned back to advance on Layla again. She stood her ground, knowing the king could not outmatch her with sheer strength. If he tried an Alteration, though... Layla pushed the thought from her mind, too afraid to imagine the implications.

Nash grabbed his father by the arm, impeding the older man's progress. "It's my fault. I crossed over to the Vanguard side, and I must have accidently attracted the attention of some soldiers. When Wil, Vespa, and Layla came in search of me, the Vanguards attacked."

A vein in the king's forehead bulged furiously. "You did this, Nash?"

Nash breathed heavily through his teeth. "Not intentionally."

"Nash." Wil called to his brother from the bed. "Don't."

"It's true, Wil. I'm to blame, not Layla."

Jesper marched up to his eldest until they stood face to face. "If I had my way, you'd be locked up in the dungeon for the rest of your days."

"It would be a welcome relief to never see you again."

"Don't test me, boy." With a parting glance that would have withered grass, Jesper stalked out of the room, slamming the door so hard the wall hangings rattled. Volton Mars hurried toward Wil's bedside, anxious to attend to the prince.

Layla stepped around the Volton and up to Nash, careful not to touch him in front of the others. "You shouldn't have taken responsibility. I could have handled your father."

"And if he'd performed an Alteration on you? Then what?" Nash's eyes burned with fury. "Besides, I think it's true."

Wil called to them from the bed, his face paltry. "Even so, we all know you didn't purposefully endanger anyone, Nash. Next time, let me handle Father."

Nash turned to the wall, away from everyone else. "You're confined to the bed with your side cut open. I did what needed to be done. Father already hates me, so adding one more failure to my list won't make a difference."

Wil remained quiet for so long Layla wondered if he'd gone into shock. He let out a long, slow breath. "Thank you for taking his anger off of Layla, brother."

"Maybe I believe in the Prophecy more than I let on." Nash left his words suspended between them all as he walked out. Wil, Layla, Mars, and Vespa glanced at one another in stunned silence.

Layla recovered first. "What is the matter with your father?"

Wil's pale face flushed with embarrassment. "I'm so sorry about all that, Layla. It's just—"

"Not now," Vespa interjected, placing a finger to her lips and pointing toward the door with her other. When she lowered her hand, the princess spoke loud and theatrical. "The Volton will fix that wound in no time. My brother would do well to remember that he's our future king. We must protect him just as we must protect you, our future queen." Vespa touched Layla's arm gently.

"Don't wish me dead already, child." A regal cadence emanated from down the hall.

"Of course not, Mother." Vespa laughed, with just a hint of nervousness. She gave the queen a quick kiss on the cheek.

"I'd like to have a moment alone with our 'future queen,' Vespa dear." False sweetness dripped from Queen Sansolena's voice. Glancing nervously at Wil, then Vespa and the Volton, Layla followed the queen out of the room.

Once they were far enough away from Wil's room, Sansolena turned her full attention on Layla. The queen's sharp stare dug into Layla, who shifted from one leg to the other under such an intense glare. Sansolena continued her silent vigil. Layla tried not to squirm.

"You know my husband desires an end to this whole Fulfillment situation," Sansolena said finally.

"I know." To Layla's surprise, she sounded steady, despite the loud, irritating thump of her heart.

The queen's brown eyes narrowed. "Just so you are prepared, I do not believe Jesper will be successful. The Elder is scheming to ensure he gets his way. It seems you may very well become my daughter-in-law whether you wish it or not."

When Layla did not reply, the queen continued, "What do you think of my son?"

"Wil is a wonderful person." She smiled in a fruitless attempt to break the tension. The queen did not smile back.

"My son is unique, Layla. He's truly the best of us all in this family, possibly in this whole kingdom. You will not break his heart, do you understand?"

Layla nodded. The queen didn't know about Nash, did she? How could she? Though the walls didn't move, Layla imagined them lumbering toward her, squeezing her into a corner from which she couldn't escape.

"I could make you love him and only him for the rest of your days. You know that don't you, girl?"

The air rushed out of Layla's lungs. She started to grab her chest but stopped, refusing to show any signs of weakness. Was the queen threatening an Alteration? Wil said there were rules for that…but he had also mentioned special situations in which a parent or a ruler could override traditional Alteration policy. Did that apply to the queen as well as the king? Or was the queen now considered to be a parental figure since Layla was bound to Wil? Either way, Layla hoped she didn't have to find out.

"We're already bound, my queen." Layla remained stoic, giving away none of her internal angst.

Sansolena's eyes narrowed farther until they resembled a cat's. "I'm not sure that's enough."

"Mother!" Nash called out, the rich sound reverberating against the walls. "Give Layla a rest."

"Nash." The queen's whole demeanor changed as her eldest son approached. Her brown eyes, which had just been narrowed at Layla with such hostility, warmed, opening wide with innocence. "I was simply having a chat with our newest family member."

The hard lines around Nash's mouth conveyed his displeasure. Layla could see he didn't believe his mother's words. Regardless of his scowl, the queen continued to smile up at her son sweetly.

"Come along with me now, Mother." Nash took the queen's hand and looped it through his arm.

About halfway down the hall, he turned to look back at Layla. She mouthed the words "thank you." When he winked, her face flamed so bright she thought she might actually combust.

CHAPTER TWELVE

Nash

Nash leaned against the castle wall, enjoying the cool midnight air. Again, he found himself unable to sleep. He knew the reason: Layla. This unaccustomed feeling, of being so profoundly affected by someone, bothered him. Since childhood, he worked very hard to keep everyone, even his family, at a distance, but for the first time, he didn't want to do that. In one of the First One's great ironies, he would *have* to push her away—no matter how much it hurt, how much he wanted nothing more than to hold onto her and never let go—because she was bound to Wil. According to the Prophecy, their marriage would serve a greater purpose for the kingdom, for the world. He couldn't be the fool who ruined the First One's plan for peace, no matter what his heart desired.

Maybe when the prophesied peace finally did arrive, he should just disappear. War would no longer impede him from leaving Etherea, escaping his father, and embarking on a new life. And seeing Layla married to Wil? Well, that would be all the more reason to go…

A small figure sneaking across the courtyard caught his attention, distracting him from his morose thoughts. Who was that? In the darkness, he couldn't make out any details, but based on the size and shape, he concluded the person must be female. Nash crept stealthily behind the mystery woman. She entered Clovis' maze, navigating the twists and turns with ease. He moved in behind her, careful to stay hidden, and decided he must be following his sister. What other girl knew her way through this labyrinth?

On the shoreline sat a lantern, which cast just enough light for the woman to see but not enough to be spotted by a sentry patrolling the area. Nash started to dash forward to confront her but shrank back when he saw a man wading across the river. A Vanguard. Nash reached for his sword.

He almost dropped it in shock when the Vanguard drew the woman into his arms, holding her in a passionate embrace. Nash's mouth fell slack as he absorbed what he saw. He edged closer. The moment before he revealed himself to the two lovers, a hand fell upon his arm. Startled, Nash swallowed down the cry of alarm threatening to escape his lips.

"Shhh," the person whispered, tugging him back toward the maze's entrance.

Intrigued, he followed, though every instinct told him to move toward the couple.

"Nash." He relaxed at the sound of her voice, the same one that stalked his sleeping and waking moments. "It's me, Layla."

"What are you doing out here?"

His tone sounded harsher than he intended. The idea of her this close to a Vanguard soldier and to the River Lars terrified him more than he wanted to admit. He still couldn't shake the image of her hanging by her hair. It haunted him.

"I followed Vespa."

He jerked back in surprise. "Through the maze?"

"No, I slipped through that gate you showed me, Holden's gate, and snuck along the wall out of the soldier's sight until I got here."

Nash smiled, appreciating her resourcefulness. "Clever."

"Well, it helps that your soldiers are more focused on keeping people out of the castle instead of in it. And honestly, if I hadn't found you and Vespa, I would be stuck out here."

He closed his eyes and took in a heavy breath. "So that really is Vespa down there?"

Layla's eyes darted around. Nash's jaw tightened. Her hesitation told him she knew more than she said, but what?

"Maybe I should go in and talk to her. Woman to woman."

"There is a Vanguard soldier in there with her, Layla. If anyone goes in, I will." He started forward.

She grabbed his arm and whisper-squeaked, "You can't."

Nash narrowed his eyes and leaned in closer. Layla swallowed so hard he heard it. Ignoring the energy that snapped between them, he forced himself to focus.

"You know something you aren't telling me. What is it, Layla?"

She glanced toward the bushes and then returned her gaze to Nash. Sighing, she said, "That Vanguard soldier is my brother, Grant, and he's in love with your sister."

Nash staggered forward as the impact of her words crashed into him. Vespa with a Vanguard soldier and Layla's brother no less.

"How long have you known?" He growled at her, angry to have been kept in the dark.

She scrunched up her face and set her jaw. "I owe you no explanation." Her flashing purple eyes both enraged and excited him.

"Vespa!" Nash screamed his sister's name, charging out of his hiding spot.

Without another glance in Layla's direction, Nash pulled out his sword, startling the lovers. His sister squealed and turned around, using her body to block the soldier behind her. Even in the dim lantern light, Nash saw the terror in her eyes.

Behind him, Layla burst through the bushes, a sword in her hand. Where had she gotten a sword? If it came to a fight, Nash calculated he would be outnumbered—two Vanguards with superior strength and one Ethereal with advanced Alteration powers. Nash sheathed his sword with an angry grunt. After a moment, Layla did the same. Only then did he notice she wore Vanguard pants instead of an Ethereal dress. In that outfit, Nash could better see her cinched waist and the gentle curvature of her hips. His mouth went dry. They stared at one another with a strange mixture of hostility and desire, the air between them practically crackling.

"Nash. Layla." Vespa stamped her foot.

"Layla?" The Vanguard soldier stepped forward.

"Grant!"

He witnessed her genuine joy. For the first time since he'd met Layla, her body relaxed. A broad smile, with no trace of strain, spread across her face. She ran toward the soldier, jumping into his outstretched arms.

"What are you doing out here, Layla?" Grant enveloped her in his arms.

Layla stepped back, her face sheepish. "I may have tried to kill Vespa when I first arrived, and she had to tell me about you to save her own life."

"Layla..." Grant admonished with a brotherly rebuke.

Nash stalked forward. "What? You've known the whole time you've been here? Why didn't you tell me, especially after the Vanguard attack?"

Layla clamped her jaw shut, her teeth clicking from the force. She knit her brows. "I promised Vespa that I wouldn't tell anyone, and I would never put my brother's life in jeopardy like that."

Offended, Nash snarled his response. "Do you really think I would harm your family?"

"I don't know what you would do, Nash. You did barge in here with your sword drawn." She crossed her arms, giving a haughty harrumph.

He almost lost the tentative hold on his anger. Layla looked so cute standing there with her arms crossed and her face bunched up in annoyance. He smirked. "Entering an unknown situation with your sword drawn is prudent. A Vanguard should know that."

They faced off, breathing heavily, both exasperated, yet also enjoying the verbal spar. Vespa's and Grant's gazes bounced back and forth between Nash and Layla.

"Oh First Ones," Vespa whispered the names more like a curse than a blessing.

"What?" Nash's head whipped to face her. Something about the way she spoke vanquished all his other thoughts. His stomach dropped straight down to his feet.

"You and Layla..." His sister placed her hand over her mouth. "I should have seen it sooner."

Before he could stop himself, Nash turned to Layla. The horror-struck look on her face rooted him in place. No matter what Vespa assumed, there could be nothing between him and the Fulfillment. He moved away from Layla, toward his sister.

"Don't try to make up stories and divert the attention away from yourself, Vespa. I demand to know what's going on here."

Grant raised his hand, pressing it into Nash's chest to stop his advance. Nash smacked it away. Sensing the escalation, Layla leapt between the two men and separated them with her own body. He noticed how careful she was not to actually touch him.

"Everyone just calm down." Despite her small stature, Layla commanded their undivided attention. "Nash, this is my older brother, Grant. Grant, this is Nash, Vespa's brother. Now, both of you shake hands."

He and Grant sized up one another for a moment before extending their hands. Vespa let out a squeal. Beside them, Layla crossed her arms with a satisfied smile.

With a friendly grin on his face, Grant said, "My sister sure can be persuasive."

"Maybe she really can bring peace to Vanguard and Etherea then," Nash replied dryly.

"Nash—" Vespa started, but he silenced her with a glare.

Layla shifted from one foot to the other, clearly agitated, while Nash moved a few steps to his left to give her more space. The farther away he got, the more the buzzing between them slowed. The more time they spent together, the stronger it grew. They didn't even have to touch to spark the flow of energy between them.

He let out a frustrated breath. While Layla made it clear earlier she owed him no explanation, Nash decided he owed it to himself, Vespa, and Layla to hear Grant out, at least for now.

Before Nash could speak, Layla burst out, "How are Mother and Father? What about Samson? Tell me everything."

Grant shook his head sadly. "It's better if I don't tell you anything, Layla. I'm not sure what Elder Werrick is capable of doing, but we can't risk it. All I can say is that Mother and Father are safe, and Mother is recovering well from her injury. As for our wayward brother, he's on a mission."

"A mission?" Layla's head jerked in surprise.

"He thinks he can free you from the Elder's proclamation."

Layla gritted her teeth, pausing a moment before she spoke. Nash caught the faint glimmer of hope on her face before she squelched it with a frown. "From what I understand, that's impossible."

"Samson believes it isn't."

Nash's mind raced. If Samson could prove that Layla was not the Fulfillment, what would that mean for her... for them? Nash shook his head in frustration. For now, he had to respect Wil and the binding by putting thoughts of Layla out of his mind.

He took control of the conversation, hoping to distract himself. "How often do you meet my sister here?"

Grant considered him for a moment before answering, "As often as I can."

"In this same spot, every time?" Nash pressed on, ignoring Layla's warning glares.

"Ye-esss," Grant drew out the word, suspicion evident in his voice.

Vespa rounded on her brother. "What are you suggesting, Nash?"

He considered the information while Vespa stamped her foot impatiently. To his right, Layla's stare bore into him. He knew neither girl would like his conclusions.

"I think you caused our security breach today, Grant." Nash spoke to the Vanguard, man-to-man.

"What? How dare you accuse him of orchestrating an attack on his own sister." Vespa balled up her fist in rage.

Grant reached out and touched Layla's arm. After giving Nash a hard look, his gaze searched his sister with care. "What attack? Are you okay?"

"I'm fine." Layla rolled her eyes and then focused them on Nash. "What are you saying?" She believed him; he could read the truth on her face, in the fierce way she set her jaw and in the flash of her purple eyes. He let out a sigh of relief, renewed by her surprising faith.

"I believe Grant is being followed."

Realization dawned in Grant's hazel eyes. "No, Nash, I'm not being followed. Vance ordered a group of soldiers to come investigate the West Wall today. He is determined to find a weak point in the Ethereal defenses that will allow him to defeat your people once and for all."

"See, Nash." Layla's eyes lit up with delight. She traced a finger along his forearm, sending a quake up his whole arm. "It wasn't your fault, and it wasn't Grant's."

He allowed himself to show only a wan smile, though relief surged through his body with surprising force. "Well, that was exceptionally bad timing for the both of us then."

Vespa laughed nervously. "Very bad timing."

Grant faced Nash, his eyes imploring. "I love Vespa, Nash. I would never intentionally be callous with her life or her heart. Maybe I can prove my loyalty to your sister by providing helpful information." Both Grant and Vespa looked at him with such hope he found it impossible to refuse. Nash nodded.

Grant took Vespa's hand before continuing. "The army is in complete disarray since Vance took over. I was able to slip away many times over the past few days to help my parents and my brother without being noticed. Besides, King Rex tasked me with monitoring the West Wall two years ago, so I can come and go from here without arousing suspicion. It's how I met Vespa over a year ago and how I've been able to continue seeing her."

Layla said, "Don't misunderstand me, I really like Vespa, but I don't understand, Grant. When we were little, you were the one telling Samson and me to follow the rules, to make the best choices. This," she gestured between her brother and Vespa, "is not following the rules."

Grant shrugged, his eyes falling upon Vespa with adoration. "Sometimes we break the rules for love."

Nash glanced at Layla, his heart in his throat. Her sad smile, tinged with hope, shredded him. He looked away.

Layla spoke again, drawing back Nash's attention as she always did. "I understand you feel strongly for Vespa, but you're a Vanguard soldier. It's what you've always wanted to be, how you've defined yourself." Nash noticed how she ground her teeth and realized she sought to understand something that eluded her. Despite their earlier kiss, he saw that a part of Layla still clung to the old notions—the separation of Vanguard and Etherea.

Grant held up his hand, intertwined with Vespa's. "Not anymore, Layla. Things are not as you remember them in Vanguard. Vance threw his father in the dungeons beneath the castle and took over as king. He's ruling alongside his mother, and they are ruthless. Right now, their top priority is killing you and continuing the war. He has offered a huge reward to the first man that brings back your head."

Nash stiffened. In a motion too small for anyone else to detect in the darkness, he brushed Layla's hand. She caught his fingers and squeezed.

He said, "If Vance is scouting out this area, we aren't safe here. I've got to get Layla and Vespa out of here. Vance's soldiers could be waiting to ambush us right now."

"What about Grant?" Nash noted Vespa's resolved posture and sighed.

"Bring him with us. We'll hide him in the tunnels for now." Nash glared at his sister and her lover. "Once we've gotten the information we need, he'll have to go back to Vanguard and gather more."

Nash placed his hand on the small of Layla's back and ushered her through the maze, scanning behind him every so often to ensure that Grant and Vespa followed. He truly hoped they'd been wise to trust Grant, or else they may have just let a Vanguard spy into Etherea.

Wil

Wil awoke with a start when Nash, followed by Vespa and Layla, burst into his room. He took a quick glance at the window and saw no hint of light. His pulse quickened. Whatever they'd come to tell him must be important given the hour. Wil struggled to sit up, wincing when his wound pulled.

"Wil, wait." Nash crossed the room in two strides. With his brother's support, Wil managed to get himself into a sitting position.

"What's going on?" he said, slightly out of breath.

Wil made eye contact with Vespa and then Layla, but they both looked away. Why wouldn't they look at him? What was going on? Exasperated, Wil turned to his brother.

Nash blew out a breath. "Wil, we have a problem."

"I guessed that. What kind of problem?"

"Apparently, our little sister has been secretly meeting with a Vanguard soldier."

"What?" Wil moved to sit up straighter, but an excruciating spasm forced him back down. He panted with pain and frustration. The gash limited him, and he didn't like being limited…especially when his family needed him.

"Wil." Vespa rushed to his side. She sat down on the edge of his bed to take his hand into hers, but he pulled away. "Wil, please."

"Why were you meeting a Vanguard soldier?"

"We're in love."

He hesitated to figure out exactly how to respond. Vespa had always been a bit naïve, and Wil feared her feelings could be one-sided. What if this soldier sought to take advantage of her to gain information about the Ethereal kingdom? But the light in her eyes stopped him from voicing those concerns. She looked…happy.

Instead of saying what he wanted to say, he chose a different avenue. "Tell me you didn't have anything to do with the attack on Layla."

"Of course not." Vespa huffed her displeasure.

Nash interceded, as he often did when Wil and Vespa butted heads. "We were attacked today by happenstance. Vance ordered his men to investigate the West Wall and look for weak spots. He plans to attack us soon, Wil."

Wil shook his head to clear it. "Let's back up. Start from the beginning, Vespa."

"About a year ago, after an argument with Mother, I ran through the maze to the river. I felt reckless, so I went all the way down to the bank, took off my shoes, and waded into the River Lars. A few minutes later, a Vanguard soldier came by. I jumped up to run, but he vowed not to harm me. We spent the rest of the afternoon talking and agreed to meet again the next week. We've been meeting as often as we can since that day. I love him, Wil."

"Vespa, you know that having a relationship with a Vanguard is punishable by death under Ethereal law." Wil tried to convey his concern, but Vespa reared back like he'd slapped her.

"Are you going to put me to death, brother?" He couldn't determine if she was teasing or being serious.

"Of course not, but I don't know how Father or Mother will react."

"They are letting you marry a Vanguard." Vespa's gaze fell pointedly upon Layla.

Wil glanced at his betrothed too. Her loveliness overwhelmed him as it did every time he saw her. He struggled to focus on the conversation, distracted by his attraction to her. "That's different."

The two siblings stared at one another, a silence falling over the room. Wil truly worried about his sister. Their father considered any fraternization with Vanguards to be an act of treason. When Wil was younger, Jesper forced him to watch the execution of an Ethereal man found guilty of having a relationship with a Vanguard woman. The man swore his allegiance to the realm, but King Jesper carried out the execution without mercy. Though Vespa was a princess, Wil wondered about their father's reaction if he ever found out. A cold sweat broke out across his body—from his wound or from distress over his sister, he didn't know.

Nash broke the stalemate. "Before Vance deposed him, King Rex assigned Vespa's boyfriend to check the West Wall once a week, so the Vanguards have never truly given up on that location as we once believed. We should consider the maze compromised."

Wil nodded, agreeing with his brother's astute assessment. "Where is Vespa's soldier?"

"We brought him to the tunnels," Vespa said.

"What?" Wil sat straight up, reopening his wound. He cried out from the pain of it and fell back against the pillows. Blood seeped through his shirt.

"Wil." Layla rushed to his side. She lifted the side of his shirt to inspect the gash with care. The stitches had torn. She furrowed her brow. "I need something to re-close this wound."

Vespa rose and walked toward Wil's dresser. Volton Mars had left some supplies behind, so his sister rummaged around, collecting the items Layla needed.

"Do you know what you're doing?" Vespa handed Layla a needle and some medical thread.

"I lived on a farm with two rambunctious brothers, so I have a lot of experience closing wounds on both people and animals." She smiled confidently as she put on a pair of gloves from the dresser.

"How can I help?" Nash stood by Layla's side.

"Hold these supplies, please."

To clear his mind, Wil focused on Layla. She touched him with hands that were both sure and confident. As calmness settled over him, he realized she often had that effect on him. Granted, Wil did not have extensive experience with relationships nor did he know Layla very well, but he desired to make her happy, as she made him.

"I'm going to start now. Try to relax." Layla pressed down on his shoulder, the material from the glove rough against his skin. Her touch made him wonder what it would be like to feel her actual skin against his when a sharp coldness on his wound interrupted his thoughts.

Wil sat back and closed his eyes as Layla cleaned the area and began to close it. He tried to keep still despite the intense pain. Her gloved hands worked quickly and efficiently, but he needed a distraction.

"Talk to me, please." He forced out the words through clenched teeth, not even bothering to hide the desperation.

She cleared her throat. He couldn't see her face, but a dreamlike quality accompanied her story. "On my family's farm in Vanguard, we had a huge blue barn behind our house." She laughed lightly. "I never understood why my father painted it blue, of all colors. Anyway, my brothers and I climbed into the hay loft to eat some cinnamon bread we'd gotten the day before on King's Day. My more adventurous brother, Samson, dared me to jump from the hayloft onto the back of one of the horses gathered below us. When I refused, he called me a chicken and leapt straight down himself. He landed in the saddle but pitched over backward when the horse took off. By the time my other brother, Grant, and I got to him, Samson's forehead had begun to bleed profusely. I sewed it up as quickly as I could, using some old supplies we dug out of a nearby shed. It's a miracle Samson didn't get a terrible infection."

Wil smiled to himself. In the library, on the night she first came to Etherea, he'd asked Layla to tell him about her family, but she'd refused. Her willingness to share such a personal story with him now touched him in a way he couldn't describe. He believed something significant had changed between them since then, and despite the agonizing burn from the needle going in and out of his skin, he felt content.

"I guess you should tell Wil the whole truth about the soldier in the tunnels." Vespa interjected herself into the conversation, interrupting Wil's pleasant thoughts.

His eyes twitched behind his closed eyelids. "What about him? There is more to the story?"

Layla let out a nervous laugh. "Well, to make matters even more complicated, the soldier Vespa has been meeting is my brother Grant." He could just imagine her sheepish grin and pink cheeks.

Wil didn't know what to say, so he nodded slightly to indicate he'd heard and understood, afraid to move too much and disturb her. When he finally opened his eyes, he noticed Nash watching Layla intently. His brother caught his gaze and then turned away. Did Nash actually look guilty? Wil dismissed the thought, chalking it up to pain induced delusions.

"So, we have an enemy soldier in the tunnels who just so happens to be Layla's brother and Vespa's suitor?" Wil repeated the information to be sure he got it right.

"Correct." Layla laughed again in that uneasy yet endearing way. "I'm finished closing the wound."

Wil relaxed, surprised to discover how tense he'd been while she worked. "When you are finished dressing the spot, I want to go see the soldier."

"I don't think you should get up." Vespa peered over Layla's shoulder. Her lip turned up at the sight of Wil's wound.

"I'm fine. Layla has done a wonderful job fixing me back up. I need to see this Grant because he may have useful information about Vance. With King Rex deposed, there is no telling what his son means to do."

"Grant does know things about Vance, and he's willing to share that information. He loves me, Wil. You'll see."

"I'll talk to Grant." Nash stepped forward. "You gather your strength, Wil. I think we'll need it in the coming days."

Wil wanted to argue but realized the wisdom behind his brother's words. The effort he would expend getting down to the tunnels would compromise his recovery. With someone as unscrupulous as Prince Vance at the head of the Vanguard army, Wil needed to be back on his feet, ready to fight, as soon as possible.

Vespa took a deep breath. "We already know that Prince Vance plans to kill Layla to avoid making peace. He wants to continue the war."

Wil looked up at Layla, who still sat beside him. She met his gaze, her face determined and brave. She'd never looked more beautiful.

"We'll keep you safe here, Layla." He vowed, sinking deeper into her eyes' purple abyss.

"I know." Her smile dazzled him. "You stay here and rest. Nash, Vespa, and I will talk to Grant and learn all we can about Prince Vance's intentions. We'll figure it out, Wil. I know we will."

He returned her smile. "I trust you, Layla."

CHAPTER FOURTEEN

Layla

Layla stared out the window, eyes glazing over at Volton Mars' latest lesson. From this spot, she'd watched autumn turn to winter and then winter to spring. She wondered about Samson as her gaze fell upon the River Lars. High up in the eastern castle tower, she could almost see into Vanguard. Was her brother still in their homeland? If not, where had he gone? For as long as she could remember, when she moved, Samson moved alongside her, an invisible string connecting them. Now, he'd simply vanished like a vapor in the wind. His absence profoundly affected her, though she tried not to show it. While she trusted his strength and wit, his mouth often got him in precarious, even dangerous, situations. Would they ever see one another again?

If only Grant would give her a clue as to Samson's whereabouts...but he kept his stubborn mouth shut.

Layla knew he met with Nash at least once a week to exchange information about Vance's movement, and even to provide updates on her parents, yet never did Grant breathe a word about their lost brother. She pursed her lips as a fresh wave of anger, pain, and sadness coursed through her.

She snuck a peek at Nash, who sat in rapt attention as Mars droned on about the invention of weaponry. A familiar twinge stabbed her stomach before flittering away. While she didn't like the idea of Nash, or her brother, risking their lives to thwart Vance's plans, she recognized the necessity. The Vanguard usurper's schemes proved unsuccessful so far, thanks to Grant's reports and Nash's strategizing. Still she worried for their safety, especially since her brother noted Vance's increased paranoia. She'd already lost one brother and refused to lose another. As for Nash...though she dreamed, and daydreamed, about her kiss with him, he never made a motion to repeat it, keeping her at arm's length.

"That's all for today." The Volton's announcement brought her back from her thoughts.

Vespa raced for the door, her glee infectious. "Thank the First Ones." Mars chuckled.

Wil slipped up beside Layla. "The weather is a bit cooler than normal today. Would you still be up for a walk after your sparring lesson?"

She ducked her head, smiling beneath her veil of hair. "I would enjoy a walk." Their daily walk, a staple in her life for months now, anchored Layla in this unsteady world. In the midst of chaos, Wil remained calm and sure.

A bright smile illuminated his whole face before he followed his sister out the door. Nash waited beside her, his gaze touching her face like a finger tracing her cheek. Despite her resolve to stay aloof, she blushed.

He picked up two swords from a table near the door. "Ready to spar?"

She grabbed a weapon from his hand. "I'm always ready to spar."

⋛⋛⋛⋛

Layla bent over, panting. Nash's sword fighting abilities exceeded all other Ethereals, and even a few Vanguards. They worked outside in the courtyard daily to keep sharp, to be prepared for any attack Vance mounted. With Nash as a sparring partner, Layla's skills improved more than she believed possible. She knew she could battle even the toughest Vanguards now, yet nothing happened to test her.

"Why do you think Vance hasn't attempted an attacked recently?" Layla posed the question to Nash as they walked back toward the castle.

"I don't know. Grant said that Vance was having trouble garnering the support of his people. Maybe that's why."

"I'm surprised he didn't just kill King Rex outright. Doesn't the fact that he's alive, locked away in the dungeons, give those loyal to Rex hope of freeing him one day?" She paused. "Not that I want Rex killed."

"Vance is in a tricky position. If he kills his father, the people will revolt against him. King Rex is well loved, as

I'm sure you know, but at the same time, you are correct. By keeping Rex alive, those loyal to him may attempt a rescue."

"I wish someone would rescue King Rex. I only met him once, but he seemed to support the idea of peace. Can you imagine a world where Ethereal and Vanguards are free to live their lives without the threat of constant war?"

Nash looked at her, his eyes full of tenderness and pain. A lump formed in her throat. She wanted to reach out to him, but she just kept walking.

"It will happen one day, Layla." How could he sound so sure? "If the fate of this world truly does lie in someone's hands, I'm glad those hands are yours."

She blushed at his flattery. "When I first came here, I didn't believe in the possibility of peace, but the more I'm here, the more I see how good the Ethereal people are. You are not the monsters we were taught about as children. If the Vanguards could escape Vance's evil influence and understand Ethereals, it actually is possible… though I still don't believe I'm the one to make it happen."

Nash laughed. "I'm glad you don't still think I'm a monster."

Against her better judgment, she stopped short and placed her hand on his arm. Her fingers came alive when they met his skin.

"I could never think that of you, Nash."

He cleared his throat, sliding just out of reach. She flinched. His simple movement—away—and the stinging rejection of it hurt more than a physical strike. When Nash met her eyes, for just a moment before looking away, Layla saw his regret.

"I'm sorry, Nash." She cradled her hand to her chest, her skin still tingling from the contact.

"No, I'm the one who's sorry, Layla. I'm more sorry than you could ever know."

Without looking back, he strode on ahead, leaving her alone in the courtyard. She sighed. How would she and Nash ever be able to reconcile their feelings for one another? She had hoped their attraction would lessen over time, but it hadn't.

At the same time, her feelings for Wil grew. He was one of the kindest people she'd ever met. How could she not like him? Even though Wil never mentioned it, she knew Elder Werrick pressured him, on a near constant basis, to proceed with their scheduled marriage. Yet Wil shielded Layla from those conversations and from the arguments between Werrick and the king. She appreciated that more than she could ever express to him. His quiet, gentle strength intrigued her.

"Layla."

She turned at the sound of her name to find Wil coming toward her, a big smile on his face. She waved and walked back to meet him. Her heart may not flutter like it did in Nash's presence, but a warm joy spread through her every time she saw the prince.

"How was the fighting today?" He smiled when she reached him.

"Nash is a tough fighter." She kept her answers vague, nervous about discussing Nash with Wil.

"He definitely is."

"Why doesn't he perform Alterations like the rest of you?"

A thousand times, Layla had wanted to ask Nash this very question but stopped herself. She knew his lack of traditional Ethereal abilities disappointed his father, and she didn't want to make Nash feel even worse than he already did. Still, the question nagged her.

"I'm not sure. He's able to do it, but he can't create vivid images like Vespa and I can. I really think he could have become proficient at it, but our father was always so critical that Nash just stopped going to training sessions. Besides, Nash has never needed to utilize Alterations. Somehow, he is just as strong as any Vanguard."

"He is quite competent with a sword...for an Ethereal." She bit her lip to keep a smile from her face.

"Hey!" Wil feigned offense. They both laughed.

"Wil," Layla grew serious, afraid yet determined to tell him, "I want you to do an Alteration on me."

"What?" He stopped walking and turned to face her. "I thought you hated Alterations. Don't Vanguards think they are evil?"

"I want to see what it's like, and I want you to teach me how to put up mind guards. I don't want to put your life or anyone else's in danger because I can't protect my mind in a fight."

He studied her face for a long while before he spoke. "You're sure?"

She nodded and swallowed hard. "Just don't make it scary." A nervous laugh escaped her throat.

"Never."

Wil stepped back and focused his blue eyes on her. Her body grew hot. Though Wil hadn't moved, a gentle sensation ran across her forehead, like a physical touch.

"Wait!"

Everything she'd been feeling vanished as Wil released her from the Alteration. He stepped forward and held his hand out to touch her, but dropped it back down to his side. "Have you changed your mind?

"No, I just need to know. You won't take any memories, right, and I won't go mad from it. Right?" She hated the scared, desperate nature of her question, but she couldn't proceed without knowing.

He smiled reassuringly. "No, it will feel like a dream."

"Okay." She pushed out a breath. "I trust you."

He smiled, such a broad smile, she couldn't help but return it as the truth of her words became clear. She did trust Wil because she would never let just anyone access her mind. Wil's blue eyes narrowed again as he resumed his concentration.

As before, heat swept over her, followed by a slight tingling sensation. Suddenly, a big open field unfolded around her. She blinked, taking in the scene. Flowers stretched as far as the eye could see. Their beautiful hue matched Wil's eye color. Layla ran forward, twirling and spinning, as the sun's warmth spread over her. It did feel like a dream...not scary at all.

In a flash, the scene changed. She stayed in the same field, but the season shifted from spring to winter. Instead of the dress she'd been wearing, a thick fur coat now draped her body. Layla felt warm despite the cold air around her. Snow, knee deep, covered every surface. She lifted her head and caught a stray snowflake in her mouth. Layla laughed with pleasure. She loved seeing and feeling the snow without experiencing the bitter cold.

She bent down and rolled a ball of snow in her hands. When she rose, Layla saw someone approaching in the distance. Wil.

"Wil." She waved.

Despite the depth of the snow, he jogged over effortlessly and stopped in front of her.

"Wil." She repeated his name like a prayer.

"Layla." He matched her reverence.

They smiled at one another. Were his cheeks flushed from the run or because he was happy to see her? Her own cheeks grew warm in response.

"It's beautiful here, Wil."

"You're beautiful." She shivered, not from the cold but from his huskiness.

She drew in a sharp breath when he pulled her into his arms. A surprising ripple of pleasure ran down her body. Had she experienced the reaction herself, or had he planted it as part of the Alteration? She couldn't be sure.

Wil cupped her face in his hands. "I'm falling for you."

With exquisite care, he brought their faces closer. Lingering a fraction above her lips, he smiled. She wiggled in anticipation. His kiss began slowly, a savory sampling, but the longer it lasted, the more she responded. She wrapped her arms around his waist. His hands slid from her cheeks, down her neck, past her arms, and settled around her waist. Their mutual passion grew, and the kiss became more frantic, more heated. Layla stumbled backward, overwhelmed by her turbulent emotions.

She lost her footing, and they both fell without letting go. The snow beneath her felt more like a cloud, soft and warm, instead of cold and harsh. Or maybe Wil's kisses made her warm…she couldn't decide. She ran her hands up and down his muscular back, and he moaned with pleasure.

"Layla." A sharp call interrupted her vision, the scene faded.

She opened her eyes, not even realizing they had been closed. She blinked to adjust to her actual surroundings. She struggled to separate reality from the Alteration.

"Wil." Heat rose to her cheeks. He stood several paces away, so much farther than she expected.

His urgent tone and troubled eyes shook her awake. His panicked face did not match the impassioned one she'd seen in the dream. She didn't understand.

"We have to go," he said. "Now."

She trotted along behind him, struggling to keep up with his long strides. "What is it?"

His jaw muscle flexed. "My messenger just told me that Vance managed to attack a small Ethereal village. Grant didn't warn us. "

"What? I'm sure my brother didn't know. He would never intentionally hurt the Ethereal people." She paused. "Not anymore anyway."

"We have to get to the meeting room to find out more information."

They tore through the courtyard toward the castle. All the questions she had about the Alteration, all the confusing feelings, would have to be set aside right now for the sake of Etherea.

�గᙢᙢᙢ

Wil and Layla flew down hallways and burst through the doors of King Jesper's meeting room. Glancing around, she saw Nash, Vespa, and Queen Sansolena had already arrived. She stepped away from Wil and flushed.

"Why didn't we know about this attack?" Jesper raged.

"As Vance has grown more paranoid, information has grown scarce," Nash argued. "Forgetting that, we have to respond. He can't attack our people like that. Father, he slaughtered women and children."

"That's enough out of you, Nash. If I wanted your opinion, I would ask for it. Since you no longer seem capable of providing useful military intelligence, sit down and shut up."

Nash raised his chin a notch, glowering at his father, before taking a seat. When their gazes met, Layla saw Nash's humiliation. She wanted to go and wrap her arms around him despite still being hurt over his earlier rejection. He dropped his gaze, focusing instead on the table and would not make eye contact again.

"Father, I agree with Nash. We can't let Vance's attack stand." Wil entered the conversation.

"You boys act like I've never been to war." King Jesper's roar echoed throughout the room. Everyone shrank back from the deafening sound.

"Well, what *are* we going to do?" Queen Sansolena addressed her husband. She held up her bejeweled hand, creating space between Jesper and his son as if her actions could somehow diffuse the tension.

Jesper's blue eyes, so like Wil's in color but so different in every other way, landed upon Layla. His lip turned up into a sneer, his disgust clear.

"When Elder Werrick came to me with this nonsense about the Fulfillment, I agreed even though I had reservations. With Rex on the throne in Vanguard, I thought this peace might actually be possible, but I don't think it will ever happen since Vance has taken over. The boy king has never actually been in a war, so he's afraid to face me on the battlefield. Given that, he'll continue to make these cowardly attacks on our people rather than take us head on."

Nash's head jerked up. "What are you suggesting?" Layla heard the razor sharp edge to his question.

"I'm suggesting we give Layla to Vance...to protect our people."

Layla's mouth fell open in shock. The king meant to hand her over to certain death? All these months, she believed she'd actually found a place, however unconventional, here in Etherea. Sure, King Jesper had never been warm, but she thought he at least accepted her enough to value her life.

"Are you out of your mind?" Nash yelled. He jumped up with such force that his chair slammed into the wall behind him. Nash closed the gap in a flash, coming face-to-face with his father. "Absolutely not."

Jesper shoved Nash, sending the younger man reeling into the table. Nash righted himself and lunged at the king. Jesper staggered into the chair behind him, a look of shock on his face. When Nash smashed into him again, the chair toppled backward with both of them still in it. Jesper grabbed his son by the shoulders, but Nash, his face bright red with rage, wrapped his large hands around his father's neck.

"Nash." Queen Sansolena, who had been watching the fray with a horrified look on her face, jumped up followed by a stunned Wil, Vespa, and Layla.

The four struggled to separate the two men. Wil gripped one of Nash's hands while Layla grabbed the other. With their combined strength, they could barely move him. Nash's anger added to his. Vespa and the queen screamed as the king's eyes bulged.

"Stop it, Nash," Sansolena pleaded, pounding on her son's back. "You'll kill him."

Layla placed a hand on each side of Nash's face, drawing his murderous gaze off his father. His jaw relaxed a little in her hands.

"Stop, Nash. Please."

His features softened. Though she knew he didn't want to, Nash let his father go and stood. Jesper crawled backward, getting as far away from Nash as he could. He rubbed his neck angrily.

"Get him out of my sight before I kill him."

Vespa grabbed her older brother's arm and pulled him toward the exit. Nash glanced back at Layla. She could see he didn't want to leave her with Jesper, but she nodded at him, indicating she would be fine. If anything, Nash's life needed protecting even more than hers now.

"Please, Nash. Just go." She didn't know whether she'd spoken aloud or just whispered the plea in her mind, but he nodded like he understood.

Nash's gaze never left hers as he backed out of the door. As soon as his son left, Jesper jumped up. He marched toward his wife.

"I will kill him, Sans, I swear it." His eyes flashed with anger, but the queen did not flinch.

"Father, you will not hand Layla over to Vance. I won't allow it." Wil drew himself up, speaking with both strength and authority.

"You're going to be a hero now too, Wil?" Jesper taunted his son, an ugly smirk spreading across his face. "You and Nash are both idiots."

"Really, Father? You would have us give into Vance rather than stand against him? Have you gotten cowardly in your old age?" Jesper's face dropped as Wil's words struck a nerve. "Besides, Layla is to be my wife. I will not allow any harm to come to her." Wil maintained a calm demeanor in spite of his father's harrowing gaze.

He crossed the room and stood beside her. Layla smiled at him, hoping to convey her thanks. Wil's faith in her and his commitment to her safety touched her. Vespa came to stand on the other side of Layla, clasping the older girl's hand with purpose.

"Father, Layla is the sister I never had. Wil, Nash, and I will stand up and protect her. We will hide her away where you will never find her if we must, but you will not give her to Prince Vance." She tucked her hair behind her ear as she glowered.

"Get out of my sight," King Jesper hissed, flinging his hand in obvious disgust. "Everyone except you, Sans."

CHAPTER FIFTEEN

King Jesper

King Jesper righted his chair and sat with a heavy sigh. His wife took a seat across from him. They stared at one another in stunned silence. So many questions raced through Jesper's mind, but he kept settling on one. The only one that really mattered—the one question he'd wondered for twenty years. One question he could never forget.

Sansolena spoke before he could open his mouth. "What just happened?" The heat of her anger singed him. "I can't believe you thought they'd actually agree to turn over Layla. And besides, Jesper, Wil is right. We can't give into Vance. If we do, he'll continue to push, asking for more and more. At what point will we say enough?" She straightened her dress primly, an action that struck Jesper as odd. "I say we make our stand now. You are a competent enough commander that you could smash this upstart into the ground without a second thought."

Jesper gawked at her, his mouth slack. He heard what she said, but the words washed over him and leaked back down onto the floor. The one thing he wanted to know dominated his thoughts, taking up residence in his mind. Everything else paled by comparison.

He opened his mouth, determined to ignore her and forge ahead with his own plans, but closed it again. Sansolena glared at him, her arms crossed. If he wanted the answer to his question, he'd have to provide one for her first.

"I don't believe in the Prophecy." She tightened her face at his admission. "Come on, Sans, you can't be shocked by that." When she didn't speak, he continued. "I won't start a battle with Vance over some Elder's irrational dream. There will never be peace between Etherea and Vanguard. If giving the girl back to Vance will prevent more Ethereals from losing their lives, I'll do it. I'm the king of Etherea, Sansolena. What do I care about some Vanguard?"

"Your sons care."

"Then they're fools."

"What if I told you I believe in the Prophecy? I believe peace can reign between Etherea and Vanguard."

"Then you're a fool too."

She unwound her arms, raising one hand to her mouth, a dazed look upon her face. He knew he shouldn't press for his answers now, but he simply had to ask. He couldn't stand not knowing.

When Jesper rose, Sansolena's eyes widened in surprise. He could see she had no idea what he planned to do, the question he had to pose. He knelt in front of his wife and took her hands in his.

"Sans, I've never asked you before, but I have to ask you now."

When her brown eyes filled with fear and dread, an invisible knife carved at his chest, straining toward his heart. Yet, he pressed on, setting his jaw in determination. The question had haunted him for years, compressing his very soul until it threatened to burst. He couldn't live another day in the dark.

"Is Nash my son?" The weight of the words choked him.

Sans snatched her hands from his and recoiled in horror, either from him or the question. His wife stared at him like a stranger, like she didn't even know him at all. He'd said and done many foolish things in their marriage, but she had never looked at him quite like this. He didn't know what to make of it. Was she offended? Simply angry? Or guilty?

"How can you ask me such a thing?" He hardly recognized the frosty woman speaking.

He almost faltered, almost wrapped her up in his arms to live the next twenty years in the dark, but the need to know gnawed at him. It'd been gnawing at him since the moment he laid eyes on Nash's thick black hair. "Oh, Sans, you know why. Just look at Nash. He isn't like the rest of us."

"Of course not. You've never treated him like our other children. You've never given him a chance."

"Because I've never known who he really is."

Sans shrank back at his forcefulness, and any small bit of warmth she may have had left in her vanished. Jesper sighed, reigned in his anger and frustration, and tried again.

"Ethereals have always had the ability to alter thoughts and memories when necessary. Wilhelm and Vespa are experts at it, while Nash still struggles. Yet he is as strong as any Vanguard I've ever met. Please, Sans, tell me the truth. Is Nash my son?"

Sans narrowed her eyes and lifted her chin. He would have given anything for a small glimpse into her mind at that moment, but his wife had always been sparing with her words. She spoke when she needed to, but more often than not, she held her tongue. On matters of state, he appreciated this quality. Today he did not.

Her frigid barrier dropped just a fraction. "I honestly don't know the answer to your question, Jesper. In my heart, I say yes, but in my mind, I just don't know. Right before we married, my father performed an Alteration. I remember the year before our wedding and our wedding but nothing in between."

Anxiety squeezed Jesper's chest. Why would Sans' father remove the memories of a full year of her life? Why had she withheld this information from him? Did she too wonder about Nash? Several breaths stuttered and faltered before he regained the ability to speak.

"Sans, your father has been dead for over a year now. His Lock on your memories is gone. If you want to access them, you can now."

Sans eyes swam with tears. "I don't want to know, Jesper. Can't you understand that? My father locked away a year's worth of memories for a reason, and I don't want to know it."

"Please do it, Sans. For me."

He placed his hands on top of hers again. She couldn't stop now, not when the answer that both haunted and eluded him lay just beneath the surface. This very question, this not knowing, had driven him mad with jealousy and turned him into a man he never intended to be.

Jesper thought back to the first moment he saw Sansolena. When she had appeared in front of him that day, her blond hair shimmering and her brown eyes glowing, he believed her to be the most beautiful creature he'd ever laid eyes on. He thought he could never love anyone the way he planned to love her.

Less than a year into their marriage, she gave birth to Nash. When Jesper saw that squalling child with black hair, a rage built up inside him. He knew deep down they could never have produced such a child together. Everyone knew blond Ethereals always produced blond Ethereals. A rare few in the kingdom had hair with brown streaks, a product of some sort of past interbreeding, but nothing like the dark puff on Nash's head.

Jesper, left with no other explanation, concluded his wife must have had another lover. The idea of another man touching Sansolena drove him to the brink of insanity. She was his wife. *His*. And every day and night since the moment of Nash's birth, Jesper had wondered, been obsessed with the idea of this other man.

He became so fanatical he demanded a daily account of Sansolena's whereabouts. Over time, he became someone he didn't even recognize. And Sansolena, his beloved, bore her husband's idiosyncrasies with grace and decorum, but he saw the toll his jealousy took on her, the constant look of sadness in her eyes. He hated himself for it, yet he couldn't seem to stop.

She squeezed his hand, returning him to the present, though he refused to completely leave the past. "Please don't ask me to do that, Jesper. We've built a life and a kingdom together. I have been faithfully by your side for twenty years. Though we didn't know one another when we married, I have come to love you more than I ever thought possible. I won't risk what we have together for some ancient memory. I won't."

Jesper sighed and stood. He had hoped she would tell him on her own. Somehow that would have been better, but since she refused, he had no choice but resort to other methods. They would not leave this room without the truth.

"Then I have no choice."

"What do you mean?" Sans' voice rose an octave. She slid back a bit in her chair.

"Forgive me, my love." He sought solace for his unforgivable act. "I invoke The King's Right."

"No. Jesper, no. Think about what we have." His whole being cried out for him to stop, to put an end to his madness, but the possessive, resentful beast inside him demanded the truth.

"I'm sorry, my dear. I can't live another day without the truth."

Jesper placed a shaking hand upon her head. His mind wandered back to the first moment he'd placed his hands in her hair. He had always loved twisting his fingers in her long, blond strands. But not today….today his touch hurt, tearing at a part of her she wished to keep secret. Possessed, he reached into the deepest section of her mind. She resisted, but he barreled through.

"I invoke The King's Right over you, Sansolena. All previous Locks and Alterations will come undone by my command." As her mind released a prism burst forth, spattering color across his vision before slipping away.

Sansolena's head jerked back with violent force. Jesper watched her with a mixture of fascination and horror as a dazed look swept across her face. In all the years he'd been in charge of the realm, he'd never once invoked The King's Right. He never could have envisioned using his power in this way.

Sans leaned forward, gripping her waist tightly. Strange moans emanated from her body. Jesper longed to hold her quaking body, but he resisted. Though a part of him wanted to undo what's he'd just done and beg her forgiveness, he still needed his answers.

"Am I Nash's father?" He whispered the question, both loving and hating it. Jesper held his breath. Today he would know, today the madness could end.

Sans rocked back and forth, still clutching her stomach. Silent tears streamed down her face.

"Please don't, Jesper. Please, I beg you." Her pain, almost a physical presence, leapt onto him, clawing at him to stop, but he couldn't. He just couldn't.

Determined, he threw off the vestiges of his wife's anguish and knelt before her. "Am I Nash's father? By The King's Right, you will answer me, Sansolena."

"No." In his frenzy, he almost missed her answer. As the life he'd built, his world, crumbled down around him, Jesper noted how powerful one small word could truly be. For twenty years, these questions had eaten away at him, chipping away more of him with each passing year and changing his very nature. He longed to hobble to his bed, yank the covers over his head, and wallow in his own misery, but he couldn't stop now.

"Do I know his father?"

"Yes." She continued her manic rocking, her eyes trained on the wall in front of her.

Jesper felt sick. With a shaking breath, he asked the final, most damning question of all, "Who is Nash's father?"

Sans stopped rocking. She caught his gaze and held it firmly, her eyes begging him to stop. Tension hung in the air, pregnant with her pause. "Do you even care what you've done to me, Jesper? You entered my mind and forced me to remember a life I didn't even know I lived."

He stared at her, dumbfounded, and tried to imagine what she must feel—to be overwhelmed by a flood of memories and emotions locked away for twenty years. But her predicament failed to move him. She knew the answer. She alone held the final puzzle piece, and he would know it too. He would learn the identity of Nash's father, and then he would kill them both—father and son. Only with their death could he finally be the man, the husband, he always wanted to be.

She narrowed her eyes, defiant even in the face of his mental assault. "You got your answer. Now stop."

"By The King's Right, you will tell me the name of Nash's father." His pain, frustration, anger, and self-loathing exploded in those words. Jesper reached into her mind, tugging for that last elusive memory—the man's name.

Sansolena grabbed the sides of her head. She screamed as he ripped. "Rex. King Rex of the Vanguards…your sworn enemy."

Jesper stumbled backward. When he hit the wall behind him, he sank to the floor. The desire to scream overcame him, dragging him farther and farther down until he almost succumbed. Sansolena and Rex?

Though he didn't want to think of Rex, images of the man floated before his eyes, and in that moment, he saw what he hadn't wanted to see for twenty years. Nash, the child Sansolena passed off as his, looked just like Rex. They had the same dark hair, the same green eyes. How had he been so blind?

When the idea of his wife in Rex's arms assailed his mind, Jesper jumped up in disgust. He took one last look at the woman he'd loved for two decades and walked out the door.

CHAPTER SIXTEEN

Wil

Wil struggled to find the right words to say to Layla. How could he ever apologize for his father's behavior? The king offered to barter her life for peace. Wil considered the notion unforgiveable.

"I'm so sorry about my father, Layla." He shook his head, embarrassed by the inadequacy of his attempt.

"Don't apologize, Wil. You stood up for me; I appreciate that." When she smiled at him, he relaxed a bit, relieved she didn't associate him with his father.

Wil stopped walking and turned to her, his face earnest. "I would never let anyone hurt you, Layla."

"I know."

He searched her purple eyes for doubt but found none.

They continued to walk in companionable silence. Wil's mind swirled with possible reactions to Vance's aggression. The crown should show a presence to those attacked, to let them know their king recognized their troubles and sought to defend them against future attacks. They had to respond, to show Vance he would not be allowed to attack Etherea without repercussions. To ignore Vance spelled the end of Etherea—the end of the elusive peace Elder Werrick and his Ecclesiastics promised.

"So, the Alteration..." Layla floundered.

"What about it?" Wil's pulse raced, though outside he remained calm.

"How does that work exactly? Do you just provide the place and situation and my mind fills everything else in, or did you create the whole thing?"

"It depends on the Alteration. Sometimes I just provide enough information to get the mind going. That can often be the best choice in a fight because people's own imaginations come up with much more terrifying images than what I can conjure. Other times, I take control of the whole vision."

She stopped walking and turned to face him. Her purple eyes glimmered in the dim hallway light.

"What about today?" she asked. "Did I make it up, or did you create it?"

Wil swallowed again. The moment he had been alternately anticipating and dreading arrived. He hoped she wasn't upset.

"I created it."

She nodded, a knowing smile playing on her lips. "I thought so."

Wil wiped his sweaty palms against his pants and swallowed the lump in his throat. If he didn't speak now, he might never again get up the courage. "Layla, I know we're bound, but I believe that my feelings for you are my own. I think I'd feel this way about you even without the Ecclesiastics' meddling."

"I—"

A nervous half-laugh burst forward. He closed his eyes, embarrassed, and wiped his palms again. He'd mess up his one opportunity, yet his confessions continued to cascade from his open mouth. Wil opened his eyes, hoping they conveyed the sincerity of his profession.

"You don't have to say anything right now…especially if you don't feel the same way. Just think about it. Think about how you feel about me and whether or not you believe you'd feel that way if we weren't bound."

"I will."

"You will?" He hadn't dared hope for such a response.

The corners of her mouth tugged upward into a smile, and she blushed. "I will."

He sucked in a deep breath. If ever there had been a time to lay his heart out, open and raw before her…"I'd like to kiss you. For real this time. May I?"

Her blush deepened, turning her face a charming shade of scarlet. He stared at the floor, certain he'd been too forward, but then she said, "Yes."

Wil's head popped up, disbelief flooding through his body. Blood pounded in his ears as he leaned in, anticipating the feel of her lips upon his. He smelled her hair, a mixture of lavender and roses. Just as he did in the Alteration, Wil paused before their lips touched, and smiled down at her.

"Wil!" Someone boomed from farther down the hallway.

He and Layla jumped back. The shock on her face mirrored his own. They turned and, to their mutual horror, found the king barreling down the hallway. His face blazed purple with fury.

"Oh no." Layla took a step back, away from the charging king. "I don't want to hurt your father, Wil, but I will defend myself if he attacks."

"I wouldn't expect anything less, Layla. But you should go."

"What about you? I can't leave you here alone to face him."

"He won't hurt me, but I can't promise the same for you. Please, Layla, go."

She hesitated for a moment longer then took off. Relief coursed through him when she disappeared around the corner. She remained out of his father's reach...for now.

"Wil!" King Jesper screamed his name again.

Wil purposefully maneuvered himself straight into his father's path, determined to give Layla all the time she needed to escape. "Father, I will not let you give Layla back to the Vanguards."

Jesper's eyes narrowed. Wil prepared for an onslaught. But his father waved his hand as if dismissing a servant.

"I don't care about your stupid little Fulfillment right now, son. We have bigger problems in the realm."

"What do you mean?" Wil blinked in confusion.

"That imposter, Nash, is to be arrested on sight for high treason."

Imposter? He didn't understand his father's ramblings. "Surely you aren't going to arrest him for what happened in the meeting room." Wil argued. Jesper and Nash clashed all the time, but their father had never ordered his eldest son's arrest.

"I'm arresting him for being a Vanguard spy."

Wil stepped back in shock. Jesper *had* lost his mind. Nash had risked his life countless times to gather crucial information from Grant. He'd been instrumental in blocking the false king's advances. Their father was mistaken.

"That's ridiculous, Father. Nash is no more of a spy than you or I.'

"He's the son of King Rex." His father's shoulders slumped as his pain and rage burst forth, finding an outlet.

Wil froze. "Wait, what?"

"Your mother just confessed it to me. All those times your brother went missing, I bet he went to see his true father. I bet the two of them had a good laugh at my expense. Well, I'll show them all who will get the last laugh. Your mother and Nash are to be tried for high treason at the end of the week. If you see Nash, seize him."

Wil's mind raced. Nash, the son of King Rex? He felt compelled to ask his mother, to hear the words from her mouth. Yet he knew the truth in his heart. With that dark hair, unusual strength, and fierce pride, Nash looked and acted more like a Vanguard than an Ethereal.

"Where is Mother?"

"She's being taken to the dungeons as we speak. Now, move aside, son. I have to find Nash so he can join her."

Wil turned on his heels and tore off down the hallway, determined to find Nash before his father did. Jesper's furious roars followed him as he ran.

CHAPTER SEVENTEEN

Layla

After Wil told her to go, Layla obeyed like her life depended on it, and given the murderous look on King Jesper's face, it might. Guilt combined with Vanguard pride nagged at her. Hadn't she once told Nash a true Vanguard never ran from a fight? Yet, she left Wil alone to face his father's wrath. She clung to the belief that Jesper would not hurt his favorite son, his heir, but still, she'd left him there. She'd run away like a coward. Layla exploded out into the outer courtyard. After slamming the door shut, she leaned against it, sucking in deep breaths. She contemplated going back and rectifying her mistake.

"Layla?" She turned to see Nash leaning against a courtyard wall. He straightened. "Layla, are you okay?"

"Your father..." She panted, catching her breath. "He came storming down the hall, and I ran, Nash. I just ran.

I left Wil. I should have fought…I've become a coward…I should…"

She wiped at the angry tears that flowed down her cheeks. Their presence, another sign of weakness, further enflamed her self-loathing. Nash rushed over and drew her into his arms. Layla relaxed against him, somehow comforted by the now familiar buzzing between them.

"You did the right thing by running. My father would never hurt Wil. Even so, Wil can handle our father. He's particularly skilled at defusing charged situations, like our mother."

Nash paused. Tightening his arms around her, he said, "I won't let Jesper hand you over to Vance. I promise." He placed a hard kiss on her forehead to emphasize his point.

"Don't worry. I won't let him either." She joked, though it fell flat, killed by her own turmoil before it took flight. Growing serious, she squeezed his waist. "Thank you for standing up to your father for me in the meeting room."

His broad chest muffled her thanks, but she didn't care. His arms ensconced her, creating a cocoon of warmth and safety. For too long, he'd pushed her away. She relished this unexpected moment of closeness and remained as still as possible lest he let her go.

"When he said he'd turn you over to Vance, I just couldn't control myself. I just…"

Nash fell silent and pulled back a bit. He grabbed her face between his hands, locking her in place, and planted kisses from the top of her forehead to the bottom of her chin, carefully avoiding her lips.

"I just went crazy at the thought of losing of you, of Vance hurting you. I couldn't stand it."

He continued to kiss all around her face and neck. Layla trembled with pleasure. The intensity of his feelings, of his mouth on her, made her weak. For months, she'd dreamed of a stolen moment like this one.

"Nash, I've wanted you to hold me and kiss me like this for so long."

"I've wanted to, Layla." His green eyes blazed. "You don't know how badly I've wanted to." He kissed her on both cheeks. "But I was afraid if I started, I'd never stop. And I have to stop, Layla. I have to. You're bound to my brother."

"But if I weren't..."

"If you weren't, I'd never let you go."

His face transformed. His jaw clenched, and he closed his eyes. When he opened them again, the hard expression he often wore returned. He moved away from her. Layla, aching for his presence, reached up to bring him back, but as he so often did when they sparred, he moved just out of her range.

However, when the door she'd just come out of flew open, Nash moved his body protectively in front of hers. They both squinted in the waning light to identify the person striding toward them. Nash's hand grazed the hilt of his sword. Though still dazed, Layla assumed a defensive posture, ready to fight if necessary.

"Nash?" Wil whispered his brother's name.

"Wil?"

Wil's postured relaxed. "Nash, we've got to get you into the tunnels right now."

"Why?"

"I can't explain it out here, but you are in grave danger. Father means to throw you into the dungeons. Now please, trust me and go."

Without another word, the trio raced toward the entrance to the tunnels. Wil went in first, followed by Nash. Nash turned around, grabbed Layla's hand, and guided her into the maze.

Wil flung open the door to the underground hideout. Vespa jumped, letting out an undignified squeak, and Grant reached for his sword.

"What are you two doing here?" Nash demanded.

Vespa avoided her brother's gaze. "I snuck Grant in through the maze."

Nash and Wil blew out frustrated breaths. Layla glared at her brother, who at least had the decency to look sheepish.

Wil closed his eyes and pinched the bridge of his nose. "You put yourselves, and the rest of us, in great danger."

Grant stood, his posture repentant. "We know, and we're sorry."

"What's going on?" Vespa's gaze bounced around between the three of them.

Wil sighed and gestured toward the table. "We should all sit."

Vespa, Wil, Grant, and Layla took seats, but Nash stood behind Vespa. He tapped his hand against the side of his leg, Layla's only indication of his distress. She almost placed her own hand on it to still his nervous energy, but refrained. The image of Wil asking for a kiss in the castle hallway, with his eyes so bright and hopeful, held her back from touching Nash in front of him.

"What's going on?" Nash dug a hand through his hair. Layla's hands balled into a fist as she forced down her rising panic.

"Father says…" Wil faltered. "He says Nash is to be tried for high treason."

"What?" Vespa tucked pieces of her hair behind each ear and then reached up to squeeze Nash's hand.

"High treason?" Nash asked.

Foreboding surged through Layla, leaving an icy trail in its wake. The punishment for high treason was death. Death.

"Why?"

Nash appeared unaffected by the news, but Layla knew better. She knew how Jesper's actions devastated Nash, yet another rejection. "Because I attacked him in the meeting room?"

"No." Wil stood and moved beside his brother. He placed a steadying hand on Nash's shoulder. "Because you are King Rex's son."

To Layla's surprise, Nash laughed. "I'm what? Is this some kind of sick joke, Wil?" He shook off his brother's hand.

"I'm not joking. Apparently, Mother confessed to it. Father thinks you've been sneaking over to the Vanguard side and telling Rex all of our secrets. He said you and Rex must be laughing at him behind his back, and you know how much Father despises the idea of anyone laughing at him."

"Unbelievable. After I risked my life to gather information that would protect Etherea, Father still believes the worst of me." Nash sighed. "This can't be right. I have to speak to Mother at once."

Layla watched, helpless to offer him comfort, as Nash absorbed the gravity of this revelation. His face flushed and then drained to an ashen color. When Nash walked toward the door, Wil rose to stop him.

"You can't, Nash. Mother's been taken to the dungeon. If you try to get to her, Father will have you arrested and thrown in there with her. He plans to try you *both* on the charge of high treason." Wil's own face lost color. "That's punishable by death. You know Father will find you guilty."

"What do you suggest I do then?" A hurt, angry sarcasm tinged his words.

Nash looked toward Layla. She gave him a reassuring smile but feared it looked more like a grimace. His green eyes sparked with unspoken angst. She longed to take him in her arms as he'd done earlier with her.

"You have to run." Wil set his jaw.

"Where would I run?"

"To Rex. To your father."

"Are you crazy, Wil?"

"Brother, hear me out…I have been thinking about it since Father first told me. You are a son of King Rex, just like Vance. If you were able to get into their dungeons and free your father, the people may rally behind you. One day, perhaps you could even sit on the Vanguard throne. If we could both rule, this peace that the Ecclesiastics speak of could really happen. We could make it happen." He glanced back at Layla. "All of us together."

Nash shook his head. "You've always been a dreamer, Wil. Fantasies aside, do you honestly think I can pull off a rescue mission and a coup? It sounds like suicide to me."

"If anyone can do it, you can. You're the best fighter I've ever seen, Vanguard or otherwise." Wil's words inspired Layla. His absolute confidence in his brother and in their ability to prevail despite the odds resonated with the piece of her that needed to believe they all served a true purpose.

Grant rose. "I will go with you, Nash. There are many men who are unhappy under Vance's rule. If we could find them and free King Rex, we could stop Vance's tyrannical reign."

Vespa overturned her chair in her haste to grab her lover's arm. "Grant…"

"Vespa, I love you, but I have to do this. I have to protect you and the Vanguards. They are my people. I simply can't stand by while Vance brings them to ruin, and after listening in on his last meeting, I know for a fact that he's coming after you and your people. I won't let that happen. As long as Vance is alive, he's a threat to everyone and everything I care about." He turned to Nash. "I'm with you if you need me."

Nash sighed. He managed to look both defeated and encouraged. "If I'm going to attempt such a mission, I'll need all the help I can get."

Layla squirmed in her seat. She wanted to go with Nash and fight alongside him. If she were with him, at least she'd keep an eye on his safety, but she knew she couldn't go. Instead, she'd be forced to wait in the castle day and night, wondering. The idea didn't sit well with her. Vanguards fought—they didn't pine away hidden behind a barrier.

So many unspoken words lay suspended between them, so much she needed to say to Nash. Would she even have the opportunity, or would he ride off leaving their relationship unresolved? She twisted her hands beneath the table, her anxiety spinning along with each twist and turn. Nash's life depended on his escape. The rest would just have to wait.

Wil nodded to Grant and Nash. "Look, I'll gather as many supplies as I can from the castle. Grant and Vespa, you search all the rooms here in the tunnels. One of them used to be an armory. If you find it, grab as many weapons as you can carry. We'll all meet back here at nightfall. Nash and Grant should leave soon after, under the cover of darkness." In that moment, Layla saw the commanding king Wil would one day be. They all stared at him in wonder.

"What about me?" Layla stood, ready to assist.

Wil's lips pursed together. "You stay here with Nash for now. Father is on a rampage. There's no telling what he will do if he finds you."

Layla stood. Stay with Nash? Though every part of her wanted to, she knew she couldn't trust herself if she did.

"I could go with you." She smiled at Wil. Nash shuffled his feet.

"I have a better chance of remaining undetected if I'm alone. I promise to be back quickly." Wil returned her smile with a huge one of his own, misinterpreting her trepidation as concern for him instead of anxiety over being left alone with Nash. A pang of guilt jarred her.

"Okay." She swallowed down the bulbous lump forming in her throat.

Within minutes, everyone else shuffled out the door, leaving Nash and Layla alone. He moved over to sit on the bed, putting as much space between them as possible.

Sitting in silence proved torturous. "What are you thinking about?" Layla asked.

He lifted his head, meeting her gaze. "I can't believe it. I mean, now that I think about what Wil said, it makes sense. I have dark hair and excessive strength like a Vanguard, and while I can perform Alterations, I can't do them nearly as well as my siblings. I just can't understand why my mother would hide my paternity from me all these years...And my father, Rex, I wonder if he even knows about me." She caught the speck of hope when he spoke of his father. She prayed for the First Ones to have mercy on Nash and allow him to find in Rex what Jesper lacked.

"Maybe she wanted to protect you. Or maybe she didn't know herself."

He frowned, his eyebrows wedged together. "How could she not know?"

"Wil told me parents have nearly unlimited control over their children's minds. Maybe your grandfather or grandmother locked away your mother's memories. I mean, Ethereals can do that, right? I've heard Wil and Vespa mention Locks."

He shrugged. "Yes, there are Locks. I guess it's possible."

"And if she doesn't know, maybe Rex doesn't either."

They fell silent. Layla concentrated on her fingers, keeping her eyes down. Though she wanted to stare at him, memorizing every inch of his exquisite face before he left, Layla trained her eyes on a spot of dirt beneath her nails. She longed to wrap him up in her arms and shut out the rest of the world, to comfort him as he processed the monumental revelation. Instead, she remained seated, watching that speck of dirt like it held the answers to all the world's questions.

"Do you think I can really do this, Layla?" Her head snapped up. "I mean, I don't know how I'm going to get in that dungeon in the first place. And even if I do, what if Rex doesn't believe me? Jesper hates me, why wouldn't Rex?"

Throwing caution to the wind, Layla rushed over and knelt in front of him.

"Nash, your father will acknowledge you as his son, and he will love you. You're amazing in so many ways. Jesper was an idiot not to see how special you are, but I have faith that King Rex will. I've met him, and you're actually a lot alike—strong and fierce but ultimately kind."

Nash's tortured expression tore at her. When he brought a shaking finger to her face, tracing the side of her cheek, she shivered at the pleasure his touch always brought.

"Thank you, Layla."

She placed her hand over his. "You're strong and smart, Nash. Remember that Vance is wild and reckless. You can use his arrogance against him."

"I'll try to make you proud, Layla."

"You already do."

She leaned into him, pressing her face against his stomach. He held her, stroking her hair. She closed her eyes, listening to the beat of his heart.

"Come with me." He murmured the words against her ear, his breath rushing down her neck.

Layla jerked her head up to look into his eyes. His earnest gaze told her he meant it, but then his face crumpled.

"No, ignore that. Your life would be in danger. I couldn't risk it. I guess I'm just saying I wish you could be with me. I don't...I don't want to leave you."

She took his hands in hers. "I don't want you to leave, Nash."

Layla stood and walked over to the table, overwhelmed by the strength of her feelings for him. He could die on this mission. Tears welled in her eyes at the thought. A life without Nash would be no life at all.

It wasn't fair for her to feel that way. She'd been bound to Wil, and he'd been nothing but wonderful. He didn't deserve to have a wife that pined for another man. Yet, she did. She ached for Nash with every fiber of her being.

"If I weren't bound, Nash…if I were truly free to choose." She faced him.

"Layla." His plea held warning and longing. "Don't. Please."

"I would choose you, Nash."

She heard the soft hitch in his throat. "Oh, Layla."

"I couldn't let you leave without telling you that."

She choked back the tears that threatened to fall. He rose but didn't move forward. They stared at one another from across the room. She wanted to run to him and take shelter in the warmth of his embrace, but she stayed rooted in place.

"Kiss me, Nash. Please…"

He drew in a deep breath. She thought for a moment he wouldn't cross the invisible barrier between them. Then Nash strode across the room and crushed his lips to hers. All the pent up emotion they'd been suppressing came rushing out in that one moment. Their mouths met again and again in a frenzied passion, unable to get enough of one another. He picked her up, and she wrapped her legs possessively around his waist. Nash staggered backward toward the bed, turned them around, and lay her down. Breaking the kiss for a heartbeat, he stared into her eyes. She pulled him closer, unable to stand any distance between them. With their faces just inches apart, he beheld her with unmatched adoration. Nash pushed back her hair.

"I love you, Layla."

"I love you too, Nash."

They smiled, lost in one another, lost in this secret passion that refused to be contained. Not willing to be disconnected from him any longer, Layla tugged his mouth down upon hers. Intense pleasure pulsated throughout her body. He consumed her whole being, shutting out everything else. Nothing mattered but him—his lips against her lips, his hands in her hair—right here, right now.

Neither heard the door when it opened, but Wil's sharp intake of breath drew them apart. They turned as one to find the prince frozen in the doorframe. He looked back and forth between them as if comprehending the scene before him.

Layla slammed her hand against her mouth, shrieking his name. "Wil."

"Don't." She shuddered at the sound of his heartache. Without another word, he walked out.

CHAPTER EIGHTEEN

Layla

Layla stumbled through the dimly lit hallways following the sound of Wil's retreating footsteps. She could hear his ragged breathing, and she recognized the sound as pain, not exertion. Guilt and remorse burrowed a gaping hole in the middle of her chest. She clamped her fist against it, a vain attempt to hold in the horror threatening to spill out. She loved Nash, but she never meant to hurt Wil.

"Wil." She squinted as she burst into the blinding sunlight.

He didn't respond to her call. He kept on running as far from her as he could get. Layla sighed, hiked up her skirts, and continued after him.

"Wil. Please." She tried to garner his attention again once they reached the courtyard.

This time, he stopped and faced her. The raw torment in his eyes chilled her.

"Wil." His name came out as a sob.

"I'm a fool. I thought we had something. How could I have been so blind?" He ran his fingers through his hair, squeezing the strands until his hands shook.

"We do have something, Wil. I am bound to you, predetermined to be your bride by the First Ones...."

"So you feel a responsibility toward me?" He spat out the words. She hadn't meant for it to come out that way. Instead of making the situation better, she made it worse. To see Wil, always calm and collected, so unraveled frightened her. Shame overtook her, spreading its piercing tentacles throughout her body until she burned from her transgression.

"How long has it been this way, Layla? Have you and Nash been sneaking around this whole time, laughing at what a fool I've been?"

"No. " The answer caught in her throat. While they hadn't been sneaking around, laughing at Wil, their feelings had begun before she met the future king. She looked down at her hands. "Nash saved me from Prince Vance's men when they ambushed my carriage on my way here. I didn't know who he was, and he didn't know who I was. We've tried to stay apart, to fight our feelings, because we both care so much about you."

He let out a disbelieving snort. "So, I never had a chance, did I?"

"We were only saying goodbye to one another, Wil. We both know that we can't be together. It isn't meant to be. Just one moment, that's all we gave each other."

Wil took a deep breath and righted himself. "Do you love him?"

"Wil." She touched her neck, strangled, an invisible noose tightening the longer she stood before him.

"Don't lie to me to spare my feelings. I want to know the truth. Do you love him?"

"Yes." She hung her head. Layla's hair fell around her like a veil and shielded her from his sight. He never spoke, but the intensity of his stare percolated around the edges of her hideout. Her Vanguard nature clawed its way to the surface, and she raised her head. Their gazes met.

"I came to the tunnels to get you because my mother wants to see you. I've made sure you will be safe coming and going to meet with her."

The gap between them widened. Layla sensed it like a physical presence. With his message delivered, Wil walked into the castle, leaving her staring at his retreat.

▽▽▽▽

After attempting to compose herself, without much success, Layla found the soldier Wil had commissioned to escort her to the dungeons. She had never seen a prison cell before and already hoped to never see one again. Though the soldier held a torch to light their way, she could barely see anything. A constant drip and the scurrying of mice made her skin crawl. When Layla tried to imagine the always immaculate Queen Sansolena down here, she couldn't. She shivered.

"Five minutes," the soldier barked as he looked down upon her with contempt.

"I'll be back when I'm done talking to the queen." Layla narrowed her eyes as she'd seen Queen Sansolena do on multiple occasions. "However long that may be." His mouth opened to offer a rebuttal, but he closed it and stepped back to allow her free passage.

She forced one foot in front of the other, careful to touch as little as possible. The farther she went, the stronger the stench became. How long had some of these prisoners been down here, and what crimes had they committed to receive such punishment? She shuddered again. The queen did not belong in this fetid, infested hole of death.

"I see my message got to you." Queen Sansolena still sounded soft and feminine, strange amongst such a dank backdrop. Though the king banished his wife from his sight and stuck her gin this dreadful place, she managed to retain her regal presence.

"Yes, my queen." Layla peered into the darkness. "Why did you ask to see me?"

Sansolena emerged from the back of the cell. Her beautiful blond hair, now dingy, hung limply at her shoulders while smudges of dirt streaked her face. Though she'd only been down there for a few hours, the queen looked ragged, like she'd been there for days.

"Tell my sons I did not know about Nash's true paternity until Jesper evoked The King's Right and forced my memories to come back to me." She sighed. "Nevertheless, Jesper wants to punish me, and I understand that."

Sansolena stepped closer to the bars. Layla could see her a little more clearly. The queen's brown eyes narrowed, employing the same expression Layla had mimicked only moments earlier.

"Here is my life's riddle, Layla Givens. Do I love my husband because I have to or because I want to? Would I have loved him if my father had not commanded me or if my father had not removed my love for Rex?"

"Why are you asking me this, my queen?"

"Because child, you are in the same position. I know you love my son, Nash, and he loves you. I see it on both of your faces every time you are together, but I also know you are bound to my other son. Wil is one of the kindest souls I've ever known, and his feelings for you have flourished."

Layla flushed, remembering the queen's earlier threat outside Wil's room. "Are you asking if I want you to Alter my mind?"

"I am capable of offering you that option."

Layla backed up a few steps, unnerved by the queen's strange grin. For a brief moment, she allowed herself to consider the odd notion. If Sansolena removed her longing for Nash, the constant ever-present ache of it, Layla could love Wil. They could build a happy life together. But it would be a lie, just like the queen's life. Eventually, the truth would force its way into the light.

Layla shook her head. "Why would you offer that? Look how it ruined your life."

"But did it, child? I lived in ignorant bliss for twenty years. I loved only Jesper, and he loved me. We raised three children together, and we were happy."

"The king hated Nash because he was different. You may have been happy in your Altered state, but your son suffered for it."

"It was just a suggestion." The queen shrugged her shoulders with her creepy fixed smile. She followed Layla's movements like an animal stalking prey. Layla's Vanguard instincts flared, agitated by Sansolena's toying. "Think about it, Layla. The Ecclesiastics bound you to Wil. They are so devoted to this notion of peace they will never let you live the life you want to live. You will marry Wil regardless of how you feel about Nash. Why not let me make those years happy for you and my son? Unlike me, you have no child to worry about…unless there is something you haven't told me."

Layla felt the warmth of her blush go from her feet all the way to her forehead. Her previous anger vanished, replaced by pure mortification. "Of course not."

The queen smiled at Layla's discomfort. "Then let me Alter your mind, Layla. Be free of your burden."

"Never." Her anger returned in a flash, joined by bewilderment and embarrassment.

The queen laughed and clapped her hands. "Good girl."

"What?" Layla shook her head, unable to keep up with Sansolena's rapid mood changes. "Is this some kind of test?"

"I needed to see if you possessed a strong enough will for what lies ahead. I did not at your age, and you're right, many people suffered for my shortcomings." The queen's whole demeanor changed. "I have a confession to make, Layla. I am a true believer. I always have been, but thanks to Jesper's release, I remembered the strength of my convictions."

Layla raised an eyebrow. "I don't understand."

"Unlike my husband, who professes his faith only when it lines up with his ambitions, I believe fully in the First Ones, in the Prophecy, and now…in you."

"Me?"

"I believe you are the Fulfillment."

Layla shook her head and placed her hand over her heart to stress her sincerity. "But I'm not."

"May I see your hand?"

With trepidation, Layla placed a trembling hand on the stinking cell door. Queen Sansolena grabbed it, pressing it between her cold palms. As with Elder Werrick, a charged wave hummed between them. Layla snatched her arm away in shock. She felt the same buzz every time she touched Nash. Werrick, the queen, Nash…what did it mean?

"What just happened?"

"It works. I knew it would." Sansolena's breath hitched in excitement.

Had the queen lost her mind? Layla leaned in to get a better look. Could someone go crazy after just a few hours in this dungeon? When the horrid smell, with a life of its own, invaded Layla's nostrils yet again, she believed a person could become mad quite rapidly in here.

Layla tried again. "I still don't understand."

"Elder Werrick insisted he felt a special spark from you, from the first moment he laid eyes upon you. That's why he pursued you and claimed you the Fulfillment without testing. I took that information to the most learned man in all of Etherea, Volton Mars. At my urging, he combed through all available material related to the Prophecy and the Fulfillment."

"Okay…" The pieces still didn't match up in Layla's mind.

"Mars found ancient texts that refer to the 'lifeblood of the First Ones.'" Sansolena's face lit up. In her great joy, she looked younger, like Vespa. Layla searched for the right words. Could she even breathe truth into this conversation? The queen's fervent belief had no reasonable basis. Would Sansolena even acknowledge Layla's assertions to the contrary?

The queen's grip on her cell bars tightened, turning her knuckles white. "Don't you understand, Layla? When I touched you, I felt the lifeblood of the First Ones flowing from you."

"I don't think that's what you felt."

"I know it is. You feel it too, don't you?"

"Yes, I feel it."

"Then how else do you explain the sensation?"

Layla gritted her teeth. While she couldn't explain the strange responsiveness that overtook her and others in certain situations, she refused to accept Sansolena's assertion. There had to be another, more reasonable explanation. Yet the answer eluded her now just as it had in Vanguard when she initially encountered the Elder.

"I can't explain it, but I know I'm not the Fulfillment."

The queen smiled. Layla wondered why her contrary answer pleased the woman. "It is believed that those directly involved with the Prophecy—like Elder Werrick—can detect the lifeblood without touching. Do you and Wil feel anything when you are together?" Her brown eyes twinkled with hope.

"No."

"Well, how about when you touch?" The queen's smile persisted, though her brow wrinkled with concern.

Layla ducked her head, embarrassed. "Wil and I have never touched."

Sansolena sank back on her heels. "Oh."

"But Nash and I have." Layla's confession shoved its way out before she could stop it.

"And does he feel the spark?" Layla nodded. The queen touched her chin, leaving a fresh spot of dirt there. "I would never have taken Nash for a true believer. Unless…" Sansolena trailed off, her mouth twisting to the side.

"A true believer?" Layla echoed the queen. Though she'd heard the phrase twice now, she still didn't know the meaning.

"According to the Volton's research, true believers—like Nash and me—can also detect the lifeblood, primarily through touch. I am glad to know Nash believes…Rex always did."

"But King Rex did not detect anything when he reached for my hand in Vanguard." The words slipped out of Layla's mouth. She silently cursed herself for blurting out pertinent information yet again.

Sansolena's face fell. "I suppose I shouldn't be surprised, given what happened to us, but I had hoped he would maintain his ardent conviction…." She trailed off, staring into the darkness. Layla continued to worry for the queen's sanity.

"Queen Sansolena, I don't wish to interfere with your faith, but I am not the Fulfillment." She needed the queen to understand, to place her faith somewhere else.

"You are, Layla, and one day you will see it. I've been watching you closely these past months, and I know that together you and Wil can change this world."

Layla bit her lip to prevent herself from speaking. She held no hope of changing the queen's mind, so set was her devotion. If only Sansolena knew how broken Layla's relationship with Wil had just become, her steady belief might waiver then.

"Time's up." A guard called from above. Both women jumped in surprise. So, Layla's attempt at intimidation had not been as successful as she'd hoped. She cast a final glance at Sansolena before heading back toward the awaiting guard.

"Take care of my sons." The queen's cry followed Layla even after she left the dungeon.

CHAPTER NINETEEN

Wil

Wil picked up the books sitting on his desk and hurled them across the room. His chambers, once neat and orderly, now looked ransacked. Though he'd taken every item he could find and flung it, his pain remained. He sank down against the wall, placing his head in his hands. Humiliation and anguish ate at him. Layla loved Nash.

A frantic knock drew his attention. At first he ignored it, but the pounding continued. With an angry growl, he pulled himself up and opened the door. Vespa's handmaiden stood before him, wringing her hands and bouncing from one foot to the other. Wil frowned, a dark foreboding tugging at his soul.

He touched the woman's arm to both still and comfort her. "What is it, Mola?"

"It's Princess Vespa. The king has her, and he's performing an Alteration."

Without gathering any more information, Wil sprinted to the meeting room. He burst through the door, blind fury giving him Vanguard-like strength.

"Father!" Wil's shout echoed throughout the room.

His heart wrenched when he saw Vespa on the floor in front of their father, a vacant look upon her face. He feared that Jesper, in his rage over their mother's confession, had been careless with Vespa's mind, permanently damaging it. He stumbled toward his sister, his distress interrupting his brain's ability to process.

"Vespa." Wil fell down on his knees in front of her. He gently placed his hands on either side of her head and guided her face to his, searching her eyes for signs of recognition. "Vespa?"

She smiled sweetly. "Wil."

Relief flowed through him. At least she knew him. He smiled back at her to hide the fear in his heart. Vespa remembered him, but she still didn't behave like her normal self.

"Father, what have you done?" Wil rose to face the king, his fists clenched by his side.

"I just found out that your mother has been lying to me our whole marriage, so I started wondering if anyone else in this family had been keeping secrets. Thanks to Vespa, I now have proof that you both have been."

"Father—"

"Enough! You've inherited your mother's smooth talking, and I don't want to listen to it anymore. Since

I've already searched your sister's mind, I'm going to search yours next. I invoke The King's Right over you, Wilhelm."

Wil tensed as his father's gaze bore into him. He tried to guard his mind, hoping to block out Jesper. Wil expected to feel the classic signs of an Alteration—the warming, the whisper light touch across the forehead as another mind forced its way in—but nothing happened. Jesper growled in frustration and tried again.

"I invoked The King's Right." Jesper focused hard. This time, Wil did not even bother protecting his mind. Again, nothing happened.

"Why isn't it working?" Jesper's face turned bright red with exertion and anger.

Wil didn't know why the Alteration wasn't working, but he was glad for it. His mind raged with an erratic array of thoughts, all of which he preferred to keep to himself. Some thoughts and feelings just weren't meant to be shared.

Unafraid to challenge the powerless man before him, Wil marched up to his father. "What did you do to Vespa?"

Jesper sneered at his daughter with contempt. "I invoked The King's Right. I forced her to tell me all the secrets she'd been hiding. So, I know about her Vanguard lover, Grant, and I know you are all helping Nash escape. I should hang you alongside your mother for that, or maybe I should hang your little Vanguard harlot."

"You will not touch Layla!" She may have broken his heart, but Wil still cared about her and would guard her against his father's wrath.

"I will do whatever I please, Wilhelm. I am the king."

"Father, I know what you are feelin—"

"You could never know that."

"I understand your heartache more than you realize, but you can't use your bitterness as an excuse to act this way. Look at your daughter. Look what you've done to her."

"I just removed all memories of that Vanguard boy. She'll be fine in the morning."

Bile rose in the back of Wil's throat. Removing memories, a delicate process, required an inordinate amount of patience and care. If not done correctly…

"Did you Lock the whole year they were together, or did you dig into every individual memory to remove Grant?"

Jesper paused. "I removed the boy from individual memories." His haughtiness faltered.

"Father, that's the most invasive kind of Alteration."

Wil looked over at his sister. Vespa remained on her knees, volleying between them with wide, frightened eyes. Wil went over and bent to her level.

"Vespa, do you remember Grant?"

"Who's Grant?" Her singsong melody reminded him of their childhood.

"Do you remember meeting a Vanguard soldier near the river?"

She shook her head. "I just like walking along the river. I never met anyone there, silly Wil."

Vespa laughed. She sounded like a little girl instead of a young woman. Fury rose up inside of him. He believed their father had damaged Vespa's mind, and all because of his own torment? Wil found the action inexcusable.

"Wil." Wil caught his father's hint of remorse but offered no pardon.

"Don't speak to me," he spoke with a quiet fury. "You are an unfit father and an unfit king. Come on, Vespa."

With painstaking care, he lifted his sister to her feet. She swayed and giggled. Wil felt sick with grief. The real Vespa—his sister, Grant's love—seemed lost to him...to all of them.

"She's not leaving this room and neither are you. You will answer for your insubordination, son."

"Haven't you done enough? She's coming with me." Wil shuffled Vespa toward the door.

"She's a treacherous whore like her mother. Vespa will go on trial with Sansolena."

"Father, you can't do that." Wil guided Vespa to a safe place behind him, shielding her from their father's madness. "She barely even knows where she is thanks to you."

"I can, and I will. You helped Nash escape. This whole situation is your fault. If you'd let me have Nash, I may have been more lenient with Vespa, but now she'll pay for your stupidity. I hope your false brother was worth it."

Wil drew his sword. "I will not let you take Vespa."

"Guards!"

The king's soldiers poured into the room. Wil settled Vespa into a corner and then swung around to meet them. He'd sparred with Nash many times growing up, and while he couldn't spar like a Vanguard, he at least knew the basics of fighting. The first man lunged, but

Wil easily avoided his charge. As his attention focused on the encroaching guards, he forgot Nash's biggest lesson…watch your back. Before Wil had the opportunity to take out another guard, from behind someone bashed Wil over the head with a heavy object. He heard the crack just before pain exploded throughout his skull.

"I'm sorry, Vespa," Wil managed to cry before he fell into darkness.

ᐁᐁᐁᐁ

Wil awoke to find Volton Mars sitting beside him. The prince's head pounded and his vision blurred, but seeing his tutor and friend by his bedside lifted his spirits. The Volton patted various body parts, checking Wil for signs of further injury without speaking a word. Mars' brown eyes shone bright with concern and a ferocious anger boiling just beneath the surface.

"What happened?" Wil dreaded the answer.

"From what the soldiers told me, your father knocked you over the head with a vase when you tried to prevent Vespa from going to the dungeons."

"Vespa." Wil struggled to sit up. Dizziness overwhelmed him, forcing him back down against the pillows.

"She's already been taken down there, Wil. There is nothing you can do right now. Try to rest and get your strength back. You'll need it if you plan to get her out."

"I will get her out." He swore a silent vow to his now imprisoned sister and mother. Wil swallowed hard, his next question stuck in his throat. "And Layla?"

"She is unharmed in the tunnels. I made sure Layla got there safely, but she may need to remain hidden until the king calms down….whenever that may be. I told her about Vespa, so she would know the importance of staying put, though I did not tell her you were injured as well." Gratitude, for Mars' constant guidance and unconditional love, washed over Wil, a salve to his aching soul. In almost every way, Mars behaved more like a father than Jesper.

Wil had not yet had the opportunity to tell the Volton about his heartbreak over Layla, yet the man seemed to know without Wil even having to say it. The two sat in companionable silence while the prince examined recent events.

After much internal debate, he selected a question to pose. "What do you know about The King's Right?"

"The same as you, that the king can invoke it. By doing so, he unlocks all previous Alterations and Locks and is granted full access to the mind. He can even compel a person to reveal secret information. This ability allowed many kings to discover traitors and foil their schemes. Why do you ask?"

"My father tried to invoke The King's Right on me, but it didn't work. Why wouldn't it work?"

Volton Mars sat back in his chair, a look of fascination on his face. He always appreciated intellectual intrigue. As he often did when contemplating a complex situation, Mars tapped the side of his head. Wil could practically see the information turning over in the Volton's mind.

"Very interesting, Wil. I've only read about this sort of situation happening once or twice in recorded history. In those cases, only a prince with a pure heart could resist The King's Right of a malignant king, making the prince the true king though his father still reigned. You could very well be that prince, Wil. I don't have faith in much, but I would believe that."

"I don't have a pure heart, Mars. My heart is anything but pure right now." Wil thought back to the tunnels, to that moment when he saw Nash and Layla locked in their passionate embrace. His own hurt and anger simmered. Right now, his heart possessed too much poison to match the prince in Mars' description.

"Wil, purity of heart is more about your overall character than your current state. It's more far-reaching than that."

"What about my father?"

"He has no power over you anymore, which gives you an advantage over him."

"Could I invoke The King's Right over him?"

"It's possible. I've never read about anyone trying it, but I can do more research if you'd like. Do you want to perform an Alteration on your father?"

"I told Layla I hoped to never be put in a position where I need to invoke The King's Right, and I meant it. At the same time, I can't let my father continue hurting people. If I must do it, I will. I will force him to free my mother and Vespa."

"And Nash?"

"Yes, I will remove the bounty from my brother's head, despite my personal feelings."

Nash

Nash bent down and splashed his face with water from the creek. He and Grant had ridden through the night and into the morning, so he welcomed the break. Nash filled up his canteen, stood, and stretched. Though he often snuck away from Etherea and explored the Vanguard side, he had never been this far. The castle, his *father's* castle, sat just a few clicks away. Anxiety gripped him. How would he get inside the dungeons, much less free his father? His father...

Thinking back to those stolen moments with Layla, Nash remembered her confidence in his success—not only in finding and freeing his father but in convincing Rex of his paternity. Layla, he missed her so much already—his brother and sister too. What if he never saw them again? He didn't want to leave those relationships so tangled, so unresolved.

"Nash!" Grant's exclamation cut into his thoughts. "A band of Vanguard soldiers is headed this way. What do you want to do?"

"You go."

Grant's mouth fell open, his expression incredulous. "What? I'm not leaving you here."

"You have to. If they find you with me, Vance could accuse you of treason, especially if he recognizes my resemblance to his father…my father. If he doesn't immediately suspect me though, perhaps I can live long enough to find a way into the dungeons," Nash finished, knowing the plan didn't sound solid.

Grant frowned. "He's more likely to kill you no matter what he notices about you."

"You mentioned there were soldiers who were still loyal to King Rex and plenty of people fed up with Vance's tyranny. Find them and gather as many as you can to oppose the usurper once my father is free."

"What about you, Nash?"

"I'll figure something out…"

Grant nodded with his lips tight, leapt upon his horse, and rode off leaving Nash to face whatever came—alone.

♥♥♥♥

For a group of men approaching a stranger, they rode without urgency. Nash stood out in the open, awaiting their arrival. If he had been a criminal or an Ethereal soldier, he would have had plenty of time to run away, hide, or prepare an elaborate Alteration before the group even reached him.

Was their pace due to laziness or apathy? He'd heard both words used to describe Prince Vance in the past, so perhaps he ran the kingdom that way. Grant's warning echoed in the back of his mind. Vance's men, or even Vance himself, might actually kill him rather than place him in the dungeon. The thought of never again seeing Layla's face pained him more than he could stand. He had to survive. He had to see her again.

"Who are you?" a large, burly soldier called when the group finally arrived.

Nash took a deep breath and tried his best to sound genuine. "I escaped from the torturous, mind-controlling rule of King Jesper in Etherea, and I seek asylum here in Vanguard. My people have heard great things about King Vance and his generous rule. I want to be a part of it."

"Take a look at this guy," the soldier, clearly the leader of the group, bellowed. Five other soldiers joined in the man's laughter.

Nash swallowed down his anger and frustration. "I was a servant in the Ethereal castle. I can provide King Vance with information about King Jesper and Prince Wilhelm."

The leader pointed at one of his subordinates and then gestured toward Nash. "Bind and gag him."

Another soldier slid off his horse with a rope and cloth. Resisting his natural instincts to fight, Nash surrendered.

They yanked a smelly sack over his head and tied his hands behind his back.

As his captor yanked him forward, Nash heard the taunt in the man's inquiry. "How come you have brown hair? I thought all Ethereals had blond hair."

Nash's reply sounded muffled inside the sack. "Most do. My mother is believed to have had an affair with a Vanguard."

A soldier lifted the sack to stuff a dirty cloth in Nash's mouth as the others laughed again. Four hands took hold of him, working together to hoist Nash onto the horse. Then they all made haste toward the castle.

As they rode along, the face covering slipped off just enough for Nash to catch a glimpse of the Vanguard palace. Its stark appearance surprised him. After growing up in well-lit, brightly-colored buildings, this one appeared dark and foreboding. He wondered if Layla, coming from this kingdom, had been equally surprised by the luminescence of the Ethereal architecture. Being in the Vanguard castle where Layla met his father, possibly walking the same hallways she walked, brought Nash a strange amount of comfort.

The Vanguards dragged him off the horse, pulling the sack back down over his face. Nash sighed, disappointed he could no longer rely on his sight. The soldiers hauled him through a series of hallways. Though he tried desperately to memorize the pathways, the task seemed fruitless. Like Clovis' maze, the Vanguard castle resembled a labyrinth.

At the end of yet another long hallway, Nash's captors opened a door and shoved him through. He fell to his knees. A soldier yanked the sack off Nash's head, blinding him with sudden light. He blinked, willing his eyes to adjust.

"What is this?" a high-pitched, boyish tenor called out from the other side of the room.

"My king." The soldiers dropped down to their knees, placing their fists over their hearts.

"We caught this man in the forest. He claims to have escaped from Etherea, and he says he can provide information about Jesper and his son, Wilhelm. We brought him to see what you would have us do."

"Information?" Vance stepped down from the throne and approached Nash.

Nash looked up to get his first glimpse of his half-brother. Applying the word "brother" to anyone but Wil felt strange; yet just as he shared a mother with Wil, he shared a father with Vance. Their common features—the same dark hair, the same strong jawline—surprised Nash, but the similarities stopped there. While Vance's eyes combined both blue and green, Nash's green ones matched their father's...or so he'd been told. The concern he'd voiced to Grant earlier hit Nash anew. What if Vance noticed the resemblance?

The self-proclaimed king stopped in front of Nash and narrowed his eyes. "What kind of information can you provide me?"

With the flick of his hand, Vance motioned for a guard to remove the cloth from Nash's mouth. Nash wracked his brain to think of a nugget of truth that would both please Vance and protect Wil and Layla. His tongue, thick and filthy, stuck to the roof of his mouth. Though he longed to expel the grime, Nash knew better than to spit at Vance's feet.

"King Jesper has had a falling out with his eldest son," Nash said. "The king placed a bounty on his head."

Vance laughed—a shrill, feminine sound that hurt Nash's ears. "While that does amuse me, Ethereal, I don't care about the son Jesper discarded in favor of Wilhelm."

He shouldn't care, but Vance's words pierced him. Nash had grown up knowing Jesper hated him, yet to have their turbulent relationship thrown in his face by a virtual stranger—no, an enemy—stung. He struggled to come up with a tidbit Vance would appreciate.

Vance provided him a lead when he said, "Tell me something of the Fulfillment, and I might let you live."

"She is hidden in the depths of the castle under constant protection," Nash lied, hoping Vance would not attempt another kidnapping. The usurper's eyes narrowed further until Nash could no longer make out any color. "But I have heard rumors that she and Prince Wilhelm do not get along." *Forgive me, Wil. Forgive me, Layla.*

At that, Vance's face and demeanor changed. He clapped his hands in glee. Nash watched him, gauging his half-brother's reaction. In the few minutes he'd spent with Vance, Nash already knew he didn't like him. The false king acted like a spoiled child playing at war—a very dangerous spoiled child.

"I like that. Tell me more."

"Some people in the castle feel the Fulfillment is in love with someone else, perhaps a Vanguard." His neck throbbed from the force of his heartbeat. To admit their mutual affection breathed new life into the depths of his feelings, not that this petulant man-child in front of him needed to know.

"I wonder if it's that boy she grew up with...." He snapped his fingers. "I can't remember his name..."

Boy she grew up with? Nash longed to ask what Vance meant, but he focused instead on the task: getting to King Rex.

"Perhaps." The lie fell from Nash's lips with ease. "No one knows his identity for sure."

"You may very well prove useful after all." Vance motioned to one of his guards. "Take him to the dungeons and keep him there until I decide what to do with him."

"Yes, my king." The soldier bowed.

To Nash's dismay, the guard placed the grimy sack over his head again and hauled him down another long, confusing series of hallways and stairs. The whole trip seemed so convoluted that Nash wondered if the guard had gotten lost. Without warning, the man cast Nash down into a puddle, pulled off the sack and ropes, and slammed the cell door. The only prison light seeped in through a small slit in the wall. Nash blinked to adjust his vision. After a cursory sweep of his surroundings, Nash found no guards in the immediate area. Hope surged.

"King Rex?" Nash whispered the name into the inky blackness.

A large lump on a bed in the cell next to him stirred. Rex sat up and squinted in the dim light.

"Who are you?"

Nash's lungs constricted. His breath popped out in short bursts as he forced the information out. "I'm Nash, your son with Sansolena, and I'm here to rescue you."

CHAPTER TWENTY ONE

Layla

The tunnels made Layla restless, yet she had nowhere else to go. Volton Mars told her King Jesper had used some horrible form of mind control on Vespa. Her Vanguard rage reared its ravenous head at the idea sweet Vespa might be permanently damaged by her father's actions. Layla stayed in the dreadful, lonely tunnels, afraid to give King Jesper the opportunity to do the same to her. After what he'd done to his own daughter, Layla knew he would destroy her mind without remorse.

When she asked about Wil, the Volton's vagueness concerned her. Mars' confirmed Wil's safety but reported little else. She wondered if Wil asked his friend to keep his responses cryptic.

Layla regretted being stuck there, unable to talk to Wil. The pain she'd seen in his eyes played over and over in her mind. She barely slept. Every time she closed her eyes, she saw his tortured face. Though she loved Nash, she still held a special place in her heart for Wil.

Nash. She prayed for his safety, chose to believe he'd survived the trip to Vanguard and Vance, but if he hadn't, would she even know it? Their goodbye kiss might be the last memory she would ever have of him. An uninvited tear streaked down her cheek. She wiped it away, hating this weakness. Vanguard women held in their tears, but she'd been far too willing to let them come of late. A knock pulled her from her self-flagellation. Layla leapt up, thrilled to have a distraction.

"Hello," Volton Mars' muffled greeting wafted from the other side of the door, retaining the soft, soothing cadence she'd come to associate with him. If Wil told the Volton about her indiscretion with Nash, the older man never gave an indication.

She opened the door to find him smiling on the other side. "Hello, Volton." She hid her disappointment. Though she liked Mars and appreciated his visits, which broke up the monotony of her days, Layla hoped Wil would come.

Mars smiled. "Wil asked me to come and get you. He'd like to meet with you in the king's meeting room."

"Is it safe?" Layla glanced up and down the hallway, half expecting the king to jump out.

"King Jesper has not left his bedroom in two days. We think you will be safe for this short visit. Prince Wil would not have summoned you without good cause. This meeting is important."

Layla's throat tightened. Short visit? Was Wil going to send her back to the Vanguards? Surely he would not send her to a certain death. He may be hurt, but he was also a kind, compassionate person, traits she valued so highly in him.

She stepped out, a knot agitating her stomach. "I don't want to keep Wil waiting then."

She took Volton Mars' arm when he offered it, and they slipped through the tunnels. When they emerged in the bright sunlight, Layla's eyes watered. Was she still crying or simply unaccustomed to the sun? Regardless of their purpose, she wiped the tears with renewed annoyance.

She needed a distraction. "How do you know about the tunnels, Volton Mars?"

The Volton laughed—a pleasant sound. "When Nash, Wil, and Vespa were children, I discovered all sorts of secret compartments and passageways during my countless searches for them. They would run and hide from me when it was time for their lessons. Once I discovered their hideouts, though, they had a bit more trouble escaping me…not that they still didn't try, mind you." He chuckled again at the memory.

She tried to imagine Nash, Wil, and Vespa as children, running away from a younger Mars. Layla envisioned Wil and Nash, pushing and grabbing to be the first one to the hideout, laughing the whole way. She could almost see Vespa's blond hair whipping in the wind and hear the jingle of her laughter as she tagged along behind the boys.

Thinking of Vespa reminded Layla of the Alteration. What had King Jesper done to his daughter? Layla worried her friend would never be the same again. Though the Volton had not been specific about the details, Layla had seen the concern in his eyes. She knew how much Mars cared about the king's children, though he tried hard to hide it and maintain the detachment expected of a man in his position.

Unlike other Voltons she'd met, Mars lacked indifference. "How did you come to be in Etherea, Volton Mars?"

"I was assigned to this kingdom by the Volton Council."

"Weren't you afraid to come here? Afraid of their abilities?"

"Like you, I had little choice."

His reply piqued her interest. "Why?"

"Do you know much about the Voltons?"

She shook her head. "In Vanguard, I had a Volton teacher in school, but he never told us about his people."

Mars nodded. "Most people don't know our history. Long ago, we were part of the Ecclesiastics. On one unremarkable day, a man named Volton Packs decided to devote more of his time to book study and medicine rather than pray to the First Ones and seek out the Fulfillment. His actions garnered much criticism from his fellow Ecclesiastics and the Elder. They ostracized him to the point where he decided to leave."

Layla listened with rapt attention, soaking up the history lesson Mars provided. "You must understand the significance of his choice. At that time, no one had ever thought to leave the religious organization. Each man had taken vows and sworn to serve the First Ones for life. Volton Packs, already an outcast, chose to make himself a permanent pariah by moving outside of the Elder compound. He relocated to the other side of the Borderlands, built a small home and school, and continued his studies."

Except for Mars' voice and their footsteps, Layla noted no other sounds as they stepped into the castle. An unusual silence permeated it. Layla's muscles tensed, her body ready to fight should Jesper appear.

Mars' unhurried walk matched his cadence as he continued his story. "Other men, fed up with the sect's rules and fanaticism, joined him. This group became the first of the Volton. Today, our size rivals that of the Ecclesiastics. We all live together in the Borderlands, but our peace is quite tentative. I believe the Ecclesiastics are still angry over the original Volton's defection." A thoughtful look crossed his face.

Layla knew if she were a man faced with the choice of life as a Volton or an Ecclesiastic, she would choose to become a Volton. Mars, so gentle and kind, highlighted Elder Werrick's horrible, underhanded ways. Her lip curled up in disgust just thinking about him.

Volton Mars cleared his throat, returning from wherever his mind had taken him. "As for how I came to Etherea…The Volton Council selected me to serve here. Some Voltons are sent to Etherea, some to Vanguard, and others remain in the Borderlands to study or teach new Voltons. Like the Ecclesiastics, we are neutral and serve both kingdoms, as well as the Outlanders. I arrived a week before Nash was born, and I helped deliver all three of Queen Sansolena's children. From the moment they were born, I loved each of them like my own children. I am supposed to maintain a distance, but I can't seem to foster the appropriate level of remoteness with those three."

Layla never doubted the Volton's sincerity. She remembered the worry in his soft brown eyes as he tended to Wil's wound tirelessly after the attack at the West Wall. In their tutoring sessions, she noted the pride on the Volton's face when Nash, Wil, or Vespa grasped a particularly difficult concept.

"Since your people originated with the Ecclesiastics, do you believe in the Prophecy and the Fulfillment?"

"I believe in the things I can see and prove, Layla. If you are able to bring about peace between the Ethereals and the Vanguards, then I will believe in the Prophecy and the Fulfillment." He smiled at her.

Layla paused, recalling her conversation with Queen Sansolena. "The queen mentioned you have been helping her research the Prophecy. Why would you do that if you don't believe?"

"The queen believes, and I am here to assist her in her pursuit of knowledge. Even though I don't believe in the Prophecy as the Ecclesiastics do, I still hope for peace. Your presence here breathed new life into this family. I think we all have hope for the first time in years."

"I haven't brought anything but pain to this family," she said, eyes downcast. The Volton just continued to smile at her, his silence compelling her to speak again.

"I'm sure Wil told you?" What started as a statement came out as a question.

"He did."

"Do you think he will ever forgive me? Or Nash? They were so close. I hate to think I've come between them."

"Wil has great capacity for forgiveness; he is not at all like his father. And Nash, poor Nash…when he arrived into the world with black hair, I knew his life would be tough, and I knew it would one day lead him away from this family. Wil and Nash will always be brothers—nothing and no one will ever change that—but they are also on separate paths now. Nash had to leave to find his true self, and Wil had to stay here to rise into the position he is meant to hold."

"Do you think Nash is alive?" Layla's voice hitched as she asked one of the many questions burdening her.

"I do. Nash received the best traits of both of the Ethereals and the Vanguards. He has always been strategic and strong. I believe he will succeed in finding Rex."

As they approached the meeting room door, Layla tensed even more. She tightened her grip on the Volton's arm. The idea of seeing Wil again, of seeing the pain in his eyes, saddened her.

"Will you come in with me, Volton?"

"Of course." He patted her hand.

The moment the Volton opened the door, Layla spotted Elder Werrick. Volton Mars stiffened beside her as she fought against her competing desires—to run or rip the Elder to shreds. Watching the two men, Layla recalled the first meeting she witnessed between Mars and Werrick and how Mars described the "tentative" peace between the Ecclesiastics and the Voltons.

"Welcome, my dear." Elder Werrick smiled with feigned enthusiasm. His smile fell as soon as his gaze landed upon the Volton. "Mars, since you did your duty and brought the Fulfillment, you may leave now."

Layla faced the Elder. Drawing upon her Vanguard nature for courage, she said, "I asked him to stay."

Mars patted her hand, still looped through his arm. "And so I shall." His warmth and kindness, in such abundance for Wil and Layla, dissipated in Werrick's presence.

"Wil." Layla found the prince standing in the corner. "What is the Elder doing here? I had hoped you and I could speak privately."

Wil pushed off the wall with his elbows, positioning himself between Layla and the Elder. She frowned at his careful avoidance of her. Her frown deepening, she glanced at Volton Mars. He shrugged his shoulders and smiled.

"I called everyone here today because I need something done," Wil said.

"I'm not quite sure how I can be of service, my prince." Elder Werrick teetered from side to side.

"Elder, is it true that you bound Layla to me in a carriage on the way here against her will?" Wil focused his withering gaze upon Werrick.

"Well…my prince…I….I simply…" Layla smiled as the Elder floundered. "I simply performed the binding which is called for by the Prophecy. Her consent was not required, and her feelings on the matter are irrelevant."

"Her feelings are not irrelevant to me," Wil said. His gaze, tight with resolve, met hers, and for just a moment, he softened. Her anxiety lightened. Maybe he didn't hate her. "Elder, the Prophecy never called for a binding."

"I'm afraid I don't understand." Werrick's mouth turned up into what started as a smile but ended more like a grimace.

"Then let me be clear. I want you to remove your self-appointed binding."

"Wil." Layla stepped toward the prince.

Elder Werrick's face drained of all color, stricken. "My prince, I most certainly cannot do that. This girl is to bring about peace by marrying a royal—you—on her opposite side. She is the Vanguard Fulfillment, you are the Ethereal prince. She must marry you or all is lost."

"Wil, what are you doing?" Layla appreciated Wil's defense, but she didn't understand his ultimate goal.

Leaving the flustered Elder to stew, the prince crossed to her. Volton Mars slipped back to give them privacy. Wil stopped a few inches from her, his eyes full of mixed emotions.

"I won't force you to marry me, Layla, especially when you are in love with someone else." He spoke slowly, as if the words were difficult to get out. "I want you to be free to choose what you want…whom you want."

Layla stared at him, speechless. Wil offered her the one thing she'd been secretly longing for—her freedom—but she wished it didn't come at his expense. Despite her feelings for Nash, Layla cared for Wil too. She'd never been so conflicted.

She whispered to him to avoid being overheard by the Elder. "But what about the Prophecy, Wil? What about the promised peace?"

"It will happen if it's meant to happen." His face set with certainty.

Layla lowered her head to hide her flushed cheeks and peered at him from beneath her eyelashes. "What about you?"

"If by some miracle you ever did choose to be with me, I want to know it's because you want to and not because you're bound to me." He moved away from her and turned to the Elder. "Do it, Elder Werrick. Remove the binding."

"I will not, Prince Wil. The whole Prophecy depends on the two of you marrying and ruling in a time of peace. I refuse."

Mars, who had been standing in the corner, thrust himself into the fray. "Tell me, Elder, when you performed the binding, did you bind her specifically to Wil or to the Prince of Etherea?" Layla recognized this voice from their studies—his thoughtful voice.

"I don't recall nor does it matter," the Elder scoffed, though his teetering increased. "Why do you ask?" Layla swung her head between the two men, searching the faces of each for an answer. What did Mars mean?

"Because if you bound her to the Prince of Etherea, there are two of them…"

The Volton's words hung in the air. For a moment, Layla couldn't breathe. She remembered. Elder Werrick had said "Prince of Etherea" in the binding ceremony.

Were her feelings for Nash a product of a mistake in the binding? Is that why they had been inexplicably drawn to one another? She wanted to believe in the strength of their love, yet Volton Mars' question planted a seed of doubt.

Wil turned to her, his face as white as she imagined hers to be. He must be thinking the same thing. He rushed to stand in front of her, obscuring her from the Elder's sight, close enough to touch though his hands remained clinched by his side.

"Do you remember what he said, Layla?"

"He said 'Prince of Etherea.'"

Wil nodded, put a hand over his face, and rubbed his eyes. "What does that mean then?"

"I don't know. I guess it could mean that what Nash and I feel is a product of the binding, but it might not be. Wil, I just don't know."

The flicker of hope in his eyes shattered her. "When I called the Elder here, I just wanted to free you, but now I need to know. If you are bound to Nash instead of me, do you even want the binding undone?"

She didn't hesitate. "Yes." Elder Werrick, the Prophecy, the binding…she needed to be free of it all, even if it meant losing Nash.

"Undo the binding," Wil commanded the Elder again.

"I will not." The Elder collected his pudgy body to its full height, which still paled in comparison to Wil's looming stature.

In response, Wil stood taller, dwarfing Werrick. "You know I can make you do it, Elder Werrick. Wouldn't you rather unbind Layla of your own free will, with your wits still intact? If I enter your mind, I can't promise you'll be the same person when I come back out. You know we Ethereals have trouble controlling ourselves when we're angry."

Layla shuddered. Though the Alteration Wil performed on her had been pleasant and beautiful, she could only imagine the horrors he could also create. The screams of those Vanguard soldiers by the river echoed in her mind. One glance at Wil told her how much he hated threatening an Alteration; yet there he stood, doing what he hated—for her.

With pure hatred in his eyes, Elder Werrick removed the locket from inside his robe. He held it high in the air as he had done in the carriage. Layla held her breath. The heaviness that befell her in the carriage reappeared, forcing her to her knees. She grunted, fighting against the Elder's bizarre power. Wil knelt beside her, panic on his face, but she waved him off.

"With this locket, I unbind Layla Givens, the Fulfillment, from the Prince of the Ethereals, and I unbind the Prince of the Ethereals from Layla Givens, the Fulfillment." The Elder dropped the locket on the floor and stomped on it with his foot. The jewelry shattered into pieces.

"Do you notice any difference?" Wil offered his hand to help her rise.

"No." She stood without his assistance, struggling to regain her footing. He dropped his hand back down by his side and sighed.

"I have done what you requested, Prince Wilhelm, but know that peace is in jeopardy now."

Wil set his jaw. "It's a risk I'm willing to take."

"What you say is blasphemous. You, and everyone in this room, will pay for what you've done here this day." With that, Elder Werrick stalked out of the door, his black cloak billowing behind him.

"Thank you," Layla said unable to convey the depths of her appreciation.

Wil exhaled slowly. "You're welcome." He motioned for Volton Mars to join them. "Volton, please escort Layla back to the tunnels for now. My father's temper has not yet abated."

Layla reached up to touch his arm but changed her mind, not wanting to give the wrong impression. "What about you, Wil?"

"I'll be fine."

"I want to talk about everything."

He nodded. "We will. I'll meet you in the tunnels soon. I promise. Now, please go before my father realizes you're here."

Nash

Nash watched his father rise to a sitting position. Even in the low light, he saw they shared many of the same features just as Layla said. In Etherea, Nash had been an outsider his whole life. To share features with someone else infused him with a sense of belonging, an unfamiliar sensation.

"You are my son with Sansolena, huh?" Rex rasped, hoarse.

"Yes," Nash replied. To his surprise, a tremor ran through his words. He hadn't fully grasped, until this moment, what it would be like to speak to his father. A familiar twisting started in his stomach. The word "father" held such a negative association.

The king scrutinized him. "You look like me. How did they do that?"

"Do what?"

Rex scratched his stubble. "Don't pretend you don't know. Montessa and Vance. How did they find someone who looked so much like me?"

Nash shook his head. "I don't understand."

"Clearly they want to expose me as a traitor, but how did they know about Sansolena? I never told anyone…" The king spoke more to himself than to Nash.

"I'm not here to frame you. I'm here to free you."

Rex laughed, a harsh bitter sound. "I'm sure that's what they want me to believe. If I'm caught escaping with my 'Ethereal son,' they would be able to hang me for sure, *with* the support of the people." His green eyes glittered with anger. "Fine, I'll play this game, Nash, but you make sure Vance and Montessa know I won't die quietly. If they didn't want a fight, they should've killed me when they had the chance. Now, I'm angry, and I'm most dangerous when I'm angry."

Nash grappled with his father's odd behavior. "I'm not lying. I am your son."

"Okay." Rex let out another harsh laugh.

Nash's fears—that his father wouldn't believe him—unfolded before his eyes. He ground his teeth in frustration. "If I succeed in freeing you from this prison, will you at least consider the possibility that I'm telling the truth?"

"Sure, sure." Nash's Vanguard ire rose in response to Rex's mocking.

CHAPTER TWENTY-THREE

Layla

Layla lay down upon the little cot wedged in the corner of the tunnels. Her mind wandered back to her kiss with Nash, how they'd fallen back upon this very bed. She sighed. Was it real? Was anything she felt toward Nash from her own heart, or had it been placed there by the awful Elder Werrick and his Ecclesiastical spells? Though their connection had been instantaneous, their feelings had definitely grown during her time in Etherea. She had come to love him of her own choosing, hadn't she? Layla wished she knew.

"This binding is as bad as Ethereal mind control," she said to the wall.

Paradoxically, she stayed in the tunnels to avoid Jesper and his mind controls, yet just being here, plagued by her own thoughts, put her at risk of losing her mind without his interference. Layla had too much to think about and too much time to think about it. When a knock sounded at her door, a welcomed relief, Layla sprang up to answer it.

"Wil." She breathed his name, pleasantly surprised to find him standing before her. Her palms, slick with nervous sweat, almost slipped off the handle.

"May I come in?" he asked, strained and formal.

"Of course." She stepped back to clear the way for him. Her heart pumped three times in quick succession, slowed, and then completed another round of erratic beats. She didn't understand the reaction. Nerves?

He entered the room, and they stared at one another. She tried to catch his gaze, to gain insight into his reason for coming. While she'd been preparing for this moment for a while, she found herself anxious now that it had finally arrived.

"Would you like to sit down?" Layla gestured to the table behind him.

"I'll stand. I won't be here long."

She nodded. Layla preferred to sit, but she stood along with him. The longer they waited in silence, each trying to observe the other without being caught, the more uncomfortable she grew.

"I'm sorry," he blurted out the words like they'd been collecting inside him for so long he could no longer contain them.

"You're sorry?" What did he have to be sorry about?

"I was hurt and angry. Because of that, I didn't handle myself well. I didn't come and talk to you before now because I'm still hurt and angry."

She softened. "You have every right to feel that way."

"I guess I just thought we had something, and I made the mistake of assuming you felt the same way. Honestly, Layla, I just feel stupid. I put myself out there, and the whole time, I never even had a chance."

"Wil." His confession and raw pain pierced her. He deserved better than what she had given. She knew that. "I should be the one to say I'm sorry. I should have told you about Nash, but I never believed it would grow into anything substantial. We fought it for your sake…because we both care so much about you."

"Please stop." He held up a shaking hand that matched his ragged words.

Silence stretched between them again. Ironically, Layla longed to be alone in the tunnel again. That torment couldn't compare to this one, to seeing him exposed and aching in front of her.

She grappled for something to say. "Thank you."

"For what?"

"For having the binding removed. Elder Werrick doesn't see me as a person, but you do. You wanted me to have freedom and a choice. I appreciate that more than I can express."

"Don't thank me, Layla. Yes, I did it to give you a choice, but I also did it for selfish reasons. I couldn't stand the idea you'd stay with me out of duty. My grandparents forced my mother to marry my father, and now he'll never know if what they shared was real. I didn't want that for either of us. If you ever do choose me, I want it to be because you want me, no other reason."

"Wil." Her hand reached out, of its own volition, to touch him, but she stopped its rise and willed it back down to her side.

"I know it's wrong, but I do want you to choose me, Layla, because I choose you. At the same time, I can't say I love you and then force my will upon you. If you want to be with Nash, do it. I just want you to be happy."

His sadness reeled her in, like a fish on a hook. She wanted to wrap her arms around him and offer him comfort, but she didn't know what would happen between them if she did. Was it really possible to care so deeply about two people at once? And if it were, did she—could she—actually love both brothers?

"I'm sorry," he said again, his angst palpable. "You know, I was thinking on the way down here that it's so strange. All of our lives, my father preferred me to Nash. My brother even explained his feelings to me once. I foolishly thought I understood what he said, but I had no idea. I do now." Wil barked out a pained laugh.

He turned and walked over to the table, tapping his finger gently on the surface. He sighed. "It's honestly the most gut-wrenching thing I've ever experienced, Layla. I can't believe Nash lived with it his whole life and didn't become a bitter person. The worst part is, while I'd love nothing more than to hate him, this knowledge just makes me respect him even more."

Wil ran a hand through his thick blond hair. Several strands stood straight up, giving him a tousled look. She almost reached up to smooth the pieces back in place. Her hands ached to touch him in a way she didn't understand.

He sighed. "I'd better go."

Wil walked toward the door, but Layla, obeying her antsy finger, grabbed his arm. Energy sprang to life between them, buzzing so loudly the sound filled the whole room. She fully expected him to pull away, but he didn't. Instead, their gazes met, holding them frozen in stunned silence.

Layla wanted to say so much to him, but she didn't know where to start. She missed the ease with which they had always been able to talk. She missed his laughter and his smile—she missed the Wil she maybe, possibly, loved. However, she didn't say anything because doing so would be selfish.

"Please let go of my arm, Layla. If you don't, I can't be responsible for my actions."

Layla knew she should let go, yet she did not. Her body acted on its own, almost independent of her mind. She tightened her grip and pulled him forward. He groaned. Absorbing her into his arms, he pressed their lips together with a force and longing that took away her breath. The spark from earlier intensified until they both shook from the force of it.

At first, she remained stiff and uncertain but then found herself responding. A part of her wanted to move away, yet another part wanted to move him closer. Just as Layla reached up to place her hands in his hair, Wil propelled himself backward, creating distance between them.

"Layla." Her name came out as a broken plea. "I'm so sorry. I knew I shouldn't have come here." He pushed his hair around again, making it stand up even more. As before, Layla longed to reach out and smooth it down, but he kept talking. "You see, the person I want to be would let you go. That person would be happy for you and Nash and want nothing but the best for you, but as much as I want to be that person, I'm not yet. I'm still selfish enough to kiss you without your consent, to want to leave you with a special memory of me that wasn't planted by an Alteration. I'm sorry I'm not a better person, Layla."

She refused to let him shoulder the responsibility alone. Though she found the quality endearing, Layla also knew he'd torment himself with it. Besides, her body compelled her to kiss him earlier, just as it drove her toward him again.

"Wil, I don't think you could be a better person if you tried. You're already so kind and selfless. And just to be clear, you didn't kiss me without my consent."

She took another step forward, sucked in a deep breath, and closed the gap between them. Layla leaned into him, listening to the sharp intake of his breath, until their lips locked together again. Wil wrapped his arms around her, squeezing her. Even with her mind conflicted, her body responded. She let out a small gasp; he matched it with a low moan.

"Layla."

His huskiness sent shivers down her spine. Wil bent down and planted a kiss at the nape of her neck. Her body ignited.

"Wil." She chanted his name like a benediction.

Overcome, Layla dragged his head back up, smashing their lips together. They stumbled backward, knocking over a chair. The more heated their exchange, the stronger the electric hum between them grew. Layla clung to him, shaking. He lifted her up onto the table, his hand lingering for a moment on her thigh. Her leg quivered.

Wil reached up, cupping her face. They pushed their mouths and bodies as close together as they possibly could. Her hands roamed up and down his back, clawing at him with a fervor she didn't even know she possessed. Mirror images, his hands copied hers.

Then, quite suddenly, Wil disengaged himself and stepped back. Everything stopped except their ragged breathing. Heat wafted around them, the air charged with their craving. His blue eyes darkened to a shade she'd never seen.

"Oh no." Some realization dawned on his face.

Before she could even reply, Wil fled. She remained in place, stunned, her whole body still tingling.

✧✧✧✧

After standing and staring at the door for quite some time, Layla returned to the bed, in the exact position she had been before Wil came. She lay down on her back, wedged in a hole on the lumpy mattress, and replayed the whole scene with Wil over and over in her mind. Her face grew warm as she recalled her wanton behavior and warmer yet as she remembered how Wil had just pulled back and left. What did he think of her now?

And even worse…what about Nash? He'd been gone only a short time, yet she'd already fallen into the arms of his brother. What kind of person did that make her? A horrible one, she decided. Nash *and* Wil deserved better. Another soft knock interrupted her thoughts. Wearily, she walked toward the door, almost afraid to answer it.

"Layla, please let me in."

She sighed in relief and flung open the door. The Volton stood on the other side, offering her a soothing smile, but she knew no amount of consoling could calm her now.

"May I come in?"

"Please do, Volton."

He shuffled in, his eyes ablaze with concern. Dread curled around her stomach. The Volton took her hand, rubbing it just like her mother used to when Layla got sick.

"Wil asked me to get you and bring you to the meeting room."

"Why?" Her words strained to work around the lump in her throat. Sympathy radiated so palpably from Mars that Layla grew even more anxious.

"I don't know why, but he acted upset. He also called Elder Werrick back."

"I thought the Elder had gone."

"Apparently not. We should go."

They rushed out of the tunnels and into the meeting room. As she entered, Layla noted King Jesper's absence, which eased her anxiety, but only the tiniest bit. Wil, the person she most wanted and dreaded seeing, sat at the meeting table. When she entered, he didn't even look up. He sat with a straight back, his hands clasped in front of him on the table. Layla glanced back at the Volton. He shrugged his shoulders.

"Thank you all for coming." Wil stood. He still refused to look in her direction. "We have a problem, Elder Werrick."

Layla swallowed, but the stubborn lump in her throat grew larger. Did Wil plan to tell everyone here what had transpired in the tunnels? He didn't seem the type, yet she couldn't read his face to know for sure.

"What problem, Prince Wilhelm? Do you need the binding reestablished? I would be happy to perform the ceremony."

"The *problem*, Elder Werrick, is that you already have."

Layla gasped.

"I...I don't know what you mean." The Elder's minor stutter gave him away. Wil's eyes narrowed as he focused on the older man.

"You performed it once without Layla's permission or mine, and you've done it again."

Werrick sniffed. "And how do you know this?"

"How I know does not matter, but your disobedience to the crown certainly does."

The Elder grinned—an evil, wicked grin. "You commanded me to unbind the girl, and I did. You gave no specific command not to rebind. After I saw how well the bonding worked between the Fulfillment and your brother, I had to try it again...with the correct prince this time." His grin could have curdled milk. "You and the Vanguard girl fail to understand the enormity of this situation. The Prophecy depends on the two of you, but you just want to throw it all away." He flung his hand toward him in disgust. "Well, I won't let you. You can rearrange my mind all you want, but the next Elder will just perform the binding again. We won't stop until we have what we want."

"You will stop." Volton Mars sounded frightening, so different from normal.

"And how do you mean to stop me, Mars?" Elder Werrick wore a smug, self-satisfied grin.

Layla's Vanguard fury flared. How dare he play with all of their lives like that? She wanted to launch forward and attack him. Only her curiosity over Volton Mars' plans kept her rooted in place, though she did take the time to consider how much force would be required to break the Elder's neck.

"You never valued learning, Werrick, and today that will be your detriment. I have been searching since the moment you presented Layla to this court, and I've discovered a way to block the binding spell. With Wil and Layla's permission, I will block them both, as well as Nash, from being bound ever again, by you or anyone else. They will be outside of your reach, free to choose their own fate."

"Do it," Wil said.

The Volton turned to Layla, seeking her permission after gaining Wil's. She nodded, a bit uneasy. Layla clenched her fists. Would she ever have control over her own mind again? The Ethereals held sway over thoughts and memories, yet the Elders and Voltons seemed to possess an equally debilitating control over matters of the heart. In the midst of such people, could she trust her own perceptions? If only the situation required brute force, she'd be prepared. But mind games and mystical spells, she didn't understand nor completely trust.

Layla glanced between Mars and Wil. At this point, she had no choice but to put her fate in their hands; judging by the stricken look on the Elder's face, this change in events deeply affected his plans. His distress alone convinced her to proceed.

"You can't do this, Mars." Elder Werrick screeched an octave higher than normal.

Ignoring the tormented Ecclesiastic, Volton Mars untied the rope around his robe and motioned for Layla and Will to stand beside him. The Elder made a move to interfere. Wil's guard snatched him back, holding him in place. The older man twisted and squirmed, his face a mask of pure rage, but he could not escape the soldier's hold.

"Do you have anything of Nash's? I want to protect him from binding as well." Mars leaned in so only Wil and Layla could hear him.

Wil bent down and retrieved a knife from his boot. He handed it over, his expression unreadable. "This was Nash's. Will that do, Volton?" Mars nodded. Without a word, he wound the rope around Layla and Wil's arms and around the blade of Nash's knife. Layla tried to catch Wil's gaze, but he still wouldn't look her way. The Elder's power reasserted itself, pressing her down without mercy. Volton Mars slipped his free hand under her armpit, supporting her, as her knees buckled. The heaviness dissipated. Had the Volton managed to ward it off with his touch?

Volton Mars raised his arms, much in the same way Elder Werrick had for his binding ceremonies, and their joined hands and Nash's knife rose too. "That which is bound, I unbind, never to be bound again."

He let go of Layla and retrieved a knife from his own boot to cut the rope in three separate places. Satisfied, he stepped back. Layla took a deep breath and felt oddly hopeful.

Wil rubbed his wrist. "Is that it?"

"According to my research, yes. When you forced Werrick to unbind Layla the first time, I knew the Elder would try something underhanded, so I've spent every spare moment researching ways to stop him. I hope this works for all of your sakes. No one deserves to be treated the way you three have been treated." He curled his lips up at Elder Werrick, an uncharacteristic sneer marring his face. "Most importantly, Werrick thinks the unbinding worked."

"I hope it worked as well. Thank you, Mars. You've always looked out for me." Wil stepped back and turned toward the door. Layla followed, calling his name.

He spun on his heels to face the guard holding Werrick. "Deposit him back in the Borderlands. If Elder Werrick ever steps foot inside Etherea again, all soldiers have orders to kill him on the spot."

Wil's proclamation pleased the most vindictive part of Layla's heart. If she never saw the dreaded Elder Werrick again, it would be too soon. Revulsion for the man and his underhanded tricks snaked through her. She thought about Nash and Wil and her feelings for them both. What kind of person manipulated the emotions of others with such callousness? Undeterred by Wil's avoidance, Layla followed him into the hallway. She wouldn't allow him to ignore her after what had transpired between them in the tunnels. Bound or not, their behavior, and its possible ramifications, had to be addressed.

"Wil." She called again. "Don't you walk away from me. We will talk about what happened. You can't avoid me forever."

He stopped in mid-stride and pivoted to face her. His blue eyes burned, and his cheeks flushed. Taking a deep breath, Wil ran his hands through his hair just as he had done in the tunnels earlier. She took a step toward him.

"Layla, please. I can't." His voice broke.

"We have to talk about it," she insisted, continuing toward him.

Wil held up his hand to stop her progress. "I said I can't, Layla. I'm sorry." She watched his retreat, hatred for Elder Werrick burning hot inside her veins.

CHAPTER TWENTY FOUR

Nash

Nash and Rex collapsed in a patch of underbrush, trying desperately to catch their breaths. After fighting non-stop—working their way out of the dungeon, through the castle, and into the woods—the effort had left them spent.

"Do you think more are coming?" Nash forced out his question, though his lungs protested.

"Probably. If we stay here, we're dead."

"If we get up to fight in this condition, we're dead."

Rex laughed heartily, with no hint of scorn or mockery. "I'd rather die out here in the woods with a sword in my hand than go back to that dungeon. To capture me before, Vance and Montessa poisoned my drink because they were too cowardly to fight me like true Vanguards. Well, not this time. If I have to die, I die on my terms, not theirs."

Nash cocked an eyebrow. Though his father's rant inspired bravery, Nash didn't want to die. He planned to return to Etherea, to Layla. Beside him, Rex sat up on his elbows, his mouth hanging open.

"What?" His father's intense scrutiny made him self-conscious.

"Say, 'You can't be serious, Rex.'"

Nash hesitated, confused by the king's cryptic request. Had his father lost his grip on reality? Shrugging, he sighed and complied.

"You can't be serious, Rex."

The Vanguard king fell back into the grass, a shocked look on his face. Concerned and still confused, Nash peered over at the older man.

Rex slapped a hand against his forehead, dazed. "I can't believe it."

"Believe what?"

"You *are* her son." Rex marveled at Nash, as if seeing him for the first time. "That look on your face…it's the spitting image of her. I don't know how many times I received that same incredulous look when your mother chastised me." Rex leapt to his feet, pulling Nash up with him. "You were telling the truth. You are my son with Sansolena."

"Yes, I am." He fluctuated between elation and dread. Now that Rex believed him, how would the king feel about having another son?

"I never knew she was pregnant. If I had…"

"You couldn't have done anything. Her parents put a Lock on her memories."

"Still, I should have fought harder for her. I loved her…I love her still. Not marrying your mother will remain the biggest regret of my life. Especially now that I know about you."

"Then we have a lot to discuss, but first, we need to get moving." He sensed a deep connection to this man, one he had never felt with Jesper.

The two men started toward the River Lars. As fugitives of two worlds, they had nowhere else to turn. Trying to stay as abbreviated as possible, while keeping an eye out for incoming danger, Nash relayed the whole story—Layla, Wil, Jesper, and Sansolena. Rex remained silent throughout the tale, though his face turned purple with rage when he heard about Sansolena's imprisonment.

"Do you think Jesper will really put Sansolena to death?" Rex pushed the words past clenched teeth.

Nash shook his head, unable to understand the manic fluxes of a man like Jesper. "I'm not sure."

"Regardless, we have to get her out of there." Rex stood tall, his figure large and imposing.

Rustling in the leaves alerted them to the presence of more of Vance's men. Nash swallowed the lump in his throat. All his life he'd felt unloved and unwanted by Jesper, and just when he had the chance to have a father, a real father, Rex might be snatched away. He sighed, saddened, but also emboldened. Nash knew he would give everything he had to this fight. He had so much to live for now.

"If this is the end, Nash, I want you to know I'm glad I finally found out about you…son." His father clamped him on the shoulder.

"Me too, Father."

Turning away, Rex roared out into the open, startling the approaching men. Nash rushed to his father's side. They stood, fearless, like two battle ready phoenixes. The first two of Vance's men lunged.

Despite their bone-weary fatigue, father and son jumped into action. Rex and Nash quickly placed the two soldiers on their backs with strategic, well-placed blows. They battled similarly, but while one set of guards distracted them, another six formed a circle around them.

Nash realized the hopelessness of their situation and stole a quick glance at Rex. How he wished he could tell Layla about his father, about the acceptance he'd finally found.

Layla…longing gnawed at him. He would never see her beautiful purple eyes again or run his fingers through her thick, black hair. The Ecclesiastics valued those features because of the Prophecy, but to him they held a different meaning. They made up a small part of the many reasons he adored her: how the purple in her eyes turned from light to dark when she concentrated hard during sparring and how she twirled a strand of her black hair while deep in thought. In these, possibly his last moments, he thought of those and a thousand other reasons why he loved her and would miss her.

At the same time, achingly, he knew his death would also release her. She loved him, he believed that, but Nash also saw how torn she was. Whether she would admit it or not, she cared for Wil too and felt a responsibility to bring about the Prophecy. Layla *was* the Fulfillment; Nash knew it with inexplicable confidence, and she would bring about the much awaited peace whether or not she believed it herself.

Despite his dire situation, Nash smiled. He had found a father that accepted him, and he'd found a woman to love him. He wished he had more time to enjoy them both, but at least he could die with the knowledge he had been given those precious gifts, if only for a moment.

"Stop!" A stranger commanded, breaking into his thoughts.

Nash turned to see Grant, an army at his back. Relief washed over him. Grant had done it. He'd managed to collect soldiers, and they'd arrived just in time to save Nash and his father. He would forever be in Grant's debt.

"Who are you?" one of Vance's guards asked as he shrunk back at the size of the group now surrounding him.

"We are the King's Guard, and we fight for King Rex." At Grant's reply, the group of men with him raised their swords and cheered. "If you leave now, we'll let you live, but if you fight, we'll cut you down."

Vance's men looked at one another, hesitating but a heartbeat, then dropped their swords and ran. Nash almost laughed, recalling how Layla scoffed at the man who'd run from them in the woods when they first met. She'd deemed him an unworthy Vanguard. Nash could only imagine what she would say about the six fleeing now. Like a man renewed, Nash walked over to his rescuer, clasping him on the shoulder.

"Grant." Nash continued grinning over his liberation, amazed by his Vanguard friend's exceptional timing. Grant returned the smile.

"I did what you asked. What do you think?" He gestured to the large group of men gathered behind him.

"I had no idea so many opposed Vance."

Rex looked around in disbelief. "These men all came out to support me, against Vance?"

"You are well loved by your people, King Rex, and Vance…" Grant paused, choosing his words carefully. "Vance is not." He placed his hand over his heart and bowed. Every other man did the same.

Rex bent down, caught Grant under the arm, and hauled him back to a standing position. "I may not be so well loved after you hear what I have to say."

"My king?" Grant looked between Rex and Nash with confusion.

"Everyone, gather around. I have something monumental to tell you." Rex motioned for the men to stand and step closer. "I am humbled by your loyalty to me, and I thank you from the bottom of my heart. But what I have to say now may make you question your choice. If you do not wish to follow me after this, I will understand."

The men looked at one another, perplexed. A worried buzz carried throughout the group.

"I need to introduce someone very important," Rex spoke over the noise. "This is Nash, my son."

The word "son" relayed from man to man, their confusion deepening. Curious stares surrounded Nash. Though their scrutiny unnerved him, he stood tall and proud beside his father as befit a prince.

"He is also the son of the Ethereal queen, Sansolena." Rex waited for the information to work through the crowd.

The murmur became a roar. The men shouted at one another, at Rex, at Grant, and at Nash. Chaos abounded. Nash took it all in—the angry, scared, and unsure faces.

Rex remained unflappable. "Quiet!" The noise died almost instantly. "As many of you well know, the Ecclesiastics found the Fulfillment here in Vanguard. She arrived in Etherea months ago to wed King Jesper's son and bring about the long awaited peace. I personally welcome this peace. Like me, many of you have spent your lives fighting a war whose origins none of us can even recall. I hope, like me, you are all tired of this war and tired of fighting it. I want peace."

Silence met the proclamation. Undeterred, Rex continued, "When I was a young man, I met and fell in love with a young woman who happened to be an Ethereal. I wanted to marry her, but her father took her away and Altered her mind to forget me. That girl ended up marrying King Jesper, becoming Queen Sansolena, and bearing my son—though I never knew about him. From what I understand, Jesper never knew the truth about Nash's paternity either, but when he found out, he put Sansolena in jail and put a price on Nash's head. He means to hang the queen in two days' time. I mean to stop him. I will fight one final battle with Jesper."

Rex let his words stand as each man absorbed the impact. "Then, I hope to lay down my sword and embrace a new peace. If you do not want to come with me, I understand. My son Vance hopes to continue a war between the Ethereals and Vanguards. If you wish the same, stay with him, but if you are willing to fight one more battle and afterward lay down your swords in peace, come with me."

The men stared at him in stunned silence before a loud murmur rippled through the group as they argued over the king's words. Nash watched as the men yelled, quarreling amongst themselves, until their shouts filled the forest.

An older man with a long scar that started on the left side of his forehead and ended at his jaw stepped out from the crowd. "How do we know this Nash is even your son? If he's Ethereal, he could make you believe anything he wanted."

Rex glanced over at Nash. "Take a good look at him. Any one of you can see without a doubt that he's my son."

"Maybe that's what he wants us to see." The man's chin rose, challenging the king.

Grant called out to the crow. "I concur with the king's story and vouch for Nash."

The scarred soldier roared with laughter. "And we should take the word of this young nobody?"

"That's enough, Rengard!" Rex's reprimand boomed throughout the forest. The argumentative guard's face flushed red, making his puckered scar stand out even more. "If you don't believe what I have to say, don't come. Go back and fight for Vance. No one will stop you."

"Forgive my rudeness, King Rex," Rengard tried again, his tone more deferential. "I fought many battles with you and respect you, but we are all just trying to understand. We left Vance and risked our lives to join with you because we believe you are the true king. Would you honor us by explaining how Vance came to sit upon the throne? As you may expect, many rumors have been passed around."

Nash watched as his father tried to calm himself, fighting against the Vanguard nature Layla often mentioned. Rex took a deep breath. "Vance and his mother poisoned me because they were too cowardly to face me in a real fight. The only person who dared a rescue attempt stands beside me—my son, Nash. Together we fought our way out of the dungeon, through the castle, and into the forest. Now, I plan to rescue his mother, Queen Sansolena, from certain death at the hands of King Jesper. You are either with me, or you're not. Decide now."

A tomblike hush fell across the forest, so quiet Nash could hear a squirrel scraping in the tree beside him. The soldiers looked back and forth between one another, their faces speaking though their mouths dared not. Nash wondered what they thought of his father and if they would choose to join the quest.

"I will stand with you, my king." Grant bowed low.

"And I," came another.

Soon a chorus of "and I" rang throughout the forest. Rengard faded into the crowd. Nash looked over at his father and felt proud to be his son.

CHAPTER TWENTY-FIVE

Wil

Wil's door swung open. Mars strode in, without his customary knock, and marched right up to the prince. In his surprise, Wil remained frozen in place, so confounded by the Volton's departure from standard decorum.

"I apologize for barging in, but I know what you're doing, Wil."

Wil regained his composure. "I don't know what you mean."

The Volton wrinkled his face. "You're planning to rescue your mother and sister, but you can't do it alone. You need my help…and hers."

Wil swallowed with great difficulty. Hers…Mars didn't need to specify. They both knew he meant Layla.

"You don't understand, Volton—"

"I do understand, in ways you cannot even begin to imagine." Wil started to interrupt, to press his teacher and friend for more details, but the look on Mars' face stopped him.

"I'm mortified by my behavior, Mars. I let things between us go too far, especially considering she loves Nash and not me." Wil ran his hands through his hair in frustration. "I can't bear to face her."

Mars pulled a chair from the corner of the room to sit right in front of Wil, as he often did during a particularly difficult lesson. While he valued his mentor's opinion, the prince suspected he wouldn't like it today. He sighed inwardly while preparing himself for the reprimand he knew the Volton had rehearsed.

"Wil, you've always been concerned about the welfare of other people, and I've believed for quite some time that you will be an excellent king because of it. I know Layla broke your heart. I know you feel shame over whatever transpired between you two in the tunnels. However, if ever a time existed for you to defer to the altruistic aspect of your personality, it is now. You must save your mother and sister, and we both know you need help to do it."

Wil flopped back against his seat. Though he'd been taught from birth that being king would occasionally demand personal sacrifice, he hadn't been able to understand how much humility certain situations required. Now he did. If he wanted to save his mother and sister, Wil needed to swallow his humiliation and go to Layla because he did need her help. The physical strength and strategic mentality of a Vanguard eclipsed that of an Ethereal.

"I'll go to her."

"You would have come to this conclusion on your own, Wilhelm. Of that, I have no doubt."

Wil grinned. "But given the time constraints, you thought you'd push me along a bit."

"Perhaps." Volton Mars smiled slyly.

⇩⇩⇩⇩

With a shaking hand, Wil knocked on Layla's door. He'd used the long walk through the tunnels to figure out what to say, but he still hadn't come up with the right words. Since his father planned to kill his mother and sister soon, Wil didn't have the luxury of finding the perfect way to express his thoughts.

"Wil." Layla's e yes lit up in surprise when she saw him on the other side of the door.

As always, the very sight of her erased every other thought from his mind until only she remained. He tried in vain to swallow his anxiety. The complex emotions he'd set aside to come here swelled back to the surface. Though he wanted to turn and run, Wil forced a smile.

"May I come in?"

"Certainly." Layla stepped back.

When their eyes met, both flushed. Memories of their last time in this room invaded his mind—the taste of her kiss, the way her hands roamed over his back, the sound of her satisfied sighs. Heat enflamed his cheeks. Layla's face responded in kind. Was she too remembering their kiss?

Wil cleared his throat, pushing past this mental assault. "I have to save my mother and sister, and I need your help."

"I'll help in whatever way I can." She peered at him from beneath her lashes, a tentative, shy smile playing at her lips.

Wil moved to take a seat at the table. The image of their entwined bodies surged to the forefront of his mind. He squeezed his eyes shut, hoping to keep the mental picture away.

"The first thing we need to do is teach you to block an Alteration." Wil refused to be deterred by his desire for her.

Layla took her seat across from him. "That sounds like a good start."

With a nervous grin plastered on her face, he couldn't help but smile back. Mars had been right. He usually was. However tenuous their truce, Wil knew working with Layla gave his family a better chance of rescue than acting alone.

CHAPTER TWENTY-SIX

Layla

Layla concentrated hard on the spot in front of her. She envisioned a wall around her mind, impenetrable to any attack, as Wil had instructed her. Though she had spent nearly an entire day working to secure her mind, she had no idea if it even worked. The only way to find out would be to test her abilities.

On cue, Wil knocked and entered. His tired blue eyes and haggard face spoke of another long, sleepless night. The Volton had told her that since the arrests, Wil spent most of his time trying to figure out a way to free them. Jesper refused to let them go, so the prince sought to defy the king and release them himself.

"You look tired, Wil."

"I am, but tomorrow my father plans to hang my mother and sister. I can't let that happen." He slumped into one of the chairs by the table, putting his head in his hands.

Layla hopped up from the bed and crossed over to him. She placed a hand on his shoulder, wishing she could alleviate some of his stress. Just like before, her hand vibrated the instant she made contact with Wil.

Ignoring the disconcerting sensation, she comforted him. "If we have to enact it, our plan is solid, Wil. They will be free by this time tomorrow."

He placed his hand over hers, sending a jolt up her arm. "Thank you, Layla."

"I had a thought last night. It's probably a silly question, so forgive me, but can't you just break them out? Perhaps you can Alter the minds of the guards or something?"

"I tried to go down there and free them, but my father had already Altered the minds of the guards. They are instructed to kill anyone who tries to get past them. When I attempted to undo what had been done, I found a Lock. I may be able to avoid The King's Right when my father tries to exercise it upon me, but I still cannot undo what he has done. Volton Mars and I are trying to figure out how extensive my powers are, but there is very little information available, and we simply don't have the time to gather more." Wil sighed. "Mars seems to think I may be able to demand The King's Right over my father though."

"What do you think?"

"I think if I can, I will. I can't let them die."

Layla placed her free hand on his other shoulder and gently rubbed them. His head lolled around, a soft sound escaping his lips.

"Thank you, Layla."

"Wil—" She stopped, unsure exactly what she meant to say, only desiring to offer him comfort.

He stiffened. After patting her hand once, he scooted away. Layla dropped her hands to her side. The tingling remained.

Wil cleared his throat. "Have you been practicing?"

Confused by his sudden change in demeanor, she nodded.

"Would you like to practice together then?"

"I would." She pushed his rejection from her mind. "I can only do so much practice by myself, and I need to be certain I can actually block an Alteration."

"Okay, I'm going to perform an Alteration, and I want you to block me."

Just as she had done earlier, Layla envisioned a wall around her mind. Wil stared. She recognized the glazed look on his face as he attempted to connect their minds. A slight pressure poked at her forehead. The sensation startled her, and she nearly faltered.

For a moment, her body warmed. She saw Wil's face in her mind. Wil's image smiled. To see his face light up like that, grinning at her as he once had, almost cause her to drop her guard. She ground her teeth. Undeterred, Layla focused on her mental wall. The image disappeared. She blinked to find the real Wil before her, his face twisted in concentration.

"Amazing." Wil marveled at her, his eyes wide and his mouth slack. He broke their mental connection and stood. Layla rocked back when the cord joining them together snapped.

"What?" Her face warmed, and she hated it for giving away her thoughts.

"You did in one day what it takes most Ethereals months to learn."

"What do you mean?"

"You not only blocked me out but replaced the mind guard when it momentarily faltered. Vespa and I spent two weeks learning that feat."

He regarded her with curiosity. Her cheeks flamed warmer under the intensity of his gaze. If only she could master a blush block…that could prove just as useful as a mind guard.

"You know, even though Nash…" Wil hesitated on his brother's name. Awkwardness enveloped them. "Even though he couldn't perform an Alteration as well as my sister and I, he always had a knack for blocking them. You do too. I wonder if your Vanguard strength is not just in your body but your mind as well."

"So, you're saying it's possible for Vanguards to be able to withstand an Alteration?"

"It's possible."

"That would be wonderful. My people could be free from Alterations."

"But then mine would be overrun. Without the ability to perform Alterations in combat, Vanguards would have an overwhelming advantage." No anger resided in those words, yet she staggered from the force of his assertion.

"Oh."

They sat down at the table, an uncomfortable silence stretching between them. Both wanted the best for their people, she knew that, but Layla wished one didn't come at the expense of the other. Could the gap between their two kingdoms ever truly be mended?

CHAPTER TWENTY SEVEN

Wil

The time he'd been dreading arrived and still no reasonable solution presented itself. His current option, to attempt The King's Right over his father, seemed unlikely. If that didn't work, he'd have to rely on the backup plan, a rescue attempt at the gallows. Even though his actions meant defying his father, the king, openly in front of the whole kingdom, it had to be done. What kind of man—what kind of future king—would he be if he let his mother and sister die at the hands of his father, a man driven mad with jealousy?

Wil looked over at Volton Mars and Layla. What a small army he had managed to assemble, but lives depended on their success. Since his father had overtaken the minds of everyone involved in the execution process, if Wil failed with The King's Right, he would have no choice but to call upon Mars and Layla for help, despite how much he worried for them both.

"Are you both sure?" he posed the question again.

Mars nodded. "Yes. The queen has been my friend for twenty years, and Vespa is like my own daughter. I would gladly lay my life down for theirs." Wil appreciated the Volton's steadfast devotion, yet dreaded putting a peaceful man in the middle of what could easily become a war.

"I am sure," Layla answered, strong and steady. "If you say I can't come with you, I'll just figure out a way to do something on my own." She raised her chin in defiance.

Wil's shoulders slumped. "Assuming I can't exercise The King's Right over my father, we will enact the backup plan. My mother and sister will be brought up from the dungeons on the other side of the southern wall. They will walk, heavily guarded, a few feet to the gallows, which have been constructed at the beginning of the meadows. My father wanted a large area for crowds to gather." He could hardly contain his disgust.

"Let's go over our roles once more to make sure we're ready. First, I will Alter the minds of everyone in the crowd, which will prove difficult without Vespa's help but not impossible. While I do that, Layla will rescue my family. Be sure to use that Vanguard strength to hold a strong mind guard. Volton, I need you to also construct an impenetrable mind guard and watch the river. When I am performing the Alteration, the guards and everyone around me will be affected by it, so the kingdom will be vulnerable to attack from the outside. If you see any Vanguards cross the river, Volton, sound the defense horns immediately."

"Won't your people be able to put up mind guards?" Layla asked.

"My Alteration will be unexpected, so most people won't have time to block it. You have to be prepared for any Ethereals that are able to withstand it, my father included. I wish I could fight beside you, Layla, but the Alteration will take my full attention."

"You will be unguarded then." He caught the waver in her words.

"Yes, but I will be far enough away that no one should be able to stop me until it's too late. You just focus on freeing my mother and sister. I'll be fine."

He made sure his smile appeared reassuring, but she didn't look convinced. She crossed the room, bent down, and whispered in his ear, "Please be careful."

Wil shivered as her breath brushed against his neck. "I will." He tore away from the enchantment she held over him and turned to Mars. "Are you both comfortable with your roles?"

Layla and Volton Mars nodded in unison.

"Ok. I'm going to confront my father. If that doesn't work, I'll meet you by the South Gate. Layla, remember to stay as far away from my father as you can. If you see him looking your way, reinforce your mind guard as much as you can. He is very powerful."

"I guess we'll find out if my mind is strong enough to withstand The King's Right." Her lopsided smile betrayed her nerves.

Wil clenched his teeth so hard his head hurt, but he kept himself from begging her to stand down. As much as he didn't want Layla involved, he knew how much he needed her help. He knew of no other sure, capable warrior with an unusually strong mind guard, except Nash. Wil frowned at the comparison. Despite his confidence in her abilities, Wil also knew the strength of his father's power. If Jesper overcame her, the plan would fail and three women he loved would die before his very eyes. The idea nearly paralyzed him with fear.

Layla laid her hand across his cheek, her touch burning into his skin. "I want to do this, Wil. We *can* do this."

He nodded once and then ducked out the door, unable to spend another minute near her, asking her to risk her life. The walk from the tunnels to the king's quarters did nothing for Wil's nerves. He obsessed the whole way, going over the plans step by step, accounting for the alternatives should something go wrong. If only he succeeded in Altering his father's mind, everyone would be safe without a fight. It would work. It had to.

"I need to see the king," Wil announced to the two guards barring the door.

"The king is unavailable."

"I need to see my father now. It's urgent." Wil heard the strain in his own reply.

"The king is not here, my prince. He's already gone to prepare for the executions."

Wil fell against the wall, crushed under the weight of his failure.

CHAPTER TWENTY-EIGHT

King Jesper

Jesper peered through the bars at the two women huddled together inside. When Sansolena lifted her head, he barely recognized her. She looked dirty and frail, two words he never thought he'd associate with his wife. Sans had always been pristine yet strong. Shame poured through his veins. His jealousy and rage had reduced her to an unkempt woman, cowering in the corner of a dark, dank cell.

"Is today the day?" Her once melodious voice sounded hollow. Jesper nearly asked her what she meant, just to hear her speak again, but they both knew. The day she would die.

"Yes."

Sans let go of Vespa, adjusted their sleeping daughter on the cot, and crossed over to him. Her brown eyes glowed black in the low light, but he still saw her anger boiling inside them.

"I don't care what you do to me, Jesper, but let Vespa go. She's already suffered enough at your hands." Sans' sharp words pierced him. "You nearly destroyed her mind. I don't recognize my girl anymore." She placed her hand over her mouth as tears sprang in her eyes.

The king glanced at his daughter, a small lump on the cot. Though his wife's muffled sobs forced him to see the monster he'd become, Jesper maintained his focus. He'd come here for a purpose. He had to get answers.

Tearing his eyes away from their child, he asked, "Did you ever love me, Sansolena? I mean, really love me?"

"Are you going to force me to tell you?"

"No." He no longer exuded his typical confidence, exposing instead a soft and broken side of his soul. "I want you to tell me yourself."

"I'm so tired of your games, Jesper." She did look exhausted. "Does it even matter?"

"It matters to me."

Sans sighed dramatically. A strange heartening befell him to see she retained a hint of her original spunk— even now, even in this place, even at the hour of her death.

"Yes, Jesper. I did." Her exasperated gaze bore into him. "I still do even after everything you've done."

Her words washed over him like a salve to his wounded soul. She loved him. He'd lain awake at night, tortured by the idea that she never really had, by the notion Rex held a place Jesper could never access. But after everything, she still loved him. The king felt whole again for the first time in…he couldn't even remember how long.

"I'm here to free you, my dear Sans."

"What?"

"You and Vespa. I am going to take you out of here."

"But you've announced our impending deaths to the whole kingdom. How will you get away with freeing us?"

"I will dress up some other criminals in your clothes. With a sack over their heads and gags in their mouths, no one will know the difference."

"But if everyone thinks we're dead…" Sansolena trailed off.

"I will get you as far as the river. After that, you're on your own. It's the best I can do."

"What will we do, Jesper? Once a Vanguard sees this blond hair, we'll be killed in an instant."

"I'm sure Rex will take you in." He hadn't meant the words to come out so harshly, but his remaining jealousy burst forth.

"You forget…Vance deposed him."

"Do you want to escape or not?"

"I do." That old fire returned to her eyes. She'd always been a fighter. She would find a way to survive, that he knew.

With shaking hands, Jesper opened the cell door. Though he desired to pull Sansolena in his arms, the king knew those days had passed. Instead, he handed his wife two robes he'd stolen from the Volton's room.

"Put these on and cover your heads."

As Sansolena wiggled into the massive green robe, Jesper crossed over to Vespa. He shook her shoulder gently until she awakened. Her brown eyes, so much like Sansolena's brightened.

"Daddy." She hadn't called him that in years.

"Hi, baby." Every part of him ached. What had he done?

"I don't like it here. It's cold and dark." She pouted, the same face she'd made hundreds of time as a child.

"I'm taking you out of here. Put on this robe just like your mother did, and be sure to cover up your hair."

Both parents helped Vespa into the robe that dwarfed her. Never had she seemed so small and fragile. He cursed himself again for harming this precious creature in the height of his anger.

"Are you going to fix her?" Sansolena shoved Vespa's blond hair into the hood.

"I don't know if I can." His unspoken regret hovered in the chasm between them. "I'm afraid I'll cause more damage."

His wife's eyes snapped. "At least remove the Lock so I can try."

"I can't risk going back into her mind, Sans. I'm sorry."

His wife gave him a look of rage and disgust. Knowing he deserved such a look did nothing to lessen the pain of it. He started to reach out, to draw comfort from Sansolena as he had done so many times over the years, but thought better of it. "Let's go."

He took Vespa's hand and led them out of the dungeons. They walked in silence past the guards at the door, through the castle, and out into the meadow. No one noticed their departure. He'd Altered them all before he descended into the prison to ensure it. Jesper wanted to say so much to Sansolena and Vespa—Wil and Nash too—but he couldn't seem to find the words. Before he could formulate a way to express his regret, they reached the entrance to Clovis' maze.

"Why are we here, Jesper? Is this a trick? You know we can't navigate the maze."

Her mistrust troubled him, but he'd given her no reason to trust him—not now, probably not ever. "Vespa can. The maze leads to the river. You can cross there to make your escape. I'm sure the Voltons would take you in if you can make it to the Borderlands. Maybe they will have some ideas about how to fix what I've done to our daughter."

His wife nodded curtly. "Okay."

"Goodbye, Sans," he said wistfully. He reached up and touched a piece of her hair. She gazed back at him, her eyes clouded with so many emotions he couldn't determine which stood out the most.

"Goodbye, Jesper."

As she turned to go, he grabbed her by the arm and crushed her to him. She leaned in, wrapping her arms around his waist, much to his surprise and pleasure. When Jesper finally let go, he lifted her head up and kissed her lightly on the lips.

"I'm more sorry than you could ever know."

Sansolena stepped back and took Vespa's hand. To-gether, they walked toward the maze, but Vespa pulled on her mother's hand, stopping their progress. His daughter turned back around to smile at him with a soul shattering look of innocence.

CHAPTER TWENTY-NINE

Nash

From the Vanguard side, Nash kept to the bushes, just out of the Ethereal guards' sight, and scanned the meadow stretching out before him. The Northern Gate stood open, allowing scores of Ethereals traveling from all over the kingdom to gather near the gallows in hopes of glimpsing such a rare event—the hanging of a queen. Never in Ethereal history had such a phenomenon occurred, and Nash intended to ensure it didn't happen today either.

A new anger boiled within Nash. In the middle of a war with Vance, Jesper allowed his personal feelings to jeopardize the safety of the entire kingdom. He not only planned to publicly execute his wife, the queen, but also left a major gate open to ensure all of Etherea could watch. Jesper's jealousy endangered everyone Nash loved. He wouldn't stand for it.

When he saw Layla, positioned atop a low-lying wall close to the scaffold, he paused to drink in her features, to memorize every curve of her face. She looked just as beautiful and warlike as the first moment he laid eyes on her, but why had she come outside of the tunnels, especially now? He surveyed the crowd again, scanning more carefully this time, until his eyes landed on Wil. His brother crouched on the roof of the South Wall, waiting. As Nash assessed their positions and their posture, he realized they meant to stop the execution just as he did.

"Wil and Layla are posed to attack," Nash whispered to his father. "If Wil performs an Alteration, you and the rest of our army will be vulnerable. I should go alone."

Rex shook his head in disagreement. "No. I spent too many years regretting the choices I made regarding Sansolena. Even if I fall to the Alteration, I have to try and reach her."

Though he didn't agree, Nash understood. He smiled. Jesper loved his mother, Nash knew, but Rex's devotion seemed even stronger.

"I'll lead you through the West Wall maze then. If you do succumb to the Alteration, you should at least be safe inside the labyrinth. Should we tell the soldiers about the risk?"

"We'll let them decide as we did before. Those who don't want to come in can stand guard near the West Wall entrance."

Rex called his army around him and explained the situation. Unlike last time, their decisions came swiftly. The soldiers separated into their groups, a vast majority choosing to enter Etherea with their king. Nash instructed those who chose to remain behind, explaining how to stay out of view from the Ethereal guards.

A small part of him felt like a traitor to Etherea—to Wil. Should he really be explaining these tricks to the enemy? Nash dismissed the thought. Nothing remained as it once had been. This day, a group of Vanguards stood poised to rescue the Ethereal queen sentenced to death by the Ethereal king. Within this group stood a Vanguard soldier who loved the Ethereal princess and a half-Ethereal, half-Vanguard prince who pined for the proclaimed Fulfillment. Traditional boundaries set by the First Ones, separating the kingdoms for centuries, now ceased to exist.

Nash motioned for the soldiers, nearly fifty in total, to follow him across the river toward the maze. Several men glanced at one another with skeptical expressions, but everyone trailed him without argument. Rex and Grant agreed to bring up the rear, ready to fight anyone who might follow them.

Once each man made it safely across the river onto Ethereal land, Nash led them to the bushes that marked the start of Clovis' maze. As he turned the corner, he smashed into someone. Nash let out a startled shout and stumbled back, trying to right himself.

"What the!" he bellowed.

"Nash?" A soft female voice, one he'd know anywhere, added to the shock.

His mother and sister stood before him, dirty and gaunt, but alive. Elated, Nash sprang forward and wrapped them both in a hug. They stunk in a way he couldn't describe, but he'd never been so happy to see them in all his life.

"Nashie." Vespa giggled with glee, muffled by the shirt.

"Nashie? You haven't called me that since you were seven."

His mother took his hand. Her mournful look made him dizzy with fearful anticipation. "Something's happened, Nash." His heart stilled, stopped in place by her grave tone.

"Wait, how did you get out of jail?" Nash interrupted his mother, delaying her revelation just a little longer so could regain his breath. Had she killed Jesper to get away? The vengeful part of him hoped so.

"Your fa...Jesper let me go." She sounded as surprised as he felt.

"Then who are they?" Nash pointed in the direction of the gallows, now hidden by the maze's layered walls.

"They are criminals Jesper already sentenced to death a while ago. He just dressed them up in mine and Vespa's clothing and put sacks over their heads, hoping to pass them off as the disgraced queen and princess."

"I'm just so glad you're safe." Overcome, he reached out and hugged them again. Vespa giggled like a child. "Wait, you said the princess...what does Vespa have to do with anything?"

The queen's eyes watered. "That's what I need to tell you, Nash. Jesper Altered your sister's mind. She's not herself."

"What?"

"Sansolena?" Rex's strangled cry interrupted their conversation.

The Vanguard king pushed his way through the soldiers. Sansolena peered around Nash, her face beaming with a radiance her son had never seen. Like one person, his father and mother stepped forward, closing the space between them, until they unified in an embrace. A lump formed at the base of his throat. They both looked… happy.

"Vespa?" Grant, close on Rex's heels, stepped into view. His face lit up with joy, but Vespa hid against her brother, pressing her cheek into his chest. Nash understood Grant's first impulse, to scoop Vespa up into his arms, but the Vanguard hesitated.

"Vespa?" Grant said her name again with less exuberance.

"Who are you?" She yanked on her brother's shirt. "Nashie, do I know him?"

Though his mother had just told him about the Alteration, Nash had not grasped its full implications. The Vespa he'd left behind had been bubbly, intelligent, and deeply in love with Grant. The Vespa that stood before him now resembled a young child.

"What happened to her?" Grant's question loomed, a truth better left undiscovered but, based on his pained expression, knowledge essential to his very existence.

The air rushed out of Nash's lungs. "Jesper performed some sort of Alteration." Vespa grinned up at him with simple innocence, but he detected no hint of a sound mind.

Grant fell to his knees in the dirt, his head in his hands. "Can we help her?"

"I don't know."

Vespa pulled on Nash's sleeve, much like she had when they were children. "Why is Mama hugging that man? Where's Daddy and Wil?"

"Vespa, this is my friend, Grant." He gestured toward the stricken Vanguard hunched over on the ground.

Grant jumped up and stuck out his hand, playing along. "Hello, Vespa. I'm Grant."

She took his hand, but her gaze darted back and forth with a nervous shyness. Pain etched itself across Grant's face, yet his smile never wavered. Fighting the lump in his throat, Nash nodded encouragingly at his sister.

"Grant is going to take care of you while I go look for Daddy and Wil." Nash forced the word "Daddy" out. To call Jesper Daddy or Father seemed blasphemous. "Ok, Vespa? So, you will stay here with Grant, right?"

She nodded. "Do you like games, Grant? Because I like games."

Nash strode over to his parents, still locked together. He hated to break up their reunion, but he needed answers. "Mother, what has he done to her?"

The queen let go of Rex and stepped back. Her face, which had only moments before been glowing with elation, fell.

"He removed Grant from her mind—memory by memory. You know how invasive that is. She's been childlike ever since."

His mother, who had always been so strong, broke down into tears. Nash drew back in surprise, but Rex stepped forward to place an arm around her. She leaned into him, a grateful smile shimmering through her tears.

"Can you reverse it?" Though he knew his mother would have already tried, Nash had to ask. He'd never felt so helpless.

"No. He Locked her mind. Only Jesper's death could Unlock it."

"Well, I'll just have to kill him then."

"No." His mother yanked on his arm with unnatural force. "He freed us."

"Look at Vespa, Mother. Does she look free to you?" He cursed himself for raising his voice. Jesper deserved his rage, not her. Softening, he apologized.

Rex cocked his head to the side. "Do you hear that?"

Sansolena and Nash stopped talking and listened. The faint clomping of hooves wafted from the distance, growing closer. In unison, they looked toward the open Northern Gate, though their position obscured most of it from their sight.

"Horses approaching...a lot of horses." Nash pushed through the throngs of his father's soldiers to better see across the river. To his dismay, he caught sight of Vance and his army only about a half mile away. He raced back toward his father.

"It's Vance. Ready the men."

Rex nodded, his face grim. "He's come to attack Jesper. I bet he has no idea we are even here."

Dawning rained down upon Nash. "He's attacking, and Wil plans to do an Alteration. It will be a massacre. I have to stop my brother."

"I'll go with you."

"No. I need you to keep mother and Vespa safe. My sister may have the mind of a child, but she can guide you and your men through the maze. If I am able to stop the Alteration, attack from the west. No one will expect it."

"What if you can't stop it?"

"I won't be affected, but the rest of you will. Once I reach Wil and stop the Alteration, you should recover and still be able to fight."

His father nodded, accepting his limited role with surprising humility. "Be safe, son." Leaning in, Rex pulled Nash into a brief hug before heading into the maze.

Nash turned to Grant. "Go with them, and please help keep my family safe."

"I will," Grant vowed, placing a fist over his heart.

CHAPTER THIRTY

Wil

When he saw the North Gate lying open, leaving Etherea vulnerable, Wil almost called off the rescue attempt. To be faced with this decision—between his family and his kingdom—left him fumbling for the right choice. Wil would never have selected this plan had he known his father planned to hold the gates open, leaving hundreds completely frozen, vulnerable. But he hadn't known, and now if he had any chance to save his mother and sister, he had to continue despite the risk. He chastised himself for putting innocent people's lives in danger, yet he couldn't stand to lose his family.

Wil glanced toward the North Gate and back to the gallows. Did he have enough time to drop the gate and still perform the Alteration? He didn't think so. He closed his eyes and took a deep breath, seeking clarity amidst the heavy weight of his decision.

He swallowed hard as he made his final choice, one he knew he'd regret on some level for the rest of his life. He gave a slight nod to Layla, hoping she remembered to guard her mind. Shaking his head and ignoring the nauseous feeling in his stomach, Wil cleared his own mind and focused on the crowd below. He could feel their hum of consciousness. Grabbing onto that, he projected a vision. Wil didn't want to scare his people like he did with Vanguards in battle, just limit their awareness.

Layla

Layla perched atop a low-lying wall, close to the gallows. She stuck to the shadows to avoid being spotted by the king or any of the guards. Though she tried to keep her vision straight ahead, Layla found her gaze wandering up to the sky. Gray skies…

The doors below opened and the prisoners stumbled out. Her nerves frayed at the sight, releasing her Vanguard beast, which she struggled to contain. Vespa and Queen Sansolena. Jesper dressed them in their finest but threw dirty sacks upon their heads. When the guards pushed them roughly toward the gallows, Layla clenched her fists to keep from leaping off the ledge early. How dare those men treat the royals with such disregard?

She looked toward Wil squatting on the rooftop directly across from her. He gave her a slight nod, and Layla erected her mental walls. Though she'd practiced with Wil, she had never before tested her ability in actual combat. What if she couldn't maintain it during her rescue attempt? Layla resolved not to falter. Vespa and Sansolena's lives depended on it.

Layla's cue—the glazed look that fell over the crowd—propelled her into motion. She leapt from the wall, landing nimbly on her feet. With a sword in hand, Layla raced toward the scaffold, reminding herself to hold the mind guard.

Out of the corner of her eye, she noticed King Jesper stand. Wil's Alteration had not affected the king, just as they had feared. She kept her eyes fixed on the queen and princess, undeterred by his movements.

"What are you doing?" Jesper's shout lingered amongst the frozen crowd.

Layla didn't answer. She kept moving toward the prisoners, checking her mental shield.

"Stop!" Jesper called to her. "You don't understand."

Nash

Nash constructed his toughest mind guard and ran along the wall toward the open North Gate, toward Layla and Wil. When no one made an attempt to impede his progress, he realized Wil had begun the Alteration. What would become of the group he'd left behind in the maze? He scanned the riverside, where he'd left the few soldiers who asked to stay behind. They stood like statues. Nash bit his lip in frustration, but he propelled himself forward. If he could just get to Wil and Layla, he'd feel much better.

As he approached the gate, Nash checked across the river, gauging Vance's proximity to the castle. Instead, something else caught his attention—Volton Mars struggling with a much larger Vanguard at the defense horns. Wil must have sent the Volton to man the horns. If that awful noise didn't pierce the air soon, Vance's whole army would breach the Ethereal land. All those Ethereals under Wil's Alteration...they would be slaughtered.

He looked back and forth between the gate and the horns. Should he make a run for the gates and close them? Or should he stop the approaching army with defense alarms? The gates took him closer to Wil and Layla, but it also meant leaving the Volton to certain death. Making a quick mental calculation, Nash decided he could make it to the horns faster than the gate. He raced toward Volton Mars, though every fiber of his being cried out for him to run to Layla.

Nash crashed into the Vanguard scout, pouring all his pent up rage into the hit. The man flew off Mars and landed on the ground with a hard thud. Before the Vanguard could regain his bearings, Nash straddled him and drove his sword straight through the other man's heart.

Nash bolted over to the Volton and then fell to his knees beside his tutor. Blood seeped from a gaping wound on Mars' head. With shaking hands, Nash ripped a piece of his shirt and pressed it against the wound.

"Volton." He shook the man gently.

"Nash?" Mars' eyes rolled around. "A scout attacked me before I could sound the alarm. Please, I can't hold my mind guard much longer."

"You have to, Volton. We need you."

Nash stood and grabbed hold of the crank as the first wave of Vance's men careened across the river, their horses rising up the river bank toward the scaffold. He spun the lever with all his might until the horns, with their awful noise, pierced the air. On the other side of the river, the rest of Vance's men writhed on the ground in agony. Nash whipped his head around, counting thirty horses riding toward the still frozen Ethereals.

Beside him, Volton Mars struggled to his feet and staggered over to the crank. "I'll continue to sound the horns. You go help your brother."

"Are you sure?" Nash asked, hesitant to leave the Volton, yet desperate to get to Wil and Layla.

Mars smiled—the same confident, gentle smile Nash had known all his life—and took over the crank. "Of course."

Nash grabbed the dead Vanguard's battle axe and ran toward the gallows, his sword in his other hand, easily wielding both weapons at once. He charged ahead, just a few paces behind Vance and his band of thirty, though his lack of a horse quickly lengthened the distance.

Wil

Out of the corner of his eye, he saw Layla jump off the wall and into the crowd. She moved toward his mother and sister. Why had his father put sacks over their heads? If this plan went awry, he may never again behold his mother's and sister's faces. He wished he could look into their eyes and reassure them. He wanted them to know he and others fought for their release, but his father had robbed them all of that. Anger welled up inside him.

A slight movement caught his attention. Jesper rose and stalked toward Layla. Though Wil knew his father would most likely withstand the Alteration, he had held out hope that the king would be affected. His father yelled, but Wil couldn't hear the words. Another sound overtook his senses—the defense horns. They whined, sending their deafening power across the river.

Layla seemed to observe the incoming army at the same moment Wil did. When she turned to look up at him—probably to warn him—she froze, and his heart stopped along with her. She had dropped her guard.

"Layla!" he screamed, terror and agony tangled up in her name.

Wil severed his connection to the collective psyche, releasing everyone at once. He scrambled to the side of the wall. Vance's men descended upon the unaware crowd—a crowd that would take at least a minute to disengage from the Alteration. The worst possible situation had occurred, playing out like a bad dream in front of him.

Wil grabbed a rope he'd secured to the rooftop. Throwing it over the side of the wall, he inched down it with great haste. Wil prayed he'd be able to make it down to the ground before Vance arrived. As prince and future king, he should be worried about his people, and he was. But three people dominated his thoughts as he slid down the rope—his mother, his sister, and…Layla.

Nash

As he ran, Nash saw Wil flip a rope over the wall and scurry down the side of it, but he couldn't see Layla through the throngs of people standing around. She must have jumped into the crowd to free the fake Vespa and Sansolena. Adrenaline swirled through him, fast and furious, as he absorbed the scene before him: a whole crowd of unmoving Ethereals. Though his lungs and legs protested, Nash's love for Layla, Wil, and their kingdom propelled him forward.

When he reached the site, people began to awaken from the Alteration, but Vance's men had already cut down several unsuspecting Ethereals. From the looks of it, they'd gone straight for the biggest and strongest. Vance's men focused so intently on the Ethereals, they failed to notice Nash.

He whipped his head around, searching for Layla. He spotted her, but the whole courtyard separated them. How could he protect her from so far away? She stood completely still. His leg shook so hard he stumbled. She had yet to recover from the Alteration, leaving her vulnerable, and he could not reach her.

"Layla!" His shout gave away his position.

Several Vanguards whipped around at the sound. Spotting him, they hesitated. He looked enough like a Vanguard to confuse them. Behind the soldiers, Nash watched as his father and the group of faithful Vanguards surged in from the west. He hoped their diversion gave Layla enough time to recover.

"He's an enemy." Vance's high-pitched whine rose from the chaos, his finger pointing in Nash's direction.

"Your father is coming, my king." A guard jerked his thumb toward the incoming group.

"How will we know which men are ours and which are with your father?" A second soldier, with wide, panicked eyes absorbed the scene.

"Just kill everyone you don't recognize." Vance's cold-hearted answer rose up from the fray.

Two men on foot bolted toward Nash. Inflamed with a deadly mixture of adrenaline, worry, and protectiveness, he rushed forward to meet them. With a battle axe in one hand and a sword in the other, Nash swung. The sound of metal meeting metal rang out in the air.

Layla

"Layla!" A scream pulled her from her pleasant vision.

She shook her head to clear it. Before she had a chance to prepare herself, a Vanguard soldier fell upon her. Layla raised her sword out of instinct and blocked what would have been a fatal blow. She shook the man's weapon off with the tip of her own and lunged. The feeling of sharp metal slicing through flesh vibrated up her arm. Without remorse, she yanked her weapon out as the man slumped to the ground.

Layla looked up to see Wil heading in her direction, shouting her name. He appeared to be fending off attackers as he went, but she knew his worry for her clouded his judgment. Given the Vanguards' strength, he would need his full attention. She glanced around to find soldiers dragging the two prisoners back into the building, apparently unharmed.

"I'm fine, Wil. So are your mother and sister," she called to him, hoping the news would help Wil focus on his own safety. She reminded herself to put up her mental guard. Though most of the Ethereals ran around, too preoccupied with escape to focus on performing Alterations, she wanted to be prepared. This time, she wouldn't allow it to drop.

One of Vance's men raised a crossbow and took aim at King Jesper. Though she had no great love for the king, Layla ran toward the bowmen. She crashed into him just as the arrow released. Landing on top of the man with a grunt, she recovered and leapt up. Layla stabbed him once in the stomach. As she pulled her sword out of his body, she glanced up at the platform where Jesper stood.

The king staggered around, an arrow sticking out of his heart. Layla surged toward Jesper, knocking down every man that stood in her path. She arrived at the platform just as the king stumbled backward, slumping down in his chair.

"My king." She knelt before him, examining his wound.

"I'm sorry, Layla." A drowning gurgle bubbled in his throat, his breath ragged. "I'm so sorry for everything. Make sure my family knows that—all of them, even Nash."

"Wil!" Layla screamed.

Amidst the sea of bodies and clanging noises, she saw Wil making his way toward the platform. Though he wasn't a Vanguard, his height and natural strength gave him the ability to hold his own. She wanted to jump down and help him, but she couldn't risk leaving the king exposed in his condition. As much as she disliked Jesper, he remained the king of Etherea and Wil's father. She fended off the few men that managed to straggle up to the platform.

"Layla." Wil called up from the bottom of the platform.

"Your father—" She hitched as the words stuck in her throat.

Wil scrambled onto the stage, his eyes wild. Layla stood, giving up her spot beside Jesper to Wil. She blocked the two men with her body, prepared to defend them both.

Wil

Wil tried not to stare at the arrow pointing up from his father's chest. He grabbed Jesper's hand, squeezing it. Jesper's eyes fluttered open, though the life ebbed from them at a slow, measured pace.

"I'm here, Father. You'll be fine," Wil whispered false assurances.

"Wil...I'm sorry."

"Don't talk now. I left Volton Mars by the defense horns, but he'll be back soon. I'll have him look at you. You'll be fine."

With his free hand, Wil wiped at the tears cascading down his cheeks. They clouded his vision, and he needed to be able to see everything clearly. With his kingdom being invaded and his father wounded, Wil had to hold himself together.

Jesper pumped Wil's hand to garner his son's attention. "I let them go, Wil."

"Let who go?" His father made no sense.

"Your mother and sister. I dropped them off by the river and told them to run."

Could it really be true? Wil's heart beat with renewed hope. "Then who was headed to the gallows?"

"Criminals I'd already sentenced to death. I couldn't do it, Wil. As mad and hurt as I was, I couldn't do it."

"Father…" Words failed him.

"I'm sorry, Wil. For everything…so sorry." Jesper wheezed, shaking violently.

"Father, no."

"Wil." Layla's panicked voice drew his focus away from his father.

He jumped up to find Vance making his way toward them, a mixture of pride and anger illuminating his enemy's eyes. Staring at the false king, Wil knew death rushed to meet him. All his hopes and dreams for the future vanished, but with his father on the verge of death, Wil would stand for Etherea even if it cost his life as well. He grabbed his sword and slid closer to Layla.

"My father is dying. Please go find Volton Mars."

"I can't leave you alone with Vance. Though he looks and sounds weak, he's still Rex's son. His position as prince gives an unusual amount of strength. He will kill you, Wil. He's here to eradicate the Ethereals once and for all." Her words tumbled out, filling the space between them. "I can't leave you, Wil. We will fight him together."

The depth of her concern and loyalty touched him, but he wouldn't risk her life. If he told her the truth—that he couldn't stand the idea of a world without her—she wouldn't go. Wil had to make her believe he needed the Volton, even though Mars could do little for the king at this point.

"Thank you, Layla, but I really need you to find the Volton."

"You go find the Volton. I'll stay and fight Vance."

"With my father injured, I'm the acting king of Etherea. I can't be seen fleeing a battle. Please, Layla, go. We don't have time to discuss it any longer." When she bit her lip, Wil knew she would go despite her objections. He spared a moment to look her in the eyes, hoping to convey everything he didn't have time to say.

"I don't want you to die."

Wil smiled at the longing in her eyes. He considered sweeping her up into a kiss but instead said, "I'll try not to. Please go."

To his great relief, she did. Wil stood to face Vance. There wasn't enough time to perform an Alteration, so he would have to battle the Prince of Vanguard, man-to-man.

Nash

Nash slammed the battle axe into the chest of the Vanguard in front of him. It landed with a sickening thud, but Nash didn't have time to think about it. He pressed on with steely resolve, toward Layla. He refused to rest until he reached her and ensured her safety.

As the path cleared, he saw Wil and Layla standing together with King Jesper lying unmoving behind them. Fear and worry seized him. He scanned the crowd, his eyes landing on Vance, who headed straight for them. Nash suppressed his rising panic, slashing and slicing through every obstacle in his path. He had to reach them before Vance did.

Soldiers streamed around him. Frustrated, Nash smashed them aside, some with the axe and others with his sword. Though the other Vanguards possessed incredible strength, they lacked his singular purpose. Men fell by the side, no more than insects in Nash's path. He never took his gaze off the platform.

When Layla ran, the vise grip on Nash's heart loosened, only to be immediately replaced by a new fear when he realized Wil now stood alone to face Vance. The Ethereal, despite his disproportionate height, didn't stand a chance against the Vanguard. Nash willed his brother to turn and run, but Wil stayed rooted in place. He recognized the stubborn set of Wil's jaw and knew his brother would fight, even surrender his life.

"Run, Wil!" Nash shouted even though he understood the futility. "I'm almost there."

With Nash just a few feet away, Vance's sword dove into Wil's skin. The Ethereal's blue eyes bulged with pain. Bile rose in the back of Nash's throat. Not Wil.

"*No!*" Nash lunged forward and knocked Vance to the ground.

Layla

Layla headed toward the horns as Wil instructed, but she skidded to a halt and turned back around. Though Wil might hate her for the choice, she would rather see Jesper die than Wil. She should never have left in the first place, no matter what Wil said. A true Vanguard didn't run. Layla sprinted toward the platform, back toward Wil, her lungs stumbling to keep up with her pace.

"*No!*" Layla cried as the tip of Vance's sword punctured Wil on the left side of his chest.

He crumpled to the ground. She exploded toward him, knocking aside everyone who stood in her way. Fueled by panic, she closed the distance in no time.

"Wil."

"Layla, go." He pushed at her. "Vance will kill you."

She looked up, sword in hand. She'd forgotten to watch out for Vance in her haste to reach Wil. The mock king leapt up off the ground—how had he gotten there? Vance hurled himself backward, managing to deftly avoid the tip of a Vanguard soldier's sword. No, not a Vanguard soldier, but Nash. Nash! As he slashed furiously at the Vanguard usurper, she longed to call out his name, but she didn't dare distract him.

Turning back to Wil, she said, "Nash is fighting Vance. You rest, Wil. Rest."

She yanked off a long strip of her sleeve. Careful not to jostle him, Layla gathered Wil's head into her lap. She pressed the piece of skirt into his wound, hoping to stymie the copious flow of blood. Her hands shook as an inexplicable buzz radiated between them.

"Nash? Here?" She heard his disbelief and pride.

"Yes, Wil. He's fighting Vance. You're safe. I'm safe. Nash will be safe." She murmured a litany of reassuring words as she stroked his hair with her free hand. His blood soaked the cloth beneath her other hand. Abject terror seized her. She didn't know how to save him, or even if he could be saved.

"They're retreating!" an elated Ethereal cried.

Layla tried to see through the tears swimming in her eyes. She looked up and spied Queen Sansolena riding in on a black steed, followed by Volton Mars, Grant, and Vespa. Charging in from the side, one of Vance's soldiers, still atop his horse, circumvented the group, knocked Nash aside, and scooped up Vance. A loud, victorious cheer arose from Rex and his men as the usurper fled. Nash righted himself, screaming curses at the retreating horse and riders.

Queen Sansolena

Sansolena, seeing her husband and son lying atop the platform, slid off the horse and raced up. With Wil attended by Layla and now the Volton, she went first to Jesper. Her whole body trembled.

Her husband's blue eyes, a feature she had always loved about him, stared vacantly up at the sky. A low moan escaped her throat. She clamped her hand over her heart, a vain attempt to hold in all the anguish threatening to spill out.

"Jesper. Oh, Jesper." She shook him, but he did not respond. Tears fell from her brown eyes.

"Jesper!" she called his name again, her voice hoarse from sorrow.

Sansolena threw herself upon her dead husband, hugging the last bit of life that clung to him. Did he know she meant it when she said, despite everything, she loved him? They both had regrets, deep ones, but they had also once had an outpouring of love. How could he be gone? Really gone?

Rex approached her, his face grim. "I'm so sorry, Sans." He spoke in a hushed whisper, giving her this final moment.

After allowing a few minutes to fully give into her grief, the queen righted herself. She kissed Jesper's forehead with aching tenderness. Stepping back, she realized he looked peaceful. In all their years together, she'd never seen his face so free from worry. His serenity brought her a small measure of comfort, but she knew the ache of his loss, within the depths of her soul, would last forever. She looked around to find that everyone, even Rex, shed tears at the magnitude of her grief.

Sucking in a deep breath, she turned from Jesper to attend her son. The Volton fluttered around Wil while Layla continued to hold his head. Nash, Grant, and Vespa kept back, trying to catch a glimpse from afar. The queen pushed her way in.

"Wil?" she asked.

"Mother, you're alive." He smiled with a sweetness that pained her.

"What happened?"

Disappointment replaced the pain on Wil's face. "Vance. I tried to stand for Etherea, Mother, but I couldn't."

She smiled sadly, so proud of her son. Did he know how much she loved him? "You did well, my son."

She stepped back, motioning for Mars to meet her. "Will he live, Volton?" She forced herself to ask the question they all wondered but feared asking.

Mars, her closest friend and confidant for the past twenty years, looked at her with worried brown eyes. His pale, tense face told her how much he feared for Wil.

"I don't know." He spoke the truth, knowing she would accept nothing less. "I think I can mend his wounds. I hope so, my queen, but I can't guarantee it."

"Do what you can, Mars." The queen fell to her knees beside her son. "The Volton will take care of you, my dear." She stroked his hair as she had during his childhood. "You will be just fine. I believe it."

She said the words he needed to hear while her eyes surveyed the blood surrounding his body. Foreboding settled around her shoulders like a shroud.

"Mother, I need to speak to Nash."

CHAPTER THIRTY-ONE

Nash

When his mother called him, Nash rushed to his brother's side. He tried not to notice the blood pooling around Wil's body, but his gaze seemed drawn to it. He knelt beside his brother and took his hand.

"I'm here, Wil."

Wil opened his eyes. His face broke out into a big smile. Nash bit back tears. "Brother, I missed you."

"I missed you too, Wil." Nash struggled to keep his voice level, but the lump in his throat made it difficult.

"You know, we've never been apart for that long. You used to disappear into the woods sometimes, but you always came home for dinner. I'm glad you're back."

"Me too."

"I need your help, Nash." Wil's intense gaze spoke volumes.

"Anything."

Wincing in pain, Wil reached up and grabbed Layla's hand. She gasped in surprise. Nash, who had been so pre-occupied with his brother's injury, finally looked at Layla. He lost his breath. Had she grown even more beautiful in their time apart? In her eyes, he saw his own fear and pain reflect back.

To their mutual shock, Wil placed Layla's hand on top of Nash's. His green eyes connected with her purples ones, both teeming with confusion. A loud snapping vibrated the air around them. His arm shook, as did Layla and Wil's. Even Volton Mars, who sat a few paces away, watched with fascination. His mother's eyes grew wide.

"Oh First Ones," Sansolena muttered a prayer.

"Wil?" Layla's gaze swung back and forth between the two princes.

"I'm dying," Wil said the words with resoluteness, shattering those around him.

"You'll be fine," Layla assured him, though the hitch in her throat contradicted her.

"The Volton will fix you up in no time." Nash willed it to be true.

The injured prince shook his head, stopping whatever other pacifying reassurances they had planned. He looked between them, his eyes burning with death's fire. Nash started to speak again but found he couldn't. The noisy buzzing, Layla's hand on his, and Wil's reason for putting it there distracted him. What was Wil doing?

"I don't know what will happen to me." Wil's face betrayed his lie—he knew, but he didn't speak the truth again for their benefit. "But I need you both to work together to save Etherea."

"What are you saying?" Nash tried to make sense of his brother's words.

"I want you to stand as king in my place."

"What? I could never…"

"You can, Nash, and you will. I trust no one else to hold my throne."

Nash glanced at everyone standing around them, expecting outrage and dissent. His mother smiled weakly, heartbroken over Wil and Jesper, while his father nodded, confidence spreading across his face. Though they had only known one another a short while, Rex's faith reassured Nash. Finally, he turned to Layla. Her purple eyes spoke the words she couldn't. She believed in him. A crackle pierced the air as the energy coursing between the three intensified.

"Okay, Wil, but only until you heal. As soon as you are back on your feet, the crown is yours."

Wil smiled. "Layla, Nash will need your support. Stand by him. Help him. I want the two of you to do whatever it takes to protect my people."

"We will," Layla promised as Wil's eyes fluttered closed. Nash turned his head, unable to acknowledge the magnitude of the situation before him.

CHAPTER THIRTY TWO

Layla

Layla tried to sort out the feelings that whirled around inside her. At the forefront, panic over Wil's condition. Volton Mars said he could mend Wil, but the blood soaking through the prince's tunic and pooling around him told a different story. She feared Mars spoke those words only to placate them, to hide the bleak reality. The thought of losing Wil…she couldn't bear it.

Why had Wil asked her to help rule the kingdom with Nash? What did he mean? Had he given his blessing for Layla and Nash to be together? If so, she didn't know how she felt about it. From the moment she'd been taken by Elder Werrick, her feelings had been the fodder for his twisted games. Could she trust her own heart, her own mind, anymore? Did she truly love either of them, or had Werrick enslaved them all in an elaborate illusion?

When she saw Nash fighting on the battlefield, she couldn't deny her attraction to him. Yet, when Wil fell to Vance's blade, her entire being shattered at the sight. What did that mean, if anything? She sat torn between two brothers, unsure how she felt about either. One minute she found herself in Nash's arms and the next in Wil's—only to realize every moment, every kiss had been manipulated by an outside force.

Upon coming to Etherea, she feared losing her mind, and perhaps she had.

Layla stroked Wil's blond hair, hoping to calm him. His eyes fluttered open, filled with adoration. Though she started to speak, nothing came out. Layla wanted to tell him she loved him, to return to him what he had so graciously offered to her. But she couldn't say the words he wanted to hear, not yet anyway. Without the ability to be sure of her feelings, she didn't dare say anything. She couldn't mislead Wil, not anymore, and especially not as he lay dying in her arms. At the same time, she wouldn't allow herself to say goodbye either. Wil would be fine. There would be time to sort everything out between the three of them...later. She repeated the words like a chant.

Nash squeezed her hand. In his eyes, she recognized his bewilderment and the questions he held back as he comforted her. She tightened her grip on his hand, hoping her gratitude flowed along the current between them. She had only that and a feeble smile to offer him before returning her attention to Wil. Praying it would staunch the flow, Layla pressed the blood soaked cloth harder against his wound.

Commotion behind Rex and the queen drew her attention. Someone, a Vanguard, rode toward them all. She started to rise, prepared to defend Etherea, but something about him looked familiar.

"Samson?" Grant squinted.

Volton Mars rushed to take Layla's place, holding Wil's head so she could stand. She pushed past a group of people blocking her view of the rider. Samson's brazen grin greeted her. He looked the same as he always had and no worse for the wear. Where had he been all this time?

"Grant! Layla!" When Samson dismounted, Layla saw the hooded girl riding on the horse behind him and grew more perplexed.

Grant rushed forward, hugging his brother. The two slapped at one another playfully and laughed. For a moment, Layla imagined herself back on the farm in Vanguard, watching them joke around. Finally, Samson stepped over to her and swept her up into his arms. She relaxed for the first time in weeks, letting her misery seep into him. He reminded her of home. Memories of their mother's baked bread and the warm fire in their Vanguard home cascaded over her.

"I've been worried sick about you, Samson. Where have you been?" She pulled back to get a better look at him.

"I wanted to find a way to get you out of this mess." He grinned with childlike excitement.

Layla thought back to Rex's castle, all those months ago. At that time, she wanted nothing more than to be free from her role as the Fulfillment, which felt more like a curse than a blessing. As a result, Samson spent months searching for a way to extricate her. She didn't even know where he'd been or what he'd done to make that a reality.

Only now, Layla didn't want to be free of it. Somewhere along the way, she'd come to accept, even desire, her role. She knew with an inexplicable certainty she would find a way—working with Wil, Nash, Sansolena, and Rex—to bring peace to Etherea and Vanguard. Elder Werrick definitely mishandled the situation, but ultimately, he'd been right. She accepted her calling, her destiny, embracing her role as the Fulfillment. Layla knew the First Ones chose her, believed it in every fiber of her being.

"What did you find?" Grant asked, breaking the extended silence following Samson's proclamation.

"Her." Samson pulled the young woman forward.

The girl pushed back her hood and lifted her head. A collective gasp arose from those around her. Her dark black hair tumbled down her back as she surveyed them all with piercing purple eyes. With great ceremony, she rolled up her sleeve to reveal a dark purple birthmark in the shape of an *F*.

"I am the long awaited Fulfillment," the girl announced.

Acknowledgements

First and foremost, I'd like to thank my fans. I would be nowhere without your love and support.

This book would never have come about without my Dream Team--Dawn Ward, Danielle, Craver, Kim Sharp, and Ginny Hunsberger. They gave freely of their time, attention, and creativity. I am forever grateful!

And to Deek, thank you for your constant support, your unconditional love, and your faith in me and my work. I would not be where I am today without you.

About The Author

Erin Rhew is an editor, operations manager for a small press, and the author of The Fulfillment Series. Since she picked up *Morris the Moose Goes to School* at age four, she has been infatuated with the written word. She went on to work as a grammar and writing tutor in college and is still teased by her family and friends for being a member of the "Grammar Police."

A Southern girl by blood and birth, Erin spent years in a rainy pocket of the Pacific Northwest before returning to her roots in the land of hushpuppies, sweet tea, and pig pickin'. She's married to fellow author, the amazingly talented (and totally handsome) Deek Rhew, and spends her time writing side-by-side with him under the watchful eye of their patient-as-a-saint writing assistant, a tabby cat named Trinity. Erin and Deek enjoy taking long walks, drinking coffee, lifting, boxing, eating pizza, staying up late into the night talking, and adventuring together.